These Precious Hours

By

Michael Corrigan

Books by Michael Corrigan

Confessions of a Shanty Irishman

The Irish Connection and Other Stories

Byron

The Filmmakers

A Year and a Day, a journal of grief

These Precious Hours

Mulligan

Down the Highway

The Dean Sisters

Cruising Paradise: Essays, Reviews, and Stories

Brewer's Odyssey

Praise for Michael Corrigan's work:

Confessions of a Shanty Irishman: "Michael Corrigan proves that the American Irish have their own magical way with words in his spellbinding memoir of growing up on the wrong side of Market Street in San Francisco…But the secularization of a good Irish Catholic boy under the too strong temptations of the later 20th century is just the bare bones of what 'Confessions of a Shanty Irishman' is about. Like all great Irish literature, this book is about death and family, what holds people together and what pulls them apart." Gerald Nicosia, *San Francisco Chronicle*.

"I found your mismarried parents and well married grandparents quite moving." Ruby Cohn, Samuel Beckett scholar.

"Michael Corrigan's *Confessions* ensconces us in the world of a typical Irish-American family, typical in that it contains all the major intrinsic elements such as love of language, the shadow of Catholicism, and sadly, the self-destructive nature of our drinking patterns…His warm, engaging style laden with humor and irony, is a fitting tribute to his familial roots making *Confessions* a virtual 'must-read' for any Irish–American worth their salt." Joe Kavanaugh, *Irish Connections* magazine.

"In the seven years between the 1st and 3rd editions, Corrigan has matured in years, voice, and experience." Laurel Johnson.

The Irish Connection and Other Stories: "Michael Corrigan channels his Irish roots with a poignant honesty. The historically accurate settings and details, as well as the true dialects and idioms of his Irish ancestors allow Corrigan's lyrical voice to transport us back to the everyday pains and joys of those days." Jamie McOuat, Publishing Consultant, Right Focus Ltd.

"These stories of the Mulligans, Burkes, and O'Learys, not only trace a passionate spine of Irish history across many continents, but along the way elucidate the passionate, complex, conflicted yearnings of all humans…Irish or not. This is the mandate of art and Michael has met it in high style." Peter Coyote, actor/ writer.

Byron: "Though the title evokes another Byron, Corrigan's multi-plotted novel draws more upon Spillane, Hemingway and even a pinch of Pynchon than the romantic style of the author of *Don Juan*. Which isn't to say the protagonist of Corrigan's novel isn't a bit Byronic, just that there's a lot more Jake Barnes than Childe Harold…non stop action, suspense, murder and plenty of sex…It's a wild ride." Sara Beitia, *Boise Weekly*.

"Corrigan brews up a potent mix of sex, violence, government indifference, survivalism, and something of the old lovelorn blues of a woman (FBI agent, Mary Goldstein) caught between two very different men, in a country that uses her for her sexuality, yet rejects her full potential as a person…*Byron* is the sort of book Georgia O' Keefe might have written, had the steely-eyed modernist turned her mind to writing Tony Hillerman and Thomas Pynchon inspired suspense novels. It's quite a book." Kevin Killian.

A Year and a Day: "Michael Corrigan's is a poignant, honest and exquisitely written journal of the year following the sudden death of his wife, Karen. It is unique to read this kind of intimate sharing of a man's grief. Because it is unique, I believe it will make a great difference to others who are in mourning." Judy Tatelbaum, author of *The Courage to Grieve* and *You Don't Have to Suffer*.

Brewer's Odyssey: In Michael Corrigan's complex psychological thriller, *Brewer's Odyssey*, his hero is Thomas Brewer, a writer of horror fiction and gifted with a dubious power: prescient dreams. Unfortunately, a future tragedy that will engulf him lies ahead unseen. Despite a dark theme, *Brewer's Odyssey* is rich with a corrosive humor. The style is clear, even lyrical, at times, and the many haunting story lines of Brewer's "Odyssey" will connect on the Aran island of Inishmore where magic can happen. (T.P.)

These Precious Hours: Audiobook read by Alex Hyde-White "Michael Corrigan has created a moving story collection about loss, grief, and recovery. Some of the stories are subtly connected. Narrator Alex Hyde-White changes locale, accent, and personality in an instant as he moves from an Idaho Shoshone reservation invaded by Mexican gangs to a Gettysburg battlefield where a relative who is a Civil War hero rests. The strongest two stories are 'The Wife and the Monk,' in which Leah Brown comes to realize that she might have a better life with a quiet and gentle monk than with her passionate and big-mouthed husband. The other, 'If I Had a Hammer,' depicts a professor who is driven to extreme behavior in the face of the changes and challenges currently taking place in academia." S.G.B. © AudioFile 2013, Portland, Maine [Published: AUGUST 2013]

"I just finished reading *These Precious Hours*, a great book by an underappreciated author, Michael Corrigan. Corrigan has the gift of the great Irish storytellers. I've read a couple of Corrigan's stories before, but most were new to me. I had different favorites along the way, but the last story, "Return of the Exiles," was perfect. The ghost of Corrigan's late wife haunts every page, along with a trio of witches, and a few other spectres here and there." Patricia Parker

"It's a beautiful book, something you should really be proud of." Gerald Nicosia.

Note: Some of these stories have appeared in online publications. "Voices Echo" appeared in *Tertulia Magazine*. "These Precious Hours" in a different form appeared in *The Irish American Post*. "Paraguay Wedding" and "Studebaker Falls" were published by *New Works Review*. *The Scream Online* serialized *These Precious Hours*.

Cover photo of Coole Lake by the author.
Author photo by Patty Healy.

Stories

"More frailer than the flowers
These precious hours
That keep us so tightly bound."

Bob Dylan, after Henry Timrod, Confederate poet

These Precious Hours

Scene One

THE therapist's office always gave Declan Mulligan a sense of comfort, an oasis from outside tensions. She regarded him intently before speaking.

"Are you sure you can travel alone?"

"I think so," he said, looking at her pleasant face. "I have to find out. I know I may see a ghost on every corner of Galway."

"Maybe seeing Kate's ghost won't be so bad," she said, writing in her notebook.

"I would welcome her ghost."

"See you in a month," the therapist said.

A week later, Declan Mulligan walked from the small Shannon airport to the stop marked Bus Eireann. He felt the familiar wet cold of Irish weather and when the bus arrived, he pulled up the bin door to place his suitcase. An older woman, bent over from osteoporosis, struggled with her bags. Declan helped her. When he pulled down the bin, his hand came away black.

"Jesus," he said. "Clean the bus, why don't you?"

Another traveler handed him a wet rag to clean his hand. The seated bus driver was a thick-set man with a dark curling mustache.

"Some old people out there need help with their bags," Declan said.

"I don't touch luggage," the driver told him in a lilting Irish accent. "You know what I mean?" He grinned.

As Declan got on the bus, another passenger remarked: "Maybe he would for a fiver, or ten Euros."

The bus started for Galway. The sky was overcast, and Declan watched the small towns and the green countryside as they passed. He thought of Kate and imagined her looking out the window at the wet green meadows and stone walls enclosing the pastures full of cattle and — more often — sheep.

"First time in Ireland?"

It was an American voice. Declan observed a young but balding man with a blandly handsome face sitting next to him. He returned the stranger's genuine smile.

"Second time. I came here four years ago with my wife."

The man nodded. He didn't ask why Declan was traveling alone and Declan didn't reveal he was a widower.

"You?"

"I've been here many times," the man said. "I have a sister in Galway who married an Irishman."

"How does she like living in Ireland?"

"She likes it. It gives me a chance to visit Galway," the American said.

"Lovely city."

"Don't drink the water," he cautioned. "There's a parasite they haven't killed, yet."

"No one told me that," Declan said. "Of course, who drinks water in Ireland? They drink Guinness."

"Don't brush your teeth with the tap water, either. Use bottled water."

"I'll remember that."

"What brings you here? Holiday?"

"Thought I'd see some Yeats country."

"You're an English teacher?"

"I have taught English, yes," Declan said.

The bus stopped many times along the way, and Declan wondered if the bus schedule matched the airline schedules. They rode on in silence. Declan was eager to see his favorite Irish city but also felt anxious knowing he'd be alone. He remembered the first time he and Kate took a train from Dublin and then a bus when they were bumped from the train, finally arriving at the Galway station. They walked through the unfamiliar streets toward the docks, pulling their luggage until they saw their hotel, the Jurys Inn. They watched the River Corrib flowing into the distant bay, and walked the narrow lanes with shops, sidewalk pubs, and street performers. When they left Galway for their return to Dublin and the airport, they took a taxi back to the station.

The station looked unchanged when Declan got off and nodded good-bye to the American. Some younger passengers walked toward a youth hostel at the bottom of the street. The pearl-colored sky threatened to open up and rain any moment. Declan walked, pulling his suitcase toward the tourist center. Inside were milling travelers, a rack of post cards, and a white-haired man behind the counter who gave him directions. "College Road is right outside. Your B&B is at the top of the street," he said in a mellow voice.

"Thanks."

Declan noticed a booth offering trips to the Aran Islands. He and Kate had taken the ferry to Inishmore, the biggest island, for what Declan later called "their Irish moment," riding in a horse-drawn cart down a narrow road. They heard spoken Irish as the driver, Pat, stopped and conversed with neighbors along the way. Declan's grandparents had lost their native language.

Declan walked outside and up the street toward Adrian's B&B. When he rang the bell, a young man answered and stared at him, mute and unsettling.

"Hello. I'm Declan Mulligan. I have a reservation."

The young man continued staring at him. He seemed puzzled and shouted in another language to someone passing in the hall.

"Maybe you know Adrian? The one I made the reservation with? I'm Mulligan."

"Mulligan?" the man said. A young woman with long dark hair and brown eyes appeared in the doorway. She was smiling.

"Hello," she said. "Fix pipes?"

"No. I'm Mulligan. I have a reservation for a week?"

"Weak, yes," the woman said. She muttered something to the young man who disappeared. They stared at one another. "Pipe broken."

"Do you speak English?"

"Yes," she said. "Much English."

"Check your books." He raised his voice. "Declan Mulligan?"

"Hello," the woman said, extending her hand. "Katrina."

They stood in the doorway. After a moment, Declan asked, "Katrina, could I come in?"

"Yes," Katrina said.

She blocked his entrance.

"Is Adrian here?"

"Adrian gone."

"Gone? Maybe you help?"

"Help? Yes. Of course."

Katrina went to a desk and came back with a wrench. "This help…for hand job?"

"I am a guest," Declan said. "I don't fix pipes. I am guest!"

Katrina saw his suitcase. She smiled again and nodded.

"Of course. Follow me," she said.

He followed Katrina into the kitchen where she opened a large book with many names and Declan saw his.

"See? There I am. One week."

"Yes," Karina said. She smiled. "You pay now."

The young man walked into the kitchen and opened the refrigerator. Declan took out his wallet and displayed a debit card. Katrina shook her head.

"Cash," she said. "Adrian want cash."

"Later," said Declan, raising his voice. "I get cash later."

Katrina nodded. Declan liked her face and expressive eyes.

"This way," she said.

She took him to a room outside the house that faced a small garden. The room was small but suited his needs.

"Adrian come," she said. She gave him the key. "You pay him."

"I will."

Katrina left and Declan examined the small room with its single bed and a mirror facing the bed. He took asthma medication and a toothbrush from a small bag, hung up a shirt and jacket, and placed a photo of him and Kate on a small table. They were kissing in a semi profile shot with the garden lawn behind them, and Declan knew it was an early photo since the roses hadn't appeared, yet. He looked at Kate's face and her sweet half smile as he whispered something, now lost, into her ear. Thinking about his late wife, Declan felt a wave of sadness.

"Jesus, Kate, what am I doing here without you?"

The wall television stared down at him like a dead eye.

"You'll be traveling alone," his therapist had said, writing in her notebook while holding his gaze. *"And you're very vulnerable right now."*

He wondered how Galway would affect him without Kate walking by his side. He also wondered if he would ever meet the mysterious Adrian. Looking out the door, he saw the cold wet day driving overhead, and decided to wear his worn Aran Island sweater and a Levi jacket. As he walked through the dining room of the main house, he saw a heavy-set man with short dark hair and light blue eyes standing in the kitchen.

"Mulligan, is it?"

"Yes. You are Adrian?"

"That's me." They shook hands. "Enjoy your stay."

"I can get cash at an ATM for the rent," Declan said.

"There's one past 'Air Square.' We pay too much interest on credit cards."

Katrina appeared and smiled.

"Katrina works for me," Adrian said.

"We've met."

"We get a lot of service workers from Poland."

Declan waved good-bye and walked down College Road toward Eyre Square where President Kennedy once addressed a crowd. He turned left and headed toward the tourist section of Galway. He walked past a statue of Oscar Wilde seated on a bench, Oscar facing a lesser known Estonian writer named Edward Wilde. Two men were drinking on the bench between the statues and waved to him. Declan liked the festive air of this medieval city, and despite the poor weather, noticed a few guitarists playing on the corners. One older guitarist with a lined face sat on the street; he wore fingerless gloves and a thin dog lay on a mat. A cap was set out for coins. Declan heard Irish music from inside the pubs as he walked toward the Spanish Arch near the river. Coming out the end of a street, Declan suddenly saw the Jurys Inn.

Declan stopped.

He could still see Kate standing on the corner, smoking a cigarette and waiting for a taxi to the station. Staring at the hotel, Declan remembered his wife's final words about Galway.

"I hate to leave this place. We'll never come back."

"Sure we will," Declan had said.

Declan did come back but without Kate.

"One good thing about Ireland," a woman friend named Molly Duvalier had told him. "You can break down and cry and no one will notice the difference with all the rain."

Declan was grateful for the light mist. He decided to walk into the Jurys Inn pub and have a drink. He sat down and ordered a small beer. The pub-restaurant seemed too bright and not as interesting as when he and Kate had lunch there four years before. Drinking his beer, Declan wondered again if traveling alone was a bad idea. He had never traveled alone, even as a young man. Now he was learning to live alone. Kate had died on a brilliant September day and he had been a widower for nearly two years. He had reached that point when friends insisted he needed a woman companion, but Declan saw Kate's warm merry eyes watching him, with perhaps a trace of pity and sadness. He missed her. There was no other way to say it.

On the television screen, Dirk Bogarde was dying on a Venice beach, a sacrifice to the plague and idealistic love. Melting black hair dye ran down the side of his aging face. Briefly, Declan recalled Thomas Mann's *Death in Venice* and an off-hand insult he received once at Walt Disney Studios. Suddenly, the bartender switched to a soccer game. Men were kicking a white ball back and forth on a green field. Outside the pub, it began raining and Declan realized his umbrella was back at the B&B. He sipped the beer slowly, reflecting on the ten years he stayed dry.

When he left, the rain had stopped and it was pleasant to walk toward the distant beach and Galway Bay. Couples passed, holding hands. He found a bench and sat with his eyes closed as the sun appeared and a slight breeze touched his face. He thought about Kate and her love of the same famous bay. Declan imagined dying suddenly, staring at the setting sun. How long would it be before people noticed the grey-haired man slumped on the bench?

Declan got up and walked back among tourists and shoppers, passing the sidewalk cafés, pubs, and shops. He heard a street musician playing a spirited version of Dylan's "Like a Rolling Stone," a favorite song. Passing crowds echoed the chorus: "How does it feel, to be on your own, a complete unknown, no direction home, like a rolling stone?" The guitarist was young with red hair and a beard.

"You do Dylan well," Declan said. "I'm like Pavlov's dogs when it comes to Dylan. I hear his music and start salivating."

"No need to salivate," the young man said. "I *do* love Dylan's songs. I even *met* Dylan."

"I never did," Declan said. He dropped some coins into the singer's guitar case and walked on. He stopped at an ATM and got cash for the week's rent at the B&B. Perhaps coming to Galway was a good idea. If he had to wander alone, this was a beautiful city to wander alone in. It had its own live soundtrack.

Declan stopped at the Forester Bar and Restaurant for lunch. As he ate, a young man wearing slacks, a white shirt and bow tie, introduced himself.

"Patrick," he said. "Proprietor. And you are?"

"Declan Mulligan," Declan said.

"A pleasure. Enjoy your stay."

Patrick rushed off. As Declan finished his lunch he thought about Kate's daughter, Teresa, who might meet him in Galway. They had much to discuss. Over the customer conversation, Declan heard a Dylan song piped into the restaurant and caught some poignant lyrics that brought back memories of Kate: "More frailer than the flowers/These precious hours/That keep us so tightly bound."

If only they had more "precious hours."

Scene Two

DECLAN MULLIGAN often tired of writing biographies for various dating web sites. It seemed absurd to put his life history into a paragraph. He grew up in San Francisco, raised by immigrant Irish Catholic grandparents after his mother left and his father died in the Korean War. He attended a San Francisco university. He chose to demonstrate against the Vietnam War when police converged on students and tear gas drifted across the campus. Declan worked with various theatres, and even authored a book about his great great grandfather, Michael Mulligan, a cavalry officer during the Civil War. Declan felt his connection to and separation from the native Irish of Ireland.

After a failed first marriage, Declan had the predictable habits of a single heterosexual man: many different women, including one-night stands or quick affairs, relationships that lasted one month or two, sometimes even a year. Any quick tryst might involve a strange woman meeting him in a stranger's bedroom, both of them sprawled on jackets and coats left by party guests, a woman he might enjoy and never see again, except for a brief wink over drinks. Occasionally, he tried to remember the memorable ones. Certainly Molly Duvalier, whom he met at an orgy staged for the San Francisco Sex Information Switchboard, was memorable. The party was given on a Sausalito houseboat. Molly could walk naked into a room of nude dancing revelers, her breasts large and Rubenesque, the hair thick and curly, the smile slightly wicked, the voice low with a slightly husky rasp, and ask one question: "Who here is not having a good time?" Declan became one of Molly's good times and he found himself experiencing a world of sexual delights with windows open to let the warm love in. When asked what she was into, Molly's answer was brief: "Everything."

But one day, Molly moved on. Declan moved to Los Angeles to study film.

"There are no seasons in the tropics," a friend once said, "so you hardly notice the passage of time."

Declan didn't live in the tropics but the years seemed to pass without any pattern or drama, yet one afternoon while pitching a film idea to a young female executive at Walt Disney Studios, Declan suddenly found himself outdated, even passé.

"This ill-fated love story you're describing, Mr. Mulligan. It happens in an old folks' home?"

"No. They're young. Why do you ask?"

"Why?"

The pretty female face observed him; she could have been the daughter of a woman he seduced at a party years before and never saw again.

"Well, no offense, but you're not a kid."

"Maybe so," said Declan. "But in the old days, I was a rogue."

He lifted his eyebrows like Groucho Marx. Sitting beneath a poster for *Peter Pan*, the woman regarded him impassively. "A rogue?"

"Yeah. Of course, I'm older, now. I used to make love all night. Now it takes me all night to make love."

He waited for a laugh or even a smile. The pitch session had turned deadly, and like a major scene in a film, it was a turning point. Suddenly, the fast life in Los Angeles with parties and Malibu beaches full of young, well-oiled bodies against a backdrop of jagged palms seemed even more illusory.

"I think we'll pass on your story," the woman said. "It feels a bit dated."

"Dated? No love story is dated."

"If we decide to do a remake of *Death in Venice* about dying, love-sick old men, we'll need a veteran *seasoned* writer — like you."

"I'm glad you at least know Mann's novel," Declan said. "Most of you younger story editors grew up on television, not the classic films."

For the first time, the woman smiled, and then asked quietly, "Who sent you to Disney?"

"Mr. Bayard Storey liked my pitch over the phone and read a spec script."

She glanced out the window at a row of Disney offices. "Mr. Storey is no longer with us. Oh, Mr. Mulligan, regarding feature films, you can pitch your ideas over the phone. There's no need to come to the office."

"Why not? I'm too old or too ugly?"

"No, you look fine. We *do* have a younger demographic in mind, of course. I just feel there's no need for you to come all the way down to our office, Mr. Mulligan."

Declan leaned forward. "What's your name, again?"

"Ms. Yumkiss."

"Well kiss my ass, Yumkiss. I ain't working for the Mouse."

When he left the small office, Declan saw a film-star handsome young man waiting to go in. They exchanged glances and a nod. Declan walked out onto the lot, knowing he had drifted outside the commercial mainstream. Despite a familiar routine, Declan still considered his life varied and interesting, though producers and agents seemed more and more dismissive. A friendly agent summed it up: "Hollywood worships youth."

Then word came to him that an Idaho friend was drinking himself to death. One afternoon during spring break, a waitress who also worked for an airline booked a reservation and Declan traveled on a rescue mission. Had he not suffered from the same plague, alcoholism? It was Easter weekend and inside the bar, Tim, facing liver disease, drank seven-up with vodka and told loud stories in a big voice while an attractive woman with blonde hair, blue eyes and a warm smile sat at the table, amused until she realized their mutual friend had spiked his soft drink. Her name was Kate. She nodded to Declan as he joined them at the table, discussing his own drying out and drinking ginger ale by the gallon to cut the withdrawal.

"Tim, it's a problem you have to confront."

"I don't have a problem with alcohol," Tim said. "I can get it any time I want."

Declan watched Kate, thin, well dressed and professional. She lit a cigarette and then offered one to Tim who took it. They smoked. Then Kate reached out and pressed her hand into Tim's. His skin had a yellow tinge.

"Tim? You're too thin. When's the last time you had a medical check-up?"

"Don't have time for doctors, Kate. What do they know?"

Kate looked away from Tim's bulging abdomen. Her eyes were moist. "They know a lot."

Declan had a soft drink and they finally talked about the past, sharing old stories. Tim had been a promising writer and he and Declan shared many a glass and even a few women when Declan briefly taught at the local university. They had indeed heard the chimes at midnight. When Declan walked Kate to her car, she stopped and looked at him, studying his face.

"Listen, Declan, I am divorced, something I never thought would happen, I have two kids, Teresa in college, and John graduating from high school, and though I have a fairly good job, I would love to do something else. You live in Los Angeles, not my favorite city."

"Nor mine. I have no kids. I'm divorced and though a bit old for Hollywood, I'm writing the great American screenplay."

"I admire artists, and I realize you've had a life of wild variety. I'm just an old-fashioned girl. I attend the Lutheran church regularly. I am not a political radical, I won't attend protest meetings or burn flags, and I love reciting the Pledge of Allegiance. I can even sing the Star Spangled Banner, if off-key."

"I can sing a little blues and some Dylan," Declan said.

"I prefer Sinatra, but I can listen to Dylan again." Kate hesitated for a moment. "I also have only one kidney. I lost it when I was thirteen. I also have high blood pressure and have to monitor it constantly."

"I see."

"Do you? High blood pressure can cause strokes."

"I know. And you smoke."

"Yes, I smoke…it's a filthy habit and I won't stop."

Declan observed her face in the soft spring light. He liked her symmetrical features and soft but resonant voice.

"Do you tell everyone about your one kidney?"

"Not usually. Just you."

"I'm impressed. Why me?"

Kate didn't answer but asked a question, watching his eyes. "What are we going to do?"

"About Tim? He has to give it up on his own as I did."

"No—what are we going to do about us?"

Declan felt a sudden thrill run through him.

"I don't know. I've never fallen in love at first sight, before."

"I never have, either."

They spent that Easter weekend talking about life, love, death, and redemption, though Kate attended Good Friday services alone. They soaked in the nearby hot springs and said nothing over the steaming water. They woke up together on Easter Sunday, and showering together, he thought she was beautiful. They were married at the Hemingway Memorial in Sun Valley with a running brook and cottonwoods and guests watching from a green hill. Kate's children were polite but distant. They traveled, including a trip to Ireland and Galway City. They witnessed her son's marriage in Mexico. They lived in San Francisco and Los Angeles while Declan continued teaching and writing unsold screenplays and Kate wrote proposals for stealth bombers. He found himself living a more structured life with a beautiful woman, and he liked it.

Then, after race riots, gang shoot-outs, and jobs suddenly ending, they decided to leave California for Idaho. On their last night in Los Angeles, something memorable happened. They dined at a Mexican restaurant named Casablanca after the celebrated film. As they left, Kate's warm connection to the staff over the years became apparent as Latino servers, bosses and kitchen help lined up to murmur, *"Adios"* and *"Vaya con Dios, Señora."* Hearing the murmured Spanish farewell brought tears to Declan's eyes. Humphrey Bogart in a trench coat watched from behind a glass cage.

Another quieter life began in Idaho with Declan teaching English and Irish writers at the local university while Kate ran a loan program for small businesses, including the Bannock-Shoshone tribe. As Kate spread the philosophy of economic independence, Declan considered writing a novel that might serve American literature. Then one bright September morning, Kate collapsed at work and was rushed to the hospital with a brain aneurysm. He was staring at Kate on the bed, a tube coming out of her mouth, color still in her cheeks. The doctor kept his eyes averted as he explained what happens to the brain with a subarachnoid hemorrhage; Declan heard the doctor's voice but not the words.

At some point, a neurologist told him what he already knew. He remembered being curled up on a chair in the visitors' room. Their life together was suddenly over as quickly as it began. There were no good-byes, no death-bed promises, no final declarations of love. It was as though a bright sunny day had turned to night and a black wind was blowing into Declan's soul, poisoning his inner being with hopelessness and despair. After 15 years, Kate was gone. The love of his life and Declan's major reason to exist had disappeared. Declan was now an older single man—a widower.

He began to cry even as the hospital assistant quietly informed him that the organ harvest team was on the way. Declan wanted to die.

It was the beginning of an understanding of a profound isolation.

Scene Three

THE second summer after Kate's death, Declan revisited Galway, a test of freedom alone in a foreign country. As he walked to the B&B, he stopped to watch a puppeteer work the crowd, the large jester-looking puppet dancing to its own tune, then rushing into the crowd to hump the legs of startled women. For the first time in months, Declan laughed. He looked at a nearby pub where a few drinkers sat outside watching the passing tourists and the puppeteer. The sign over the pub read what looked like "Tis Coili," but Declan knew it was in Irish and written Irish wasn't always phonetic.

He remembered Tim who died of cirrhosis two years after his attempted intervention, and then Declan entered the pub and ordered a short beer. A Celtic group was setting up. He listened to their lively Irish music for an hour, and when he came out, the puppeteer was working another part of the street. Declan noticed the young, red-haired guitarist sitting at a sidewalk table.

"What's this place called? Tis Coili?"

"The T.I.S. is actually T.I.G and is pronounced 'Chee' for house. This pub is 'Chee Coili' or the 'House of Coili.' You don't know your Irish?"

"No," Declan said. "Why don't they just spell it C.H.E.E.?"

"Then it wouldn't be Irish."

Declan saw the guitar case. "You're taking a break?"

"I gave my spot to Emily."

The young man pushed back his bowler hat and lifted a pint in salute. "And you are?"

"Declan Mulligan, American Irish."

"I gathered that. Jamie McDonagh, native Irish. And here comes JP, the great puppeteer."

Wearing a black cap, dark glasses, tee-shirt and fatigues, JP came up to the table, put his large puppet into a black suitcase and sat down.

"I need a cider," he said in an American accent.

"This is Declan Mulligan, another Yank," Jamie said.

JP tipped his cap as Declan sat down.

"Apple cider?"

"Yes, but fortified with alcohol."

"Where are you from?"

JP looked at him. "Are you a journalist?"

"No, but I *am* a writer. Thought I'd do a little Yeats tour."

"I'm not a writer," JP said. "But I *am* from Florida."

"You visit Florida often?"

"No. I cut all ties." JP took out a cigarette. "We're buskers. We travel to different countries, cities — we perform on the streets." He lit the cigarette. "Yeats, eh?"

"You need to visit Sligo for Yeats," Jamie said. "It's a quiet town. Galway is a lively town full of blow-ins. All of us are from somewhere else."

"So one doesn't have to be Irish to play Galway streets?"

"We have all nationalities here. Emily's an American."

Others came up to the table, and it became obvious to Declan that JP and Jamie were local celebrities.

"Watch what you say," JP said. "This man here is a journalist."

Declan bowed to the gathering. Jamie stood up.

"We are all a rootless generation," he said.

"I'm a bit rootless myself," said Declan.

"I'm Steve," a large man said in a nasal English accent. He had a round bullet head with thinning hair on top and his eyes bulged slightly. "I'm a builder. This here is Trisha, my fiancé."

Trisha, a pretty woman with dark hair, smiled at Declan. "Pleased to meet you."

Steve touched her breasts. "My puppies," he said, grinning.

"What do you do, Trisha?" Declan asked.

"Right now, nothing. I was a secretary, but my boss, an English Muslim, thought he was a bloody king. I got tired of that. I'm not even a royalist," she added, laughing.

"Nor am I," said Declan. "We dumped our king in 1776."

"I knew Steve since early school days. We met again, and bought a place in Galway. Lovely city, wouldn't you say?"

"Beautiful," Declan said.

"Our English pound goes farther than the euro," Steve said. "I'll get us a round." He looked at Declan's glass. "You need a pint," he said. "Why are you drinking those little beers?"

"You don't want to see me drunk," said Declan.

When Steve returned, he carried pints and shots of whiskey. The patrons drank and Declan nursed his small beer as more rounds were bought. Occasionally, JP grinned at Declan, the dark glasses hiding his eyes.

"Those Muslims should learn what it means to be English and integrate," Trisha argued. "He expected *me*, a white English woman from Leeds, to wear a veil."

Declan was about to reply when Steve leaned close.

"What do you do, again?"

"I write and teach."

"Teach what?"

"English and Speech communications," said Declan.

"I never was good at public speaking," said Steve. "I'm a builder. I build things."

Steve gulped a shot and then lifted up his pint to drink. Declan swallowed his beer and stood up. "I need to get some food," he told them.

"Wait! You should get a round," Steve bellowed.

"A what?"

"That's all right, I don't speak English either," said JP.

"We need another round," insisted Steve, looking at Declan.

"Maybe later."

"We'll be still here when you come back," said JP.

Declan walked up the street through the crowds that were growing larger. Declan passed more buskers on the way to Eyre Square and the Forester restaurant. After a pleasant meal, he walked back toward the medieval district as the light faded. The group still sat outside the Tig Coili, drinking and very drunk. JP waved to him.

"Hey journalist, we're going to Sheridan's Wine bar after this place closes."

"Then the Roisin Dubh," Jamie said, his eyes red.

"What's a 'Roosen Dove'?" said Declan. "A Russian bird?"

"It means, 'Black Rose.'" Jamie shot him a glance. "The black rose is symbolic of Irish resistance and romantic love. You need to learn some Irish."

There was a Celtic fiddle group playing at Sheridan's Wine Bar. Declan felt a familiar loneliness though surrounded by people. Steve and Trisha drank in a corner of the crowded bar until Trisha danced to the rapid music and shook her "puppies" at the cheering crowd. Jamie and JP stayed together, drinking and talking. It was hard to hear over the loud music and bar noise. Three older women began dancing an Irish jig, hands frozen at the sides, legs kicking. A curly-haired buxom woman who reminded Declan of Molly stood in another corner drinking a pint of Guinness. At one point, their eyes met.

Declan finally stepped outside. He glanced at a big ship moored in the docks. It had been a long time since he'd stayed up this late drinking in crowded bars. Perhaps he would skip the Roisin Dubh. He thought of Kate who would be having a cigarette and watching the ships on the water.

"Jesus, Kate, where are you?"

Suddenly, the curly-haired woman stood beside him. She held a cigarette.

"There's a poetry reading tomorrow," she said. "At BK's wine bar."

"Excuse me?"

"Bring some original poems."

"I'm not a poet," Declan said.

"No? You have that dark poet look," the woman said.

"I only write novels about the human condition."

Declan was about to tell her his name when she asked, "Do you like Yeats?"

"Of course. Who doesn't?"

"The poets at BK's. He's too classical for them."

"Actually, Yeats is one reason I'm here."

"I thought so."

He looked at her face, at the thick dark curly hair and the wide sensuous mouth, and guessed her age in the mid thirties.

"Coole Park is close, isn't it?"

"It is," she said. "Take the bus to Gort. Then take a cab since it's a good walk to the park."

"Maybe you could drive me," Declan said, feeling suddenly bold.

The woman smiled at him, but didn't answer. A young man with short hair appeared and without acknowledging Declan, lighted her cigarette. Together, they walked off, and for a moment, Declan felt invisible.

The music continued inside. Declan strolled along the waterfront, recalling his earlier walk with Kate from the station to the Jurys Inn. The ships moored at the docks were large and appeared empty. No muggers lurked in the alleys. He stopped at an internet cafe and heard people calling long distance, talking loudly in foreign languages. When he checked his e-mail, Teresa wrote that she was taking a Dublin train to Galway at the end of the week. They would spend time together after all.

Scene Four

IN the morning, Declan took a bus to Gort. From there, he walked two miles along the highway toward Coole Park, enjoying the beautiful green countryside. He wanted to see Coole Lake that inspired the poem, "The Wild Swans of Coole." Declan imagined the swans flying overhead in noisy profusion. On the highway, Declan saw the Coole Park sign and turned down a narrow road lined with pastures. Gradually, the paved road became a shaded forest path.

Declan crossed a parking lot and found the tourist center. After looking at videos and hearing a history of Lady Gregory's house, no longer standing, he found the "autograph tree" and peered at the faint initials of famous Irish writers who had gathered here in another century: W.B.Yeats, John M. Synge, and George Bernard Shaw. Though numbered, they were hard to read. Then he found the wooded path leading to Coole Lake. He followed the dirt road until he saw the lake through the trees, the water low, boulders exposed, a single swan in the distance. The trees were "in their autumn beauty" when Yeats beheld the wild swans "scatter wheeling in great broken rings." Declan stared at the famous body of water and recalled a stanza:

> Unwearied still, lover by lover,
> They paddle in the cold,
> Companionable streams or climb the air;
> Their hearts have not grown old;
> Passion or conquest, wander where they will,
> Attend upon them still.

That's what I need, he thought: *passion and conquest*. Even now, the voice of his therapist echoed in his mind: *"Will this be some kind of a writer's pilgrimage…or a way to connect with Kate?"*

Declan couldn't answer at the time. Perhaps it was both.

He meditated on the lake and where the swans had flown. An old man in boots, rain-coat and cap, walked along the water's edge. He wore rimless spectacles and suddenly turned towards Declan, laughing briefly. Slightly disturbed, Declan watched the old man continue down the rocky shore. Then he took his time walking back along the path, enjoying the dark forest and dappled meadows. He could feel Kate by his side, stopping to examine each tree, the beeches, sycamores and others he didn't recognize in the light-split gloom. He imagined them having lunch at the park restaurant and taking an expensive taxi to Gort. It would be convenient and give Kate a chance to talk to an Irish cabbie.

But he was alone.

Many families were enjoying the park. After some apple pie at the small restaurant, Declan walked back to the highway and continued toward Gort, facing the traffic which was on the left. What would he ask had he met the ghost of Yeats back there in the forest shadows? Would he write something that would last a century? When would young writers scoff at Declan Mulligan for being "too classical"? It was an amusing thought. The bus to Galway arrived and Declan rested, his eyes closed, thinking of wild swans, not falcons, flying in a widening gyre.

When he got to Galway in the late afternoon, he stopped at the Tig Coili. JP and the English couple sat outside, drinking and smoking.

"Sit down. Have a drink," JP said. "Do you good."

Declan sat down. "Where's Jamie?"

"He went to Dublin to try his luck on Grattan Street."

"Up late, last night?"

"Until four in the morning," JP said. "I took today off."

Steve was asleep. Trisha examined Declan, as though she were analyzing him.

"How are you?" Declan asked.

"I'm trying to figure you out."

"Really?"

"You seem so…so tight."

"Tight as in cheap?"

"Maybe — but I meant, tight as in dark."

"All writers are dark," JP said. "Hemingway killed himself."

Trisha leaned forward, her eyes focused and hard.

"What do you write?"

"I'm working on an expose of expatriate English people hiding in Ireland."

"You're joking, right? Why are you here?"

"Why are *you* here?"

"We *moved* here, but we are also on holiday."

"So am I."

"And?"

"I came alone."

"And?"

"It was a bit of an experiment."

"And?"

"I am doing well."

Trisha stared at him. "After what?"

Declan lowered his voice. "I got hurt in the war," he said.

JP laughed.

Trisha shook her head. "You're not telling me something," she said. She guzzled her pint. Then she wiped her lips and said, "Something is missing."

Declan was about to stand up and declaim that he was a widower and a dark wind had blown through him, sucking out all life, that this voyage was a journey to find a new reason to exist, and why didn't they all just go fuck themselves, but then a young busker with a guitar sat down at the table. He was cursing.

"Damn, I hate it."

JP sat up. "Hate what, Richard?"

"When drunk hecklers tell me to get a job. I yell back, 'Get a life.'"

Trisha sat back, watching Declan. Then they heard more cursing. Two policemen struggled with a drunk, scruffy-looking young man. Vomit soiled his tee-shirt.

"That's the earbasher there," said Richard. "What never-never land is he from?"

The drunk struggled as the officers wrestled him to the ground.

"I've never seen this kind of violence in Galway," said JP. "Never."

Steve suddenly stirred and opened his eyes. He looked at Declan.

"Jesus Christ, you're like a bloody ghost. Everywhere I look, I see you."

"Funny, I was just about to disappear."

Declan waved good-bye. Trisha waved back.

"You can stay here. You're with your mates," said JP.

"Maybe later."

"We need a round," Steve said.

"Sure." Declan walked into the pub and approached the bartender.

"You know JP's table?"

"I can hear them from inside."

"Here's 50 Euros. Use it to buy the next round."

"I will," the bartender said.

Declan stepped out the back of the pub. He saw Saint Nicholas Church and wondered briefly if Christopher Columbus had, in fact, prayed there before plundering the new world. Then he walked toward his B&B. At the top of Shop Street, a familiar red-faced drunk sat between the two bronze Wildes.

"I'm a bit wild, meself," the drunk said, waving a bottle at Declan. At one time, Declan might have joined the drunk for afternoons and late evenings of drinking and philosophizing about the world's tragedies.

Lying on the bed in his cramped room, Declan felt a powerful fatigue, even as the black wind of past longing and regret sank into to him. He looked out the window at the small garden. The sun was still bright. Declan pulled the curtain and closed his eyes. Kate had not visited his dreams in over a year. Perhaps this afternoon would mark a beginning. He slept. When he woke up, it was still light outside. Kate had not appeared.

I need to be with other writers, he thought. *Poets, even bad ones.*

He got up and walked toward the commercial district. The drunk was still there, joined by another drunk, sitting between the two statues.

"What state are you from?" the first drunk asked.

"California and Idaho," Declan said.

"Well—which one is it?" asked the second drunk.

They laughed, each holding a can of ale. Declan walked on. When he passed the Tig Coili, the same people sat around the same table playing a familiar game. A coin was balanced on an upright cigarette on a coaster covering a pint glass. The object of the game was to get the coin into the glass without touching it. One of the men leaned down and blew on the coaster from below; the coin shot into the air, then fell into the glass. Everyone cheered.

Declan walked on to BK's wine bar located across from the new museum. They had a poetry reading going with Irish poets reciting loudly from the lighted stage. A handsome middle-aged man with silver hair introduced the poets. Patrons sat at tables with pints and glowing candles. One poet growled and bit his arm. Another poet recited an angry poem about a "fooking freeloader named Jack." An American woman recited a poem about her lover who could "fuck but not love." Later that night as the readings ended, Declan discovered the mysterious woman from Sheridan's sitting near him.

"I don't know about the literary value of these Irish poets, but they *are* entertaining. We usually read poetry in America, we don't recite. What's with that barking poet who gnawed his hand?"

"He's British."

"I liked the woman who wrote about her sexual frustrations. She just needs a tune-up."

"And maybe you got just the right tool?"

"Please…she *is* a bit young."

"And you care? Or is it fear of rejection?"

"Neither. I'm a gentleman."

Her guttural laugh sounded like a catarrhal cough. Declan looked at the large blue eyes, observant, inquisitive. "What's your name?"

"Maeve."

"Declan."

She sipped her red wine. "Can I buy you one?"

"A beer," said Declan. "Are you married?"

"Never married."

"Children?"

"No."

"Almost everyone gets married at least once and has at least one kid."

"I'm not everyone," Maeve said. "Why didn't you read?"

"I have noting prepared."

"This is Ireland, a land of poets. Make something up."

"I'm not that confident."

They drank and talked until closing time.

"I have had a few one-night stands, but not tonight," Maeve finally said. "You understand?"

Declan looked again at the sensuous lips, the wide face, the handsome features, the eyes that seemed amused at his expense. "Sure, I understand."

"Do you? There's something dark inside you."

"An English woman suggested that. Do I have a sign, 'Beware, dark existentialist on the prowl'?"

"Maybe."

"Actually, I *am* carrying a burden."

"Tell me later."

"When?"

"We'll meet again."

"Where?"

Maeve shrugged. "How many pubs are there in Galway? I'll be in one of them. I like Knockins pub."

Declan noticed a guitar on the stage. Some patrons were leaving, but a few of the poets were still in the pub, drinking and discussing slam poetry.

"Dylan had a birthday recently. I play a little guitar, myself."

"Play a song, then."

Declan walked to the small stage and picked up the guitar. It was in tune. He stepped to the microphone.

"Apologies to the owner of the guitar but I thought I would sing a song in honor of America's greatest song writer who just had a birthday."

The writers cheered. Declan played "It's All Over Now, Baby Blue" with a dropped C tuning to create a throbbing bass. It felt good to play and sing, again. He felt the lines, "Leave your stepping stones behind, there's something that calls to you/ Forget the dead you're left, they will not follow you." He finished the song and the small audience clapped. Maeve had left.

"Next time, bring a few poems," the master of ceremonies said.

"I will."

"You might donate to the readings."

Declan gave the man five Euros and finished his beer. Then he walked outside and stood by the Spanish Arch, looking at the flowing River Corrib. At one end, many swans floated on the dark water. There was a breeze, and he could smell the distant bay. Declan looked up at the glowing sign for Jurys Inn. He remembered lying next to Kate in their hotel room above the river and hearing the flowing waters at night. It had been a happy time. He looked away from the Inn and down the river.

For just a moment, he wanted Kate's ghost to come walking toward him. He would accept a ghost. He would accept any apparition, even if he didn't believe in the afterlife or ghosts. She would appear and there would be a wind between them and she would smile her radiant smile.

The Galway streets were empty when he walked home. It gave him a strange peace to walk past closed pubs and the bronze Oscar Wilde with no drunk waving at pedestrians. He might find a few people in sleeping bags on Eyre Square's lawn. Then he saw three women wearing hoods and capes walking toward him. As they came closer in the slight mist, he saw the lead woman had painted her face and bare breasts red and green. She stared at him, chanting: "We are the three goddesses of Galway, and those who have polluted our water will die!"

"Die," the other two women echoed.

They skipped by Declan and down the street toward the bay. Declan decided to have one last beer at a pub that played the old Irish songs about lost battles and martyred Irish heroes.

Scene Five

DECLAN left Galway for Yeats country and Sligo Town. He walked from the Sligo bus station through the quaint city to the river, passing a statue of Yeats before a bank. Something about the statue disturbed him; there was the familiar patrician face, the spectacles, one hand uplifted on a body that looked like a cross between an insect with manta-like cape and a stork on thin legs. Continuing on, Declan found his B&B at the top of a hill. It had an Irish name sounding like "cruzkeen" that meant "full jug." Liam, the proprietor, was polite and quickly stated the rules.

"There's no breakfast served after 10:00 AM," he warned. "Make sure you have your key since I don't answer the door after 10:00 PM."

"Okay," said Declan, always annoyed at a disapproving tone.

Once again, he would sleep in a cramped room, though this time, Declan shared a hall bathroom. He put up his garden shot of himself and Kate. Then he called an Irish woman he had met online named Josie who had agreed to show him around Sligo. Josie picked him up and drove him through heavy traffic to Yeats's grave. Declan read the familiar epitaph, and snapped a photo of the headstone while ravens cawed overhead.

"So this is where the greatest English speaking poet of the 20th century lies for eternity?"

"That's himself. I used to read his 'Stolen Child' poem to my kids," Josie said. She was a small woman with dark but brittle-looking hair. "It's set at Glencar Falls."

They drove past the flat Ben Bulben Mountain to Glencar Falls which looked like a special effect, the falling water full of light like a painting of a gossamer waterfall. The surrounding woods had a mystical ambiance. It seemed an appropriate setting for Yeats's poem about fairies stealing a child from the "weeping world."

Josie drove him to a small house to meet her mother, daughter and grandchild. Declan found himself shooting photos of four generations of women in a rural Irish scene. The seated white-haired woman smoked a cigarette and peered at Declan.

"Do I know you?"

"I'm visiting."

"Oh. Having a good visit?"

"Yes."

"Want a smoke?"

"No thanks," Declan said. "I might get lung cancer."

The elderly woman laughed. "I'm ninety-six," she said.

Josie joined her mother with a cigarette. Megan, her granddaughter, ran into another room. Outside the window lay the wet valleys of Sligo County, with its herds of loose sheep grazing on green hills.

"You've come during a bank holiday so I'll be busy with my family," Josie said. "I can't spend more time with ya."

"That's okay," Declan said. "If I need to go somewhere, I can rent a car. You've been very helpful and friendly."

"We live in the country," Josie said. "We are always friendly."

"The city folks aren't friendly?"

"You're an outsider," Josie said. "A blow in."

Declan noticed the elderly woman staring at him over her cigarette. She had many wrinkles in her face but her eyes were blue and clear.

"By God, are you John?"

"No, no," said Josie. "That's Declan. John is dead."

The old woman nodded to herself. "Oh yes…dead."

"Killed one night riding on his motorbike."

"Oh yes," Josie's mother said. "I remember. He was English."

Josie took Declan on a ride around the country. The roads were narrow and cut through green meadows encircled by rock walls. He had never seen so much green: hills, fields, and distant low mountains. The light was soft and misty.

"Who was John?"

"My late husband."

"I'm sorry to hear that."

"It was four years ago. He may have had a drop taken."

"Do you miss him?"

"Oh sure, but I have a daughter, a granddaughter, and mum to care for."

"No other man in your life?"

"God no," said Josie. "It gets better with time." They took a turn, passing a man on a tractor. "You'll find peace eventually."

"I hope so," said Declan.

Josie drove him back to the B&B.

 "I'll try and call you before you leave," Josie said.

Declan had dinner at a local pub and tried to make conversation, but the waitress brought him his food without comment. Customers watched a horse race on television. He sat reading Yeats's collected poetry, but no one noticed. Later that night, he stood in a packed pub and listened to recorded music. At the B&B, he studied the photo of himself and Kate, wishing he could talk to her. He made entries in his travel journal. Then he went to sleep.

The next day, Declan walked around the town with its river and visited the Yeats center. He saw the library and walked through a pedestrian area, but no buskers sang on the corners. That evening, the streets emptied early. He found another pub and watched the drinking patrons until a group of young women wearing pink bunny ears entered. They were shouting and dancing to the recorded music and demanding drinks. A young man at the bar picked up one of the women and hugged her. The others cheered. Then the woman, wearing rabbit ears and a tiara, waved a small pink object which Declan recognized as a rubber penis and testicles.

"What's going on?" Declan asked.

A man leaning against the wall laughed and said, "It's a hen party."

"And what is that?"

"That girl is getting married, soon, so she goes out with her girlfriends to have a wild time. You can kiss the bride-to-be. Maybe even hump her, Yank."

The man's friends shared his laugh.

"Don't listen to him," another man said. "He's just taking a piss."

Declan retreated to another corner and ordered a beer. Moments later, a woman tapped him on the shoulder.

"You're the tallest in the room," she shouted. "You get to run the gauntlet."

"And what's that?"

"Run through us hens." She touched the inside of his thigh. "Don't be afraid."

Declan looked at the intoxicated young women lined up, waiting for a man to run between them. At the end of the line, the bride-to-be kissed her rubber toy and drank a shot. She motioned to the men in the pub, winking and smiling. The line of rabbit-eared girls looked at Declan, urging him to enter the line. One of them fluttered her tongue.

"I better pass," he said. "I'm in therapy."

"Give it a try," the first man said. "You might get a feel."

"Where's the husband-to-be?"

"At an all men's party getting drunk…or laid."

The girls shouted over the music and laughing customers; suddenly, another man bolted through the line, the women grabbing his thighs and buttocks. He got to the end and lifted the chubby bride-to-be, kissing and pressing her against the wall. He made humping motions. The patrons clapped. The girls cheered. Two women grabbed at his belt. Though packed together, they moved to the loud music.

Declan finished his beer and left. He stood outside, breathing rapidly, feeling a meaningless panic. A woman not connected to the hen party came out to have a cigarette.

"You might have enjoyed that gauntlet," she said. "Except their real goal is to get a man's underwear."

"Maybe I should go back in," said Declan. "They can have mine."

The next day, Declan's therapist sent an e mail praising his reluctance to participate in the local customs. "Feeling uncertain, and given your vulnerability, it was the right decision."

"On the other hand, I may have gotten lucky," he wrote back.

Declan contacted Adrian who had a room available, and then informed Liam he was leaving Sligo early.

"If I didn't have someone else to take your room, you'd be liable for it," he said.

"I have seen what I had to see," said Declan.

When the bus pulled into the Galway station, Declan felt as though he were back home. He walked to Adrian's B&B and saw a no vacancy sign. He wasn't surprised when a strange woman answered the door and looked at him puzzled.

"Good afternoon," she said.

"You speak English?"

"Much English," she said.

"I'm Declan Mulligan. I made a reservation online."

"I'm fine," the woman said.

Declan indicated the kitchen. "Book with names—in the kitchen?"

"Kitchen closed. Guests only."

She began to close the door.

"I am a guest."

The woman regarded him. "No," she said. "House full."

"Is Katrina here?"

"Katrina gone," the woman said. "Poland."

"Adrian?"

"At work," she said. "Galway."

Declan pointed to his suitcase. "Internet booking."

The woman suddenly understood.

"Internet?" she asked. "New guest…just arrive?"

"Yes. Just arrive."

He followed her into the kitchen and they looked through the book, finding his name. Declan found himself in a bigger room in the house, with a view of the garden and the distant city. The woman gave him a skeleton key.

"Susan," the woman said. Her hair was thick and blonde.

"Pipes good, Susan?"

"Pipes good, water still no good."

"No need for hand jobs, eh?"

Susan returned his gaze.

"Call the girl from Donegal—Jurys Inn on weekends," she said.

Declan tried to explain the joke but Susan had left.

He walked down to the Forester hotel and bar and ordered their lunch special. Patrick smiled while passing. The short blond man was always moving, always cheerful. "Mr. Mulligan. We've missed you. And where have you been?"

"Sligo Town."

"Sligo Town is it? Quiet."

When Declan finished lunch, he checked his e-mail and saw a familiar name. Declan walked through the square and down Shop Street toward the bay. He passed a few buskers but didn't recognize anyone. Then he saw her walking toward the Jurys Inn. Though she had blonde hair, Teresa didn't resemble her mother in any way, her body heavier, her face lacking make-up, her walk that of a person who had hiked across many countries. They met and embraced.

"So you got in this morning?"

"Finally," Teresa said.

"I had lunch but are you hungry?"

"I could have a nosh."

They walked into McDonagh's Fish and Chips. The place was busy inside; they stood in line to order, and then sat down.

"McDonagh's is famous for their fish and chips," he said.

While Teresa ate lunch, they talked about Teresa's pleasant train ride across Ireland. After a moment, she looked at him carefully.

"The day my mom passed, I heard she was agitated at a meeting. What was that all about? She wasn't feeling well? She was angry?"

"She was angry over cell phones. The company was too cheap to furnish them. Now it's standard practice."

"I happened to get a cell phone the day before it happened. Dad called me."

"When she collapsed, it was over quickly if that's any consolation."

"Tell me what happened."

Declan told her the details, about hearing the news, about seeing Kate at the hospital unconscious but fighting for life, then the emergency team placing a tube down her throat. They took Kate to be x-rayed and Declan waited in the crowded emergency room, the doctor not answering questions, except to say it was "serious." Much later, another doctor was informing him that his wife "had passed." He recalled the doctors and nurses giving him cell phones to call relatives, but his hands were trembling and he didn't know any numbers. On a ventilator, Kate's skin color appeared normal, though she would never speak again.

Declan almost enjoyed telling the story, wanting to bring Kate back, unaware of his tears as he spoke about the arrangements and his grief at seeing Kate for the last time on this earth before cremation, kissing her cold lips, then the subsequent days and nights spent in an empty house waiting for Kate to return, the dark wind blowing through him even when he stood in the garden tending to Kate's beloved roses.

Teresa listened without speaking. It was always hard to read her expressions.

"You had a long plane ride from England to think about it."

"Yes, but I was prepared," she said. "Did you ever ask her to stop smoking?"

"Yes, but she wouldn't hear it." Declan remembered their big arguments over her tobacco addiction. "I understand addiction," he said. "It might have made a difference if she quit smoking but we'll never know."

It was the old "What if?" scenario. What if they had discovered her heart problem? What if she had quit smoking? Would the fatal brain hemorrhage have been delayed, giving them more time? Or was Kate fated to die young?

"We had plans to meet in London," Teresa said. "My expensive apartment's cramped but mom would have liked it."

"You will get half of the house, you know, you and your brother."

"You need it. I'm not into money. People are slaves to money — to buying things."

"Tomorrow, we'll go to your mother's favorite place, the Aran Island of Inishmore. We can meet at the tourist office in the morning."

"Sounds good. I'd like to hear some Irish spoken."

"They speak it there."

Teresa finished her dessert.

"Maybe we could walk around," Teresa said.

They walked to the red-colored Tig Coili. Outside, JP was just finishing his show and Declan saw Jamie at the table. Steve was asleep in front of his pint. Down the street, Declan saw Trisha dancing to the beat of many drummers. She moved her hips and breasts in a sensuous grind. Teresa sipped a beer as Declan motioned to Jamie.

"My stepdaughter, Teresa, wants to hear Irish," he said.

"Do you? Well, say anything and I'll repeat it in Irish."

Teresa spoke some sentences in English that Jamie repeated in Irish. JP picked up his puppet. "Buy us some shots of whiskey, we'll even do a show."

"Sure," said Teresa. "I'd like to see it."

She went inside the bar. Moments later, Teresa emerged with two shots of Irish whiskey. Jamie played guitar while JP's puppet danced, moving its hips from side to side, beckoning to passing tourists until a young woman shrieked as the cap-and-bells puppet advanced on her. Then the puppet stopped and danced and more tourists gathered. Jamie kept strumming, a steady beat. When the show was over, Teresa gave the performers their drinks.

"You want another beer?"

"No," Teresa said. "I need to go."

"I'll walk you back to the B&B," Declan said.

"I can find the way," Teresa insisted.

She waved good-bye and walked down the brick-laid street. Declan stood among the passing crowds. JP and Jamie sat down at the sidewalk table and ordered another pint with shots.

"I had a good day, today," said JP. "My puppet was well received."

He opened the box for his heavy puppet. It lay there like a corpse with the coffin lid open. Suddenly, it was three in the afternoon in a Pocatello mortuary and Declan was staring at Kate's dead face.

"We are all puppets," Declan declared. "We have a few precious hours, and one day, fate cuts the strings."

Declan saluted with his glass. No one commented on his remark. The day was fading to twilight. Trisha sat at the table and shook her fiancé. Steve stirred and sat up, blinking. He saw Declan staring at him. "Jesus," he said. "You again!"

Scene Six

DECLAN bought two tickets to Inishmore the next morning and they boarded a bus to the ferry. Many trucks were still in the Galway pedestrian section, unloading supplies until 11 AM when the trucks had to leave. It would be a pleasant ride to the docks where the Aran Island ferries departed.

The day was unusually warm, and Declan enjoyed the ferry ride to Inishmore. As Teresa sat upstairs looking at the bright bay and foaming wake, Declan remembered sitting downstairs with Kate four years before, and their shared excitement at a new adventure. He was still thinking about Kate when a stocky bearded man with salt-and-pepper hair sat next to him. "Hello. I saw you at Adrian's. I'm Chris."

"Pleased to meet you, Chris."

"I'm from Texas," Chris said.

The Inishmore dock looked the same with a pub, tourist center, restaurant, large hotel, and a wool factory. There was a rocky beach with sand and seaweed. The sea was blue-green with a bright silver corridor from the glare. They saw men in horse-drawn carts and minivans. A heavy-set man approached them as they got off the boat.

"Ten Euros for a tour of the island," he said.

"Sounds good," Declan said.

He and Teresa boarded the van. When it was full, the driver drove up into the hills on a narrow road, driving past a closed pub with roosters and hens sitting on a fence.

"Those roosters are waiting for the pub to open," he said. He had a sharp loud voice. He continued his historical narrative as he drove. "We have one policeman, one priest, one nurse, and one doctor. No one ever gets sick since we drink Guinness."

The van took some sharp turns, with other cars pulling over.

"Today, we'll see an old stone fort that goes back to about 500 BC or more. They weren't Celts. Who knows who they were? Cromwell may have used the same fort to launch his attack on Galway to massacre Irish Catholics."

Chris started talking to the driver. They stopped and walked around an old graveyard with Celtic crosses. Declan felt in a reflective mood; graveyards and headstones held a fascination for him. Teresa read the inscriptions in English and Irish.

"Boy, a lotta stone on this island, wouldn't you say?"

"Yes, Chris, a lot of stone," Declan agreed. "An island of stone."

They drove to the prehistoric fort called Dun Aengus.

"You have to pay a fee and walk to the top," the driver said. "Be careful. Don't fall. The rocks are treacherous."

Declan and Teresa walked up the rocky hill. It was a difficult climb. At the summit stood a concentric stone fortress facing the slope, and Declan wondered what pre Celtic warriors defended what ancient Helen on this cliff. Past the walls, he walked into what looked like an ancient Greek Amphitheatre. Declan walked to the back of the fort and stood on a cliff facing the Atlantic. For just a moment, he had a fantasy. He was Paris and Kate his Helen, and as the invading hordes surged over the remaining wall, the lovers faced the ocean for the last time. There would be a brief glance, a whispered "I love you," and then they would step into space and plunge hundreds of feet to the raging sea.

Declan imagined the orgasmic rush of air as they plummeted to death and freedom. A strong wind blew over the cliff. He was close to the edge.

"Declan!"

He turned around. Chris was facing him.

"Why does the back of the fort face the open ocean?"

"I suspect over the centuries, half the fort fell into the sea. Maybe it was a place for rituals and not a fort. I've heard stories of ancient prehistoric tribes sitting around a fire. What rituals did they enact is what I want to know."

"Let me take a picture of you on the wall. I'll use your camera."

"Okay."

Declan climbed the first level of the stone-block wall and Chris snapped a photo. An island ranger appeared and ordered him down.

"This is an ancient site," she said. "You need to keep off."

"Okay," Declan said. "Sorry."

The resulting photo was striking, Declan standing on wind-polished ancient rock silhouetted by vaporous clouds and the open dim sea.

"Nice shot," Declan said.

Chris peered at the image. "Look at this. There are angel-looking clouds in the photo but not in the sky."

Chris was right. Facing west over the fort's layered rock walls, carefully cut and placed, it was hard to tell the sea from the blue sky.

"Maybe it's a flaw in my camera," Declan said.

"At least you're visible, or I'd think you were a vampire."

Declan studied the photo again. The clouds had a female shape. Chris shot another photo of Declan and Teresa together. When they descended the rock-strewn hill, Teresa struck her leg on a boulder and sat down, holding her knee.

"Are you all right? Need help?"

"I can make it," she said. "I should have been more careful."

Teresa limped back to the van without assistance. Then they stopped at a small restaurant and sweater shop.

"I'll be back in an hour," the driver said.

Chris talked about his past travels in Europe while Declan and Teresa had lunch. He talked about his early retirement and his plans to spend at least a year traveling. He talked about his grown sons back home. He talked about his future itinerary.

"I even got a free place for a month in Amsterdam," he said. He looked at Teresa who had remained silent. "Declan said you know a lot of languages. How many do you speak, anyway?"

"Not that many. A little Rumanian."

Declan was going to list the others but stopped. When Teresa left the table, Chris had a comment. "She's quiet, isn't she?"

"Sometimes. She doesn't brag about her linguistic skills." After a moment, Declan said, "We lost her mother a little over a year and a half ago."

"I'm sorry to hear that," Chris said. "I'm divorced, and it wasn't pretty."

"They usually aren't very pretty," Declan said.

When the van dropped them off, they paid and Declan took Teresa for a walk down a road lined with stone walls. Teresa had bought some tape and wrapped her knee. They could hear passing islanders speaking Irish.

"We took this road in a horse-drawn cart," Declan said. "Your mother loved it. The driver was a guy named Pat. His horse was Jack. He told her all about his life. He was planning to go to the Philippines to find a wife."

"I'm sure Mother loved his stories," Teresa said. She looked at Declan. "This is a great place. Thanks for bringing me here."

Declan felt another wind blowing over him, but this time, it was a warm steady breeze off the bay. "She really loved it here," he said.

"I wear black on my mother's death day," Teresa told him. "In Europe, that's recognized as a sign of mourning."

They had the ferry ride home. Chris stayed on top, shooting photos. In the morning, Teresa would take a train back to Dublin, and the short flight to London and her university. That evening, they had dinner and Teresa told him of a recent affair that had ended. Normally, she didn't discuss her private life. Declan was impressed.

"He was an egotistical jerk," Teresa said. "His sentences often began with 'I can't believe this incompetence.'"

"Was he incompetent?"

"About some things," Teresa said. "I'd rather not elaborate."

They went to the Tig Coili and heard Irish music, packed in with other customers. After a while, it was as though the fiddle and banjo melodies ran through his blood. He saw Chris with an Irish woman and a handsome, long-haired Frenchman at the bar, though the Frenchman had limited English. Declan did not see any of the familiar buskers. He did not see the mysterious Maeve from Sheridan's pub.

Chris joined them. "That Irish lady is really fine, but I think she likes that pretty Frenchman."

The noise made conversation difficult. Teresa observed the musicians and dancers and then motioned to Declan. They walked outside the pub.

"I need to sleep."

"Let's meet before you leave," Declan said.

"At the Jurys Inn," Teresa said. "Tomorrow morning."

She shook his hand and walked back to her B&B. Declan looked past the bouncer into the packed pub and the few people dancing to the fast Irish music. He could see Chris drinking coffee and talking to another young woman. Declan walked up the colorful ancient streets through Eyre Square to the Forester, where he ordered a whiskey and seven up. He knew it was risky drinking hard alcohol. He could hear his therapist. *"If you drink again, ask this: Were you an alcoholic or someone who abused alcohol?"*

Perhaps a man who once abused alcohol could drink wisely. An alcoholic had to stay dry forever. He looked at the bartender and asked a question.

"What's better, Catholic Jameson or Protestant Bushmills?"

"I have nothing against religion, but I think both taste like shit," he said.

In bed, that night, Declan hoped for Kate to appear in his dreams. She didn't. In the morning, Declan waited at the Jurys Inn for Teresa. When she arrived, they found a sidewalk cafe to have a light breakfast. A young man washed down the alley and lane. Declan saw the taxi stand up the street near the brightly-painted Tig Coili.

"I'm so glad you took the time to come here," Declan said. "I know we were never that close." He laughed to himself. "Your mother once said we were very much alike."

Teresa said nothing.

"When I first met your brother that first summer, he was shocked when he saw me in my battered car with my long hair and floppy hat. I felt the same way about him. Here was this geeky teenager staring at me from the porch. We laugh about it, now. Kate had talked a lot about you, and I thought we would hit it off."

Declan remembered the defiant young woman who ignored him with a spectacular indifference. Summers passed and they rarely spoke, except out of forced politeness.

"Yes," Declan said. "I'm glad you came here."

Teresa finished her coffee. She wasn't looking at him. Perhaps she wasn't looking at anything, except pedestrians. Declan knew she was listening.

"I'm glad I came, too," she finally said. "I leave for Rumania next week, but I'll be in touch."

They walked up to the taxi stand and embraced. "I saw how devastated you were at mom's funeral."

"You seemed so in control."

"It was an act," Teresa said. "I *will* stay in touch. That's a promise."

Moments later, Declan watched as Teresa waved good-by through the taxi widow and the driver turned toward the train station. Their last moments were behind them.

Good-by, Declan said to himself. *You are the flesh and blood of my beloved Kate.*

He spent the rest of the day singing on the street with the buskers, including Jamie. Often as they harmonized together, particularly on Dylan songs, people at the cafes watched and listened. There seemed to be no age barrier, though Declan was much older than the young musicians.

"You should consider busking yourself," Jamie said.

"I like steady paychecks and health insurance," Declan replied. "I'm used to a safety net."

"We buskers have each other," Jamie said. "Life is for living."

That night, he searched for Maeve, and though the pubs were packed, he couldn't find her. He asked people in the street about 'Knockins' pub, and though they gave directions, he couldn't find any place with that name. In the morning, he would take a bus to Shannon for the long plane ride home. Declan was about to have a final beer when he saw her. Maeve was standing in a doorway smoking a cigarette. He looked at the pub sign over her head: *Neachtain*. Of course, an Irish name that wasn't spelled phonetically. He crossed the street.

"Hello, Maeve."

"Declan." She smiled, and then dropped her cigarette. "We have a lot to discuss. Let's go inside."

The pub had many small rooms off the corridors, and two bars inside to order drinks. Though packed, they found a seat in a cubicle that gave them some separation from the pub traffic. She took his hands.

"I just graduated with an art degree so I'm celebrating. It's nice to see you."

"And you," said Declan.

Talking loudly over the music and voices, he told her about his day.

"You spent time with your stepdaughter? How nice. Where is the mother?"

"I lost her," Declan said.

As he explained, Maeve's eyes moistened. "I understand a lot, now. I'm sorry. Has the trip been difficult?"

"Yes and no. Some nostalgia, some exploration."

Maeve touched his face.

"I am glad I connected with Kate's daughter," Declan said.

He could feel Maeve's intense gaze.

"How old is your stepdaughter?"

"Late thirties."

"Late thirties? How old are you?"

He told her. He could see Maeve retreat slightly, as though a bond of intimacy had been broken. Then she laughed. It was a laugh mixed with a cough. "Excuse me."

"It's okay," Declan said. "I understand. You might read Hemingway's *Across the River and into the Trees*. Wonderful novel about a May-December romance."

"Excuse me—but Ted wants to buy a round."

"Who's Ted?"

Then Declan saw the same young man from Sheridan's standing near the crowded corridor. He lifted his glass and smiled.

"We're going to an after hours place," Maeve said. "The band might be a bit loud for you," she added.

"Yes, of course," Declan said. "My hearing aid distorts loud music. I forgot my cane and it's past my bedtime."

Maeve regarded him with a look, serene and compassionate.

"The greater the love, the bigger the sorrow," she said.

When the couple left to hear the live band, Declan walked home. He got undressed and lay in bed, thinking about Maeve. Wasn't there a female warrior in Irish mythology called Maeve of the Friendly Thighs? She tempted even the great warrior, Cuchulain. Surely this Galway Maeve wanted him, and had possibly followed Declan home, ready to burst into his room and strip, showing her beautiful breasts in the moonlight pouring through the window. A morning breeze would dry their exhausted bodies at dawn.

He stared at a clock he had bought in Galway. Before sleeping, Declan thought he heard distant music and a man and a woman arguing in the garden, but he didn't understand the language. The woman may have been Susan.

Finale

HE woke up at five in the morning. The bus for Shannon left at seven, but Declan felt restless so he dressed and left the B&B. It was still dark outside, and he knew it would be some time before he had coffee and breakfast. He walked through Eyre Square, empty except for a few transients sleeping on the lawn, and headed toward Galway Bay. The town was deserted. Declan felt a calm finality walking past the closed shops and pubs, past the double bronze statue, stopping to view the Jurys Inn and the distant bay for the last time, and then walking back through the narrow lanes of the colorful medieval district. He had the ancient silent streets to himself.

He should have felt isolated, but didn't. He had not dreamed of Kate and walking these empty streets affected him with bitter-sweet nostalgia, but nothing more. When he came to the square, he realized he wasn't alone. Through the soft morning air, three female apparitions seemed to float toward him, the tallest with painted bare breasts leading a trio dressed in hooded capes and black skirts. They chanted Irish. The first woman stopped and stared at Declan, transfixed, holding his suitcase.

"The sewage man is dying," she said. "Don't *ever* antagonize the three goddesses of Galway!"

A fat woman standing behind her grinned. "He's being devoured by foul bugs. Let him rot for a change."

"After polluting our water, he deserves it," the third woman said. "He'll turn black and die."

"Die," they chanted together.

The three goddesses cackled. The fat woman confronted Declan. She grinned, exposing bad teeth, and though shorter, her head seemed to hover over Declan's. From her cape, she produced a short breadstick.

"Eat this," she said. "I rolled naked in the dough before baking it. It will cure you of all pain." After looking at the others, she added, "Nothing else will work, Yank."

Declan backed away.

"Sure he's afraid," shrieked the first woman, thrusting forward her painted breasts. All three goddesses laughed and danced chanting in a circle around him. Then they held hands and skipped down the lane past the seated statues of Oscar and Edward Wilde. Declan could hear their echoing voices as they came to a fork at an intersection and disappeared into the ancient part of the city.

Declan walked through Eyre Square to the station. As the morning light grew brighter, he saw other passengers gathering. When the bus arrived, it had an electric side door for passengers to place their baggage. At the small Shannon airport, Declan had a full breakfast with coffee and bought an Irish newspaper. He saw the strange headline: *Superintendent of city sewage treatment plant stricken with flesh eating bacteria.*

Declan put down the paper.

"Jesus, so the wicked sisters were right."

He told no one of what happened except for an e mail to his therapist. When Declan sat in the familiar office a week later, the whole trip seemed to be a distant dream.

"Back in my womb," he said. "My little oasis."

The therapist sat opposite him and took out a yellow pad. She smiled, her eyes warm, watching him. "I am dying to hear about these Celtic witches you described. Weird."

"They were weird, all right. Maybe I should have eaten that breadstick"

"You think it would have helped you?"

Declan wasn't sure if the question was serious. "I don't know."

His therapist regarded him. "You made it there *and* back, you made some connections — *and* you traveled alone."

"Yes — alone," he said.

"Was it good for you?"

"It proved I could do it."

The therapist watched him, waiting. Her gift was to know when to speak and when to listen.

"Yeats's grave is impressive," he said.

"You felt a connection to a great poet, then?"

"Yes. But the statue of Yeats in Sligo town? Hideous. He looks like a cross between a manta ray and a stork. Awful. The Irish call the statue the 'wank at the bank.'"

"But you liked the Irish poets and musicians?"

"Yes. Art is what I have in place of religion."

She waited for him to continue, but Declan was unusually quiet.

"It *was* strange going back without Kate."

"It must have been."

"Galway is a lovely city," he said. "Kate loved it."

"Meeting Kate's daughter? That was good?"

"It was."

"Good."

"I won't let her go. Or her brother."

"This could give you a connection to Kate."

"Yes."

Declan sat with elbows on his thighs, his chin resting on folded hands.

"You seem more focused, confident."

"I do? I feel a bit scattered."

"But you have come this far."

The sun was bright outside the office, the light filtered through the curtain.

"I met an attractive woman."

"That shows you're human."

"I think I liked her more than she liked me."

"Welcome to life."

"Maybe she was my black rose."

"I don't know what that means, Declan."

"I believe it's an Irish myth about dangerous romances."

"Was she dangerous?"

"I didn't have a chance to find out. Maybe she was a witch, too."

For a minute, Declan was silent.

"I don't understand anything," he finally said.

"Don't you think you've actually grown a lot?"

"Maybe…but what a time it's been. I missed Kate and sometimes I *didn't* miss Kate…when I had to *do* things….I mean, I can always *function*."

"You can. That's crucial. And you *have* to move on and be good to yourself."

"But what a time it's been," he repeated. "I finally did dream about her."

"Tell me."

"I had written some article praising a place I didn't really like, but a teacher criticized it and she gave me a 'C' for not being honest. Then I walked out into the backyard and there was Kate, dressed in white but not like an angel, and she was lying on her stomach on this table, reading my essay. Always the editor, she looked up and said, 'Your teacher's right. This is crap.'"

"What did you do?"

"I rushed to kiss her. I remember touching her back and then kissing her neck and cheek as I did so many times…and then she was gone. I woke up."

"But it is significant that she appeared in your dreams."

"What does it mean?"

"Maybe she was making a real connection…on some practical level."

"Practical? She comes back from the dead to criticize some stupid paper I never wrote? I go to kiss her and she disappears?"

"What do *you* think it means?"

"You tell me."

"Perhaps it's her way of telling you that you'll find peace."

"If I hear that word one more time, I'll commit a crime," Declan said, standing suddenly. He slammed a fist into his palm. Declan realized he had startled the therapist and quickly sat down. There was a deep breath, and then a tear. Declan had never cried in her office, before, but suddenly he was crying, softly and openly. The therapist offered him a tissue but he refused it.

"I want her back," he finally said.

He put his face in his hands. The therapist remained silent. They were like two statues sitting in the quiet room. "It *will* get better," she told him.

Declan lifted his head and looked at her. Then he laughed.

"I never got a Goddamn 'C' in my life," he said.

The session ended. At the door, he paused.

"Tomorrow is our July wedding anniversary. I'm going to put roses from our garden into the little brook that runs beneath the Hemingway Memorial where we were married."

The therapist nodded in approval. "That's a *great* way to honor her—and yourself."

The next morning, Declan cut some garden roses and put them in a cooler with ice. He drove through the Arco Desert and past Craters of the Moon, stopping at the Hemingway Memorial in Sun Valley. Declan carried the cooler down the familiar path toward the bust of Hemingway and the plaque with words he had written for a hunter slain in 1939. Declan put the chest on a stone bench and remembered the wedding guests from years before. Many were gone or sick. Did hidden sprits live in the trees and the water, despite the golf course below and the many tourists who snapped photos and the cyclists who rode by? Would the spirits appear after he left? Would Kate be among them? *Maybe she knows I'm here*, he thought.

He opened the cooler and tossed the various colored roses into the running stream. The flowers vanished around a bend before he turned back with another rose. Then he took out the last two, a white Princess Diana and a dark red Mister Lincoln rose. They had been Kate's favorites. He placed a rubber band around the two roses and dropped them into the narrow, swiftly moving brook beneath the bust of Ernest Hemingway. Sunlight came through the cottonwoods. He watched the bound roses float away.

"For you, my love," he said softly, "and for us."

Paraguay Wedding

IT didn't seem to matter they were late since the priest didn't show up for the wedding rehearsal, but Greg was still concerned about where he should stand during the ceremony.

"After all, according to the Paraguayans, I'm the fake father," he said. "You're the real father."

"It will work out," Sean Dineen said. He winked at Priscilla who smiled back. "I guess the so-called real parents stand in front of the altar and you, the stepfather or *padrastro*, get to stand in the front pew."

They looked out the side door of the old church and saw Carson Dineen standing with his bride-to-be, Paola, a beautiful Paraguayan woman who spoke little English but knew Portuguese, Spanish and the native Guarani Indian language. Carson was striking in a tux. Time in the Peace Corps had led to his meeting with Paola. She was now watching a pet monkey chained to a tree branch. It was a spring night and the temperature still high. Wearing a tuxedo, Sean could feel the heat, wet and oppressive. Only early morning gave a brief relief. They could hear the heavy Asunción traffic.

"We can meet here in two hours," Priscilla said. Sean could see she was tired.

"Never thought our boy would get married in Paraguay, right?"

"No, Sean, I never thought that…even though Carson is adventurous."

"A Paraguay wedding is an adventure for all of us."

Watching Priscilla in yellow streetlight, Sean Dineen remembered the young woman he had once loved. She had lost weight, the dark spiked hair now streaked with grey, her face lined with age and recent pain. Greg had gained weight and his once thick curly hair had turned white. The eyes were still dark and always seemed to hold a sardonic humor. Though they had raised Carson through his teen years in England, they both missed the spring cherry blossoms of Washington DC, their new home. Paola approached Priscilla.

"We go to do the makeup job and…" Paola searched for the word. "Dress," she said, smiling. "Makeup and dress."

"I'll need a lot of makeup," Priscilla said. Sean was suddenly aware of Carson at his side.

"There's a great pizza bodega near here. Let's grab a bite."

Sean looked at the handsome face of his twenty-four-year-old son.

"Son, I don't like pizza. I *hate* pizza!"

Carson nudged him playfully. "You'll like this place. It's got ambiance. The guy who runs it fled during the Stroessner dictatorship. His pizza is to die for and he has a lot of stories to tell. I can translate."

"Then let's hear them."

"I like pizza. You need a third party?" They looked at Greg. He was sweating.

"I need to talk to dad alone," Carson said.

"Dad? What am I, chopped liver?"

"Of course not. I just need to talk with…with Sean for a minute."

Greg nodded. "You guys want time alone, I understand that. I'll meet you back at the house."

"We can meet at the church."

"You also need to spend time with your mother," Greg insisted.

"I will. And you need to get dressed."

"Yeah, I guess it's time to put on that penguin suit."
They felt the furnace heat of Paraguay. "Let's hope it cools
down, tonight."

"It won't," Carson said. "Not until what we call
summer."

They watched as Greg helped Priscilla into a cab and
drove to the house where Paola had put them. It was a large
white house with a red tiled roof and a swimming pool in the
courtyard. Broken glass lay imbedded in the top of the garden
wall and armed guards manned a station down a short path to
the street. Paola waved to Sean and joined her sisters in
another car.

"We need to talk about mom," Carson said.

"Sure."

The pizza-bodega was small with a bar and an oven,
the front door facing a busy street. Outside were modern
houses and small shacks. An occasional palatial palace from
colonial days lined a major boulevard. Inside the bodega, a
poster of Bogart from *Casablanca* was on the wall and a section
of an epic poem about a rebel gaucho called Martin Fierro.
Carson sat on a stool and ordered.

"I know that poem," said Sean.

"I think Martin Fierro eventually sold out in the end
and became a government man. Even after Stroessner was
deposed, he kept his Colorado party in power and had secret
police."

"He also harbored Nazis."

"Yes, he did. A few descendants might be still around."

Carson spoke in Spanish to the owner who shook his
head and replied. He was gaunt with missing teeth and
strands of hair combed over a bald scalp.

"He says he was tortured by Stroessner's secret police
and fled to Argentina. He might have some stories for your
potential novel."

"Maybe. I gave up political cartoons. Real life just got
too bizarre. I have to create something."

"Maybe a graphic novel," said Carson.

Two beers and the pizzas came and Sean was impressed. He stopped in mid chew. "I, who loathe pizza, love this. It's great."

Carson watched his father's face as he sipped his beer. "What?"

"I thought you quit drinking."

"Since losing Rachel, I decided to have a beer or a glass of wine now and then."

Carson nodded. "No gambling, these days?"

"None. Not even bingo."

"I'm glad you and mom are reconciled and you approve of Greg."

"He's okay," Sean said. "I think he loves her. Your mother and I weren't meant to be husband and wife, only crazy lovers."

"I was so sorry to hear about Rachel."

Sean could still see the young cop's neutral expression while reporting the accident.

"It was terrible," Sean said. "Two years later, I still think about her — but life goes on."

"I liked her."

"She liked you. In a world of fiber glass, she was a gem." Sean winked. "I borrowed that line from a song."

"Well, it's true," Carson said. "She *was* a gem." His eyes had the same brilliant rich brown of his mother's, the hair thick and brown, the perfect teeth white enough to give Carson what others called a "wicked grin."

"You know, Carson, your mother reached out to me after Rachel died."

"I know."

Sean was thinking about his late fiancé when the thin proprietor asked how the pizza was and they agreed that it was excellent. Then he told stories about the ruthless dictator called Alfred Stroessner, speaking in rapid-fire Spanish which Carson translated. Sean was able to recognize an occasional word.

"They executed his son," Carson said, "and imprisoned his wife. He finally got out but he never saw her again."

"Well, Stroessner is gone."

"And so is the economy. It takes 4,000 Guaranis to make one dollar. It will get worse."

They finished the pizza. Sean had noticed a store across the street with a German name. He wondered if some of the stories were true: dispossessed Aryan Nazi tribes, golden-haired and blue-eyed, living in the jungle and enslaving the natives. He had heard other stories that such Nazi colonies existed but they finally succumbed to tropical diseases. Sean ordered another round of beers.

"What's on your mind son? This should be your happiest day…or evening."

"It will be. But I'm worried about mom…and Greg."

"She was very ill, but she's here. I think it would have broken her heart to miss your wedding."

"I'm glad she made it," Carson said. "I was just thinking. You lost a beloved woman."

"True."

"Greg worked hard to be a good stepdad. Maybe you could help him when—"

Carson's voice went silent.

"Greg's a nice guy but he makes me nervous. All he thinks about is money."

"We can't all be artists like you," Carson said.

"True, again. And who said I was an artist?"

"Greg might be a little jealous. He knows what you and Mother had."

"And lost."

"And lost."

He touched his son's face. "I'll be there for you."

Sean felt a sudden rush of sorrow. He was seeing the cop's face, again; the cop was telling him that his fiancé had been struck by a drunk driver while returning from shopping.

"She did not survive the accident," the cop simply reported. The radiant woman who had suddenly appeared and given Sean a new reason to live was just as suddenly gone.

"We've known mom's inevitable outcome for some time," Carson said, "but when it happens, it will be difficult for me and you…and Greg."

Sean could see moisture in his son's eyes and on this happy occasion, wanted to ignore future sad vigils. "We'll get through it." They both stared at Bogart on the poster. He was looking at a radiant Ingrid Bergman. "Don't forget, Paola. She'll be strong for all of us."

"She has to learn English, first," Carson said. He suddenly lowered his head and laughed. "And you need to learn better Spanish. Do you have any idea what you said to her sister, yesterday?"

"Tell me on the way back," Sean said.

They left the bodega. Traffic was heavy, with many motorcyclists without helmets driving down the crowded lanes. Sean saw a crippled dog lying on the sidewalk. Carson began to tell the story of Sean's language mistake. They were still laughing when Greg and Priscilla met them outside the church. Priscilla's face was white with makeup, the eye liner and lipstick layered on thick. It was 10 PM, dark but humid with sweltering heat.

"What's so funny?" Greg asked.

"Yesterday, my dad was complaining about his Jesuit education. You know, the Jesuits settled Paraguay and actually helped the local Indians. Anyway, dad was telling Paola's sister that the Jesuits were always warning him about sin when he was in high school, but he used the wrong word."

Priscilla smiled, watching Carson's animated face. It was nice to see him so happy.

"Wrong word?"

"The Spanish word for 'sin' is *pecado* and the word for 'fish' is *pescado*. Dad used the word for 'fish.' Basically, he told Paola's sister that the Jesuits warned him he would go to hell over 'bad fish'."

Greg's face went dead. "I guess that's amusing."

"Paola's sister is concerned since there will be fish served at the wedding party."

Everyone else started laughing.

"I can handle the fish. I might even handle a little sin," said Sean.

Hours later, Sean Dineen sipped champagne and stood on the balcony of a luxurious hotel, staring across a river at a well-lighted boat anchored in the darkness. People on board were also having a party, but Sean remembered the double wedding ceremony in Spanish: first came the church wedding while he and Priscilla watched Carson and Paola exchange vows, and a tenor sang Ave Maria, and then a Paraguayan official performed the civil ceremony in the massive basement of the Yacht Club. All the *testigos* or witnesses signed a huge book beneath the ornate chandeliers. At one point, Sean's eyes met Priscilla's and she nodded, near tears. Greg was moved, watching his stepson marry.

And of course, Paola was radiant, Sean thought.

He finished his champagne. A Mariachi band began playing, and turning, Sean saw a very drunk Carson singing in Spanish while Greg shot photos. Beautiful and sensuous, Paola lifted her bridal gown exposing many multi-colored elastic leg bands which her new husband slipped down and then tossed to prospective brides and grooms in the audience. Plates of food were everywhere, including fish. Waiters carried trays of champagne glasses.

Sean walked over to an empty table to rest. A moment later, Greg joined him.

"Our boy is married," he said.

"That he is."

"Beautiful couple," Greg said, slurring his speech slightly. "You like the pink stuff, eh?"

"I do," Sean said. "Perhaps too much."

Priscilla sat down. Her powered face gleamed and she breathed heavily. "I'm out of shape," she said. "Well, Sean, our son got us *both* into a church."

"Maybe you can get a Rabbi to do another service in the States."

Priscilla nodded. "I'm beat," she said.

"We have that El Monte resort place to rest, tomorrow," Greg said.

"Yes. Then Carson wants us to travel with him to Iguaçu Falls. We have the Brazil visas," she added. Priscilla glanced at Sean. "You wanna go?"

"Won't it be a bit crowded?"

"For you, maybe. I just think he wants to be close to his mom," Greg said in a loud voice.

They heard cheers. Couples were comparing leg bands and laughing. A few men cheered and lifted their glasses. One young man waved a garter belt like a trophy. Carson tried to stand and fell, a laughing Paola catching him.

Greg said, "I think that's more fun than the bride tossing her bouquet or whatever it is to the bridesmaids, don't you?"

Priscilla watched silently. Sean felt a sudden combination of sorrow and happiness.

"I'll get us more champagne," Greg said, rising unsteadily.

"I have some," a voice said. A short stocky man with light-colored skin and blue eyes served glasses of champagne from a tray which he then gave to a waiter. He had a handsome face with blond streaks running through his thick dark hair. He sat down.

"Your son is a good looking boy. I like his new bride. Nice thighs, heh, heh."

"Excuse me?" said Greg.

"I am Pablo Escobar," the man said. A beautiful woman sat next to him, holding a plate of cake. Pablo leaned back, spreading his legs.

"Escobar? Like the drug dealer?" asked Sean.

"Yes — except I'm a television star." He laughed and the woman fed him some cake. Chewing, he asked, "What do you *blanco hombres* do?"

"I used to draw political cartoons," said Sean. "Now I plan to write the great American novel."

"And you, *señor*?"

"I'm a pig-dog capitalist," Greg said. "I have a plantation in Chile. I exploit brown people."

"Good idea," Pablo said. "They should be exploited! Except what do we have in Paraguay to exploit? Nothing. The Chaco desert is worthless except to Mennonites. The jungle is disappearing with these damn cattle ranchers. The Guarani Indians have no place to go. They are killing our Paraguay panthers. *Que lastima.* What a shame! I need to do a show about our endangered panthers."

"I'd like to visit the Guarani," said Sean.

"The Indian women are beautiful and wear nothing but black paint. They are *always* available. The men wear black and red paint and some gold arm bands and that's it. They are a simple people of hunters, like the old days, before the Jesuits, before the wars."

"Wars for what? You have no resources," said Greg.

"You're right. This country has been ruined by wars…and for what? The government is corrupt. We need to turn *communista*," Pablo insisted. He gulped his champagne. "Or bring back Stroessner. He was cruel but we had *order*."

"And a haven for Nazis."

Sean could feel Pablo's hard gaze. "Who invested in Argentina, Brazil, and even Paraguay after World War II? France? No. England? No. America? Hell no! Germany did. My grandfather was a German farmer and not a Nazi." He turned to his adoring female companion. "*Comida, mujer.* Food!"

The dark-haired woman went to fetch a plate of food for Pablo, and Sean marveled that despite the poverty and often meager diets, Paraguay produced beautiful women.

"She wants to be a star on my show," Pablo said. He turned to Priscilla. Sean found something disturbing in Pablo's pale blue eyes. Pablo used a soft suggestive voice. "Madam, your boy and his bride are a handsome couple."

"That they are," Priscilla agreed.

"But I hope they don't settle here. He doesn't want his bride to be ugly like a squat Indian woman cooking all day."

"They won't settle in Paraguay," Priscilla said.

"Good. I love beautiful women to stay beautiful, and being a television star has benefits. Paola, now. Very talented girl, heh, heh."

"What do you mean by that?" asked Greg.

"She speaks in many tongues. I hope your boy can tame her," Pablo said.

"He can take care of himself."

"Good. She needs a man."

"He is a man," Sean said.

Pablo lifted his drink. "*Bueno.*"

"I need some air," Priscilla said.

"There's a nice view of the river from the balcony. I enjoyed it."

Greg helped her up and they walked to the balcony. Sean closely observed Pablo. His woman was feeding him chunks of meat. Sean began to sketch the scene on a napkin.

"So when does the revolution start?" Sean asked.

"Not in my lifetime," said Pablo. "If anything, thieves will overrun the country. Why do you think there are armed guards at your place?"

"I don't know. Why *are* there armed guards?"

"No order." Pablo and the girl watched him sketch. "You like my show?"

"I haven't seen it. I don't speak Spanish," Sean said.

"You don't need to. We just trap men who are cheating on their wives. They get caught and the wife beats the cheating husband's bitch up, heh, heh. Sometimes both women beat the husband up. The live audience loves it. Some of it is staged, of course. Next week, a man finds his wife sleeping with a Jew."

Pablo laughed and finished his drink. The woman asked him to translate the joke. Sean continued sketching.

"Why don't you do a show on the Paraguay panthers?" he asked.

"Who would watch that?" said Pablo. He opened his mouth for another serving. After a while, Sean got up and slid the napkin portrait across the table. Pablo and the woman examined it. The drawing showed a beautiful woman feeding meat to a caricatured bloated Pablo.

"I like it," Pablo said. "Maybe it's a bit ugly, but it's correct. I *am* an animal!" The woman laughed. Pablo smiled at Sean, who saw a flash of malevolence in his eyes. "You want another drink, *señor*? The pig can buy you a drink."

"I have to go," Sean said. He left the table.

"*Bonita*," the girl said, pointing to her image. Pablo glared at Sean walking away, making a gun with his fingers.

It was early morning when Sean said good-bye to Carson and Paola; he found Priscilla and Greg, slightly drunk.

"I'll see you later," he said. "I think I can find our apartments."

"Don't get robbed," Greg said. "I left my guns at home."

"I don't need a gun, Greg."

"Think about Brazil," Priscilla said, touching his arm. He nodded and left.

Sean walked through the still crowded dark streets of Asunción toward their secure apartments. A group of seven Mormon missionaries passed him, six men and one woman. He found the right street and the guard station. The guards carried automatic weapons and nodded to him. They could hear many hidden frogs. In the courtyard, the swimming pool was flat and reflected the bright moon; the warm air was heavy with moisture. Sean changed and went for a moonlight swim. He thought of Priscilla and decided that traveling to see the famous falls was a good idea. Then he closed his eyes, enjoying the cool water and the feel of the slight, late night breeze. The frogs went silent. He felt a chill in the water. When he opened his eyes, Sean realized a man was standing in the shadows of a palm tree.

"*Quien es?*" the man said.

Sean stood up. "Pablo?"

"*Quien es?*" the man repeated. He had an edge to his voice. His face remained in shadow.

"Who am I? Dineen," he said. "Sean Dineen. I came here for a wedding." He peered at the stranger and saw the .45. The intruder pulled back and released the slide. His voice was louder: "*Quien es?*

"*Yo soy Americano,*" Sean told him, staring at the gun.

"*Americano*?" The man turned and shouted. "Jose!" Jose appeared and they spoke in Spanish. "Who are you?" Jose finally demanded. "My friend is nervous to find a half naked American man in his pool."

"*His* pool?" Sean told them who he was and why he was there. "A wedding," he said.

The armed man spoke in Spanish. Jose translated. "What daughter of Paraguay is marrying your son?"

"Her name is Paola."

"Paola?" They put the accent on the first syllable. "You know Paola?"

"Yes. I am her new husband's father. *Comprende*? We are renting this place. How did you get past the guards?"

Jose repeated this to the other man in Spanish and both of them laughed. "We pay the guards," Jose said. "There are a lot of bad people on the streets, understand?"

"They've been good to me."

"Let's hope they stay good. We also have dengue fever, here," he said. "Crocodiles in the river. The Guarani devour white people."

"I'll remember that."

"Enjoy the city," Jose said. "*Buenas Noches*."

As they were leaving, Priscilla arrived, holding a very drunk Greg. He saw the two men.

"Hey, when do we get breakfast? The room service in Paraguay is terrible."

"Be quiet," Priscilla said.

The two men stared at him and then walked on, laughing quietly. Priscilla wiggled her fingers at Sean and led Greg to bed. "I'll put on a bathing suit and join you later," Priscilla said.

Sean could hear the stranger and Jose shouting at the guards. Moments later, Priscilla joined him in the small pool. The once lovely breasts sagged, her face still holding some of the old beauty in the soft moonlight. Sean remembered earlier days when they were in love, and it was raw and passionate. He told her about the armed visitor.

"Those guys demanded to know who I was. What was *that* all about? The guy with the gun scared me."

"Maybe Paola forgot to tell the owner about our presence." After a deep breath, she said, "I am so tired these days. One minute you are strong and healthy, and the next, some silent killer like ovarian cancer enters your life." She smiled at Sean. "But, Goddamnit, I am here."

"You are here," Sean said. "And what a day we had." After a pause, he asked, "Is the chemo that bad?"

"You don't want to know. I won't do it again."

They looked at the bright stars. Even with a full moon, the southern sky seemed more black, the stars more brilliant. The chorus of frogs had started, again.

"It would be nice to float here forever," she said. Priscilla turned toward him. Then she was staring into his face, holding his eyes for a long time. "Boy, we had a nice run for a while, didn't we?"

"As Shakespeare said: 'We have heard the chimes at midnight'. Am I forgiven for being a drunken, gambling slob?"

"Sure. Do you forgive me for running off with our son?"

"Absolutely. I was a bad father."

"You know, I had a sexual fantasy about you last night."

Sean grinned and looked up at the apartments, waiting for Greg to appear. He imagined them as two aging lovers suddenly stranded in an exotic tropical region. It would make a good soap opera. "There might be life in the old war horse yet," he said.

"Please," Priscilla said. "I'm a married woman. Greg is a pain in the ass, but he adores me."

"We *all* adore you." They gently kissed. For a brief moment, Sean imagined them tearing off their suits and making quick love in the pool, a farewell coupling. They parted and heard Greg. He was standing on the balcony in a bathrobe, blinking and peering down at them.

"Jesus, Priscilla, I woke up and you weren't there! It scared me. Come to bed."

"On my way," she said.

Sean and Priscilla went silently to their separate apartments. She had once used the metaphor of the same bus stop but different buses for both of them. Sean lay on his bed and after a while, went to sleep. Rachel came to him in his dreams. There was sadness in her face.

"*You need a woman,*" she said. "*Keep those old bones warm, big guy.*"

"*Who could follow you?*"

"*Not just anyone, I guess, but you need a woman to care for you, Sean. I'm gone.*"

"*Where are you?*"

"*At peace,*" Rachel said. She was like a silver image at dusk, suddenly fading. "*Good-by, Sean. I miss you.*" He woke up in darkness, hearing the hum of the air conditioner. Staring at nothing, he felt like crying but finally drifted back to sleep.

*   *   *

THEY spent two days at a resort 30 miles outside of Asunción. The restaurant and pool overlooked a thick jungle, including palm trees, and they stayed in small bungalows. Red dust lay on the roads. Sean found it an exotic place to keep a journal with the sounds of the jungle birds at night. During the long afternoons, they rode ponies, raising the red dust of the roads that ran between rows of palm trees. They drank wine and hard drinks or swam in the pool. Food was served at random times and Greg was often hungry.

"There is no time in Paraguay," Carson told Greg. "Sun up, sun down is time."

Priscilla leaned against the pool's edge. "What happens if someone gets sick? You're in a remote place."

"We just push them off a cliff," a blonde woman said carrying a tray with snacks. She laughed and walked on.

"No emergency medical help here," Carson said. "Why? Do we need it?"

On the third day, they drove toward the Brazil border and stopped at a roadside café where sheep grazed outside. The distant hills and plains looked like a range Sean had seen in America. When they approached the Paraguay-Brazil line, Sean felt a nameless anxiety in the dusty tri border town of Ciudad del Este. There was the Friendship Bridge with hoards of people crossing, traveling to and from Paraguay, Argentina and Brazil. He saw a distant shopping center, and men stared at them from the crowded dirty sidewalks as they stopped just past the border check. Sean knew he could easily buy drugs and weapons. A few ragged children were begging.

Carson stood in the street, bartering for Brazilian currency. A small man in cheap clothing held a roll of money and spoke in a high pitched voice. Paola sat in the car. Behind them, Priscilla rode with Greg and two of Paola's sisters. Greg got out of their car. A line of cars waited in the heat, honking.

"We're holding up traffic," he said.

A deal was reached and then both cars were moving.

"I got a good deal on the money exchange," said Carson.

Sean saw a man walking with an AK 47 over his shoulder. "Why do I feel like I'm in some movie about drug thugs?"

"All border towns are evil," said Carson. "It will be worth it. We'll stay at a wonderful resort and then take a bus to the Iguaçu Falls."

They drove through the small towns of Brazil and then found a large resort with tennis courts, golfing, a large restaurant, a Jacuzzi bath and luxurious cabins. It was cheap enough for Greg to notice.

"This is ridiculous. They could charge more than $75 dollars a night."

"Brazil is also poor," Carson said. "We're paying top dollar. Let's visit the famous falls."

They took a special park bus. Paola talked to the driver in Portuguese.

Late that night, Sean remembered Priscilla's shouted voice over the roaring of the powerful flowing waters as they watched the massive multiple falls. Ducks walked around on the lawn outside his cabin and there was a small pond he could see through the window. Sean wrote in his journal: "Iguaçu Falls is like ten Niagaras, and while standing over one falls, you can feel the rain from another above you, and the thick mist comes up from the deep gorge, wetting your face. Coili raccoons scavenge for food. If one falls in the current, death is certain. It's a sure thing for potential suicides."

They had a night out at a local night club, hearing a clownish MC barking in Spanish and Portuguese, with muscular men doing acrobatic routines and half naked beautiful women dragging drunken male customers up on the stage. Carson and Greg joined in the fun, pointing telescopes at the crotches of beautiful dancers or blowing long trumpet-shaped kazoos between spread female thighs as Paola watched impassively. To Sean's surprise, Priscilla found enough energy to join the drunks and girls on stage for a kicking dancing conga line. Priscilla began a sensuous dance by herself and the other dancers swirled around her. Greg lost his balance and fell off the stage. Sean Dineen declined to join in the festivities.

The next morning, they waited at the border while passports were passed up to Paola who sat in the front seat. Sean Dineen and Priscilla sat in back. Greg rode in another car, agreeing to let Priscilla spend more time with Carson. Sean was about to speak when they heard a slapping sound on the left side of the car and a young boy reached through the right window and snatched Paola's purse. She cried out. Then Carson bolted from the car and chased the two boys. "Passports," he screamed.

"Oh my God," Priscilla said.

Sean pushed his way out of the car, afraid Carson might get hurt. He heard Paola behind him. Greg was standing outside his car, blinking and holding a flask. "What's going on?" he said. Sean turned around and saw Priscilla was crying.

"Greg—stay with her!"

He ran through the thick traffic and saw Carson gaining on the boy with the purse. The youth dropped the purse which Carson picked up, then dropped while running. Not breaking his stride, Sean retrieved the purse and saw the money and passports were gone. With the heat and exertion, he felt a pain in his chest, his breathing suddenly rapid. *I'm too old for this shit*, he thought. He heard Carson's angry voice as he caught the running boy by the hair and, still running, struck him in the face. The boy fell heavily.

"Where are the passports?" Carson screamed.

The boy kicked at his face and then stood up, holding his ground. As Sean reached them, the boy pulled out a knife. He was thin, around 14, and light reflected off the tiny blade. Then they saw other boys converging, many with knives. The young thief began screaming in Portuguese, still waving the blade.

"I think we better get out of here," Sean said. Feeling chest and side pains, he tugged at Carson. "Son, let's go."

"If we don't get our passports, we'll be stranded."

"Or dead."

Carson spoke in Spanish to the advancing boys, but they didn't understand. The youth he struck had a rising welt on his cheek. Dust covered his young emaciated face. They would remember the blazing hatred in his eyes for a long time.

"Let's go," Sean said, blocking his son from the gang closing around them. Sweat stung his eyes and he felt dizzy. Then they heard Paola's voice in Portuguese. She handed the passports to Carson. The two men continued to back up, walking toward the traffic jam at the border while Paola screamed at the young boys. She spit once. They looked at each other, some smiling, but they backed away.

"*Vamos,*" she told Sean and Carson. "Hurry! *Apurate.*"

They walked quickly ahead toward their cars, Paola giving orders in Spanish. Sean felt his chest pain subside. Carson said: "I'll take the passports to the gate. You and Greg drive the cars through. We might get stopped by the border guards."

"Why? We're the victims."

Greg was waiting. "What the hell happened?"

"It's all right," Sean said. "We got our passports."

"Passports?" Priscilla's eyes were full of outrage. "Carson might have been killed!"

"You put him in danger?" demanded Greg. "Huh?"

"That's a stupid question, Greg. Of course not. We made it, thanks to Paola."

Priscilla stared at him. "Jesus, you're white as a sheet."

Sean shrugged and got behind the wheel. An old woman with missing teeth shouted about *ladrones*. "Follow me," Sean said and drove toward the station while Priscilla took deep breaths. Cars were honking and drivers shouted at them.

"Did you hear his tone?" Greg asked. "What arrogance."

"Just drive and shut up," Priscilla said. Angry, Greg followed Sean. The guards waved them through but another guard motioned that Sean pull over.

"They want us in that office," Carson said, pointing.

"Is a purse snatching that big a deal?"

Sean followed Carson into an office, but guards stopped Paola. She protested as Greg parked his car and got out. "I sure would like some information here," he said. Priscilla was silent. Inside the office, a customs official addressed them, first in Spanish, then English. He had a pock-marked face and intense, dark eyes. "Did you beat up a Brazilian boy?"

"He was a thief," Sean said. "The punk had a blade."

"That was not the question," the officer said. "Did you knock down a Brazilian boy?"

"Yeah," said Sean. "I knocked him on his keister."

"What is 'keister'?" the officer asked.

"I hit the boy," said Carson. "I thought he stole our passports."

The officer held up their passports. "They are here," he said.

"I guess they were in the car the whole time," Carson said.

"Then why did you hit that boy? They want us to send you back for a trial."

Sean got up. "Trial? They should be tried for robbery."

"Let me handle this," Carson said. "Sit down."

Sean sat down.

"Explain what happened," the officer said.

In Spanish and English, Carson told the officer what had happened. Sean felt the pain coming back. His skin color turned grey.

"Why did you have your car window down?" the officer asked. "That was stupid."

"*Si*," Carson said. "Stupid. *Muy estupido.*"

"Don't apologize," said Sean. He was sweating. The officer watched his face.

"You ran far?"

"Maybe a half mile," Carson said.

"And the old man ran that far…in this heat?"

"I am not old," Sean insisted.

"We both ran. Then the kids pulled knives and cornered us."

"Your wife stopped the boys?"

"Yes," Carson said. "She did."

"Bring her in."

They brought in Paola who spoke rapidly in Spanish and Portuguese, explaining again what happened. The officer seemed amused. "You scared the boys."

"*Cobardes*," she said.

"Not cowards, *Señora*, poor young boys."

They could hear the anger in Paola's voice as she answered. "*Ladrones. Niños con cuchillos.*" She glared at the officer. "Boys with knives."

Paola took out a switchblade and stuck it in the desk. Then she spoke in a furious stream of language. The official turned away, smirking.

"What's she raving about, Carson?"

"Paola says she took the little thief's knife and threatened to cut his balls off." He pulled at Paola. "*Calmate.*"

Paola went quiet. The officer pulled out the knife, no longer smiling. "They are very poor and theft is a border problem. We don't want an incident with Brazil." He noticed Sean's sudden deep breathing. "*Señor? Infermo?* Are you well?"

"Of course I'm well."

"You don't look good, dad." Carson handed his father some water.

The officer opened the door. "We don't want an incident in Paraguay, either. *Medico.*"

A doctor came into the room and checked Sean's pulse. He listened to his heart and gave Sean an aspirin. Then he spoke in Spanish. Carson listened, his expression grave. The customs official translated.

"He says he thinks you may have suffered a little heat stroke, but you're okay now. Maybe your heart needs to be checked. Do it when you get home. I don't want any dead bodies in my office." He coughed. "That will be two hundred American dollars."

"Two hundred?" Sean and Carson looked at the official. "What for?"

"My time for interrogation, and the doctor's fee. Pay and you can go. Unless you want to be sent back to Brazil." They paid. The officer handed them their passports. "*Adios.*"

Outside, Priscilla embraced Carson. Sean explained to Greg as they drove back to Asunción. Greg was impressed.

"God, they were just kids," Sean said. "What a life."

"What a place, eh?" Greg passed him the flask. The whiskey tasted sharp but gave Sean's heart a little lift. They were driving fast.

*   *   *

FOR their last day in Asunción, they stayed in their former apartments and it was quiet. Sean gave the guards a sketch which they found amusing. They also knew about the landlord pulling the gun on Sean and found that story amusing. Everyone had a gun in Paraguay, so it was nothing.

An American physician listened to Sean's heart. "Your pulse and circulation are good," he said." You might consider an EKG back home. Your cholesterol is elevated, and don't ever run in this heat," the doctor said. "Especially at your age."

"My age? Sixty is not old."

"And you better watch your diet…because high cholesterol will cause a heart attack."

That evening, they sat around the pool. Sean drew a group portrait of them, though Paola had gone shopping with her sisters. Greg drank bourbon with 7-Up and was soon drunk. Though tired, Priscilla had remained cheerful during dinner at an all meat restaurant, a carnivore's paradise. A marker with red on one side and green on the other signaled the waiters whether feeding should continue or stop.

"Terrific," Sean said. "All I have to do is flash the green side at a waiter to get any meat I want on a skewer, but I'm supposed to lay off red meat. I don't like lettuce and spinach. I could get e coli in this country."

"You have a point," Carson said. "Let's take a walk. Get some exercise."

"Sure," Sean said.

"I'm going to bed. See you in the morning."

Carson kissed his mother. "Okay, mom."

Greg saluted with his drink. "I'm staying right here."

"Suit yourself."

Out on the street, Carson was disturbed. "Mom looks a bit drawn, and you aren't so healthy, either."

"We'll get by," Sean said. "We have a little time, and you'll be together in Washington, DC."

"That's true. I hate that we are all so damn vulnerable."

"So live life while you can. We're happy that you're happy."

"Thanks for that."

They returned to the pizza-bodega. On the movie poster, Bogart still wore his iconic trench coat. The old proprietor described more horrors from the former dictator's regime. No longer threatened by secret police, now poverty and government corruption was the enemy. For Sean, it was good to drink with his son and tell and hear old stories. He sketched his son talking to the proprietor. Later, they moved to a corner of the small bodega as other customers came in.

"I met your mother at a theatre audition for a one man show."

"A one *man* show? What was she doing there?"

"A mistake, I guess. But it was love at first sight. Boy did we fight. Just because I almost lost the house in a crap game. Then she took you and left me. Appalling."

"I know that story, dad. We found each other."

"Your mother was beautiful. A kind of sensuous Saint Joan — but not too saintly."

Carson held up his hand. "I don't need any details."

"I guess not." Sean added details to his son's face. "We will want grandchildren — and soon."

"We'll see." They left the bodega and stopped at the guard station. "Tomorrow," Carson said.

"*Mañana, hijo.*"

Carson walked away, taking the charcoal portrait with him. Sean saluted the guards.

"Time for a swim in the pool," he said. "*Piscine.*"

He pantomimed swimming. One of the guards brandished a pistol and laughed, shaking it in Sean's face. Sean could hear the familiar loud croaking of many frogs in a nearby pond. When Sean reached the crest of the driveway, he saw Greg sitting by the pool, a single light reflecting off the water and the broken glass driven into the top of the adobe wall. It was cooler and a steady breeze stirred the palm tree. Jagged shadows covered the patio. Greg was still drunk and held out the flask. "Drink," he said.

Sean sat down and took a drink.

"What a weird country, eh, Sean?"

"It's different. Surreal."

"She's asleep," Greg said. "Priscilla was worn out, today."

Sean looked at the apartment where Priscilla was sleeping and remembered a time in Hawaii when she straddled his lap and threw back her hair and arched her back, naked breasts lifting, a warm breeze and surf sounds coming in the window; Priscilla had suddenly laughed and murmured that she wanted this moment to last forever.

"She will be more tired, now," Sean said.

"She loves her boy. We love her boy."

"You'll all have time when they join you in DC. How are you feeling?"

"Drunk."

"Good."

"I love her," Greg said. "Did you?"

"Yes."

"There's a lot to love, isn't there?"

"Yes," Sean said. "There is."

Without warning, Greg started to cry. The tears seemed to spring suddenly from his face.

"I love her and she's going to die."

"We have time," said Sean.

"She's going to die."

After a moment, Sean put his arms around the sobbing man and began to rock him gently. Bull frogs serenaded them from their dark watery places.

Stonehenge

DURING afternoon tea at the historic Pump Room in Bath, Molly Malone noticed an attractive middle-aged woman sitting alone at a table. She had long hair, porcelain skin and clear sculpted features, but Molly recognized something in her eyes. It was the frightened harried look of a traveler on the road escaping despair back home. Molly guessed the woman to be European, but her clothes and a slightly arrogant confidence suggested American. The woman got up and left, possibly to visit the Roman Baths in the adjoining building. Molly had observed the dead green pools and Roman artifacts dedicated to the goddess, Minerva. Surrounded by visitors in the Pump Room, Molly finished her tea and scones with clotted cream and jam. While leaving, she caught her image in a hall mirror, an older woman, now, a bit plump, her hair white.

In the plaza stood three statues of hairy upright creatures with camel faces and jackass ears, thin statue dogs frozen in place around them. Street entertainers often performed before the adjacent Abbey Church, and Molly imagined her granddaughter playing Mozart for the tourists. Molly photographed a monk talking on a cell phone before the massive church doors. Around the corner was the point of departure for Stonehenge. A middle-aged Englishman with a dated shag haircut was collecting passengers. A traffic officer in uniform scowled, and the driver and officer exchanged words. When Molly Malone boarded the bus, she saw the woman from the Pump Room get on and sit up front. Finally, the driver got behind the wheel.

"I have to move, ladies and gentlemen, or the traffic officer, Smiley, will get all upset."

Passengers laughed as the bus pulled out and "Smiley" glared at them from the street. As they drove along the narrow English roads, the driver kept up a running narration.

"The French bought most of our bridges, if you can believe that…and these Eastern European drivers only use the satellite system and don't know about our narrow English roads, so they often end up in a ditch. If we see a Polish truck in the river, we'll just carry on."

Molly enjoyed the British countryside, but saw rain clouds through the window.

"First stop is Laycock," the driver said, "an ancient town of stone houses, and where a lot of period films are shot, including the Harry Potter series."

They crossed over a bridge and Molly saw locks along a river. The driver stopped the bus.

"This is an engineering marvel built by the British to control the level of water, like the Panama Canal, but guess who owns the bridge?" He paused for dramatic effect. "The French!"

A few snapped photos and then they drove to the town of Laycock where the first photograph had been taken and the first negative created. The town did have a quaint 14th century feel with many stone buildings, tea gardens and modern pubs with coats of arms over the doors. The driver signed them out and pointed to a stone cottage that seemed vaguely familiar.

"That's the house where Harry Potter lived in the first film. Good movie extra work for the locals. You can't own property here unless your family has a Laycock connection or history. The name of Laycock comes from a Saxon word. Take a walk around, explore. We leave for Stonehenge in 30 minutes."

Molly walked to a nearby pub but saw that they were closing down. Photos of actors from past films shot in Laycock hung on the walls.

"I was hoping for some lunch," she said.

The young bartender shook his head. "We close the kitchen by three O' clock, but you can order a pint."

"Maybe just a glass of wine." She then added some beef jerky to the purchase. "We'll be hungry when we visit Stonehenge," Molly said.

"British pubs close at three," the young bartender repeated. "We serve dinner at six."

"Terrible hours for us," a female voice said. Molly turned and saw the attractive woman from the tea room. She was still pretty up close, her accent American. "A shot of whiskey and a small glass of beer might do."

She sat next to Molly who offered her some beef jerky. "Thanks."

"There's a concession at Stonehenge," the bartender said, "though they will soon shut it down and take out the highway. More authentic, you know."

Molly introduced herself as they chewed the jerky. "Hello, Molly. I'm Susan."

"I'm looking forward to seeing those ancient stones."

"I think they will make us feel very mortal and short lived," Susan said. "How long have they been there?"

"At least four thousand years. Maybe more."

"Suppose over three thousand years ago some worker was crushed to death hoisting a stone, and his wife and kids mourned. Maybe the wife committed suicide. What difference does that make now?"

"Little difference, except we have the stones," Molly said.

"Right." Susan threw back the shot, sipped her beer, and turned to examine the photos on the wall. "I knew him," she said, pointing to the photo of a veteran actor who had died recently.

"I liked his work," Molly said. She felt slightly tipsy as they walked to the bus and the driver checked off their names. A light rain was starting.

"Next stop is County Wiltshire and Stonehenge," he said.

It struck Molly as they drove that the driver never mentioned details of Stonehenge.

"So you're traveling alone, Susan?"

"Yes. I was planning to visit England and Stonehenge with my husband, but here I am…alone."

Molly wanted to ask about the absent husband but didn't.

"My husband declined to join me," Molly said.

They rode along the highway of Salisbury Plain and then turned off the road where they saw concession and souvenir stands in a tourist car park. The bus driver addressed them: "Here we are folks, the famous Stonehenge. I hope you got an umbrella. Walk around the stones and be back in 45 minutes or so…that's about all you'll be able to stand with this weather."

"I don't have an umbrella, only a rain hat," Molly said.

Molly and Susan exited the bus with the other tourists and walking up a hill, suddenly glimpsed the concentric stones arranged and erected over a millennium by three different unknown peoples. Molly had seen many photos of Stonehenge but was unprepared for the sudden sight of the actual iconic monument. They joined a line of visitors walking toward the megaliths which grew more massive as they approached, the first path taking them close to the outer stones. Rain fell and lashed them in a biting wind. The visitors looked like pilgrims in the rain. Molly snapped some photos, imagining lost tribes dancing and singing within the circle of stones, celebrating life, death and obsolete gods. Despite her 70 years, she could easily envision herself in a remote time dancing around a fire half naked, flashing her breasts at dancing warriors nobly erect. Where had these invisible people gone?

"Was this a place of burial or healing, I wonder?"

Wearing a long black coat and a white scarf, Susan remained silent. Then she took a picture of Molly with Molly's camera, a giant stone in the background. In the gray light, Molly's face was moist and clear in the frame.

"Let me photograph you."

"Sure," Susan said. "I didn't bring a camera, but go ahead."

Molly snapped Susan's photo, catching a frozen look of sorrow. For a moment, Susan could have been a magnetic actress in a dramatic scene. A tourist then photographed them together. The rain blew against them as they walked, feeling the cold wind, the path taking them farther from the circle of stones as they walked behind Stonehenge. A man ran toward the stones to retrieve his rolling hat. People held umbrellas against the wind and steady drizzle. Susan ignored the weather and listened to an audio recording, pointing out details as they walked.

"There's the so-called Altar Stone. It's all still a mystery, of course."

"They'll remain mysterious long after we're gone."

The rain stopped. They circled Stonehenge and headed toward the highway and the distant bus. Green fields stretched toward the horizon. Susan stopped to take a final look and Molly saw the moisture in her eyes, spilling over darkened lower lashes. Molly imagined tears freezing in the numbing cold, even as a ray of light illuminated the monument.

"Oh Brian," Susan said. "I'm so sorry."

Susan glanced at Molly who said nothing. They nodded to the driver and got on the bus, clothes dripping. Susan lay back, her eyes closed. They drove directly back to Bath and got out near the Abbey Church. The two women walked into the crowded plaza, and Susan suggested they have a drink.

"Sounds good," Molly said.

They found a pleasant bar that also served food, so they both ordered a late lunch. They sat in silence, eating and drinking white wine. Susan avoided eye contact and was deep in her own thoughts. Molly finally spoke.

"I saw a young black woman at the Holiday Inn who, despite her English accent, reminded me of my daughter back home."

"Really?"

"Thanks to her, and through no fault of her, I had my white children taken from me. Women who had biracial children in Florida during those days were considered unfit mothers."

"That is shocking. We have a biracial President, for God's sake."

"Exactly. Recently, my sister in Ireland found my white children and they found me. Twins, a boy and a girl. We had a nice reconciliation."

"And their father?"

"Dead. Good riddance."

"And your" —Susan hesitated —"black daughter?"

Molly put down her glass. She had not told this personal family story to a stranger, before, but it seemed appropriate.

"Kenya has some issues: drugs, violence, manic depression, but she won't take prescribed drugs like lithium. Kenya could also be schizophrenic, like her father. She has two delightful daughters by different absentee fathers, and a judge, citing the need for children to be with their biological mother, awarded her custody of the girls instead of me and my husband. My grandchildren, Sonya and Jenny, left a luxurious three story house to live in a homeless shelter. It's a tragic mistake."

"I'm sorry to hear that." Susan met Molly's eyes. "Why isn't your husband here?"

"Tom doesn't travel well, lately."

"Why is that? Because of losing the girls?"

Molly sipped her wine and looked around the restaurant. It had many empty tables but a nice view of the street. For just a moment, she seemed to age even more.

"Tom lost his son last year and won't give up his heavy work schedule for the time being. David was a lovely young man on a fast track in business. Then he met some druggies in New York and overdosed on heroin in a run-down hotel. Two men were arrested. I identified the body."

Without warning, Molly began to cry. Susan reached over and stroked her shoulder.

"My God," she said. "I'm so sorry."

"David was my stepson but I loved him." Molly recovered and finished her wine. "I know I have a look of grief in my eyes. I think grieving people find each other. We carry the same darkness, don't you think?"

She looked at Susan who looked away and ordered bourbon and seven for herself and another glass of wine for Molly. Susan placed her hands on the table and stared ahead at nothing. To someone watching from a distance, they could have been a mother and daughter discussing an intimate issue. Susan was about to share another nightmare in black and white.

"You want to hear about Brian — my husband?"

"Only if it's not too painful."

After a moment, Susan began. "Brian White was a promising actor and did a few guest spots on TV. He was your classic white Anglo-Saxon protestant and I was this spoiled Jewish princess named Susan Finegold who came into his life. We had a great marriage of opposites. We had a son. Then a year ago late January, it all ended. Brian was an avid skier and got caught in an avalanche. I waited for two agonizing days for the recovery team to dig his body out. I'm told victims suffocate and the snow is like cement."

Molly took her hands. "You don't have to continue."

"It's all right. Anyway, for a year I was like the walking dead, sobbing one minute, catatonic the next. Eventually, I did visit some of the places we had visited in the hopes of bringing back something of him. Then I remembered we had often discussed seeing Stonehenge." Susan seemed to enjoy telling the story. "If I was trying to recover somehow, my son, Jimi, was angry at losing his dad. He would cry and scream and then act out, often running away."

"How old is he?"

"Twelve. One day, he took off in a park and I sat on a bench and started crying. I just gave up. 'Let him run,' I thought. 'I'm just too tired to chase him.' Then I looked up and saw Jimi watching me. He was also crying. 'I'm sorry mom,' he said. Now we are in it together."

"That's something. Where is he now?"

"At a rock guitar camp."

"Good for him."

For the first time, Susan smiled.

"My son, the rock and roll star."

"How long are you staying in Bath?"

"Tomorrow, I'll meet a friend from southern Cornwall…she lives in Polruan, a lovely town on a deep-water bay. There's a daily ferry that crosses over to Fowey. Daphne DuMaurier had a house down the cove. I'm a writer, myself," Susan continued. "I want to write plays. Maybe someday, I'll write a dramatic monologue about all this."

"That might be a start toward some relief." After a moment, Molly said, "Susan. I'm sorry to hear about Brian."

Susan felt sudden tears, her face beautiful despite the sorrow.

"It's a big hole in my life, and I can't fill it with dating…not yet."

"You're not ready," Molly told her.

"No, I'm not." She peered at Molly. "I'm here on a weird pilgrimage. Why are you here? Just to see Stonehenge?"

"I wanted to see Stonehenge, but I'm here for another reason. After much fighting, Kenya agreed to let me take Jenny, her oldest daughter, to a great violin teacher in London. I'll meet her tomorrow. We got hit pretty hard by the economy crashing, but I was determined Jenny studied with a classical teacher."

"That's what we do." Susan paid for the fresh drinks and took a swallow. "Oy vey, when does this pain end?"

"Never, but it does lose some focus. You have to create a new world. It's tough."

They finished lunch and their drinks. A few customers were coming into the restaurant and sitting at the many wooden tables and booths. They could hear clipped English accents.

"Molly? What's your last name?"

"I've had a lot of last names. Right now, it's Malone."

"Molly Malone? In Dublin, I saw the busty statue of Molly Malone, the famous street walker."

"The tart with the cart. I may have looked like that once."

"Well, you are well endowed, I'm sure, but not a street walker." For a moment, Molly thought Susan had blushed. "At least, I don't think so."

"I've explored a little," Molly said, "but not that. Of course, we're all whores on some level. Now I'm getting old, and my breasts are heading south."

"You look fine, girl." Susan watched her face and then dropped her eyes. "What did you explore?"

"Life…love…with men…and women."

Susan blushed again.

"I guess I'm old fashioned. I love men, and the best one of all had to *die* on me."

"Let me help you if I can."

Outside, they began walking.

"I'm staying at the Pratt hotel. I have a picture of Brian on the dresser. It's comforting, but not the same."

"No, it isn't" Molly said.

They caught a taxi. Traffic was heavy.

"I'm having a hard time with the traffic on the wrong side," Susan said.

"I'm used to it since I grew up in Ireland."

Susan took her hand. "Why don't we have dinner on our last night?"

Molly agreed it was a great idea.

"We could have a few drinks."

"I have to be careful," Molly said. "I'm diabetic."

"I'm sorry to hear that."

"It's managed. I'll call you at your hotel," Molly said.

They embraced, and after Susan left the cab, the driver turned and smiled at her. He had long yellowish-white hair and missing teeth.

"You got an address, Miss?"

"Holiday Inn."

At the Inn, Molly tipped the driver and entering her room, clicked through her photos in the digital camera, admiring Susan's classic face with its latent sadness. Once again, she saw the impressive iconic megaliths that would be standing centuries after they were dead. The massive stones did put human lives into perspective. What did their little transitory dramas matter? And yet they did matter. Molly thought about Jenny and their final week in London, and her concerns about Kenya growing more dangerous. Decisions would have to be made back home. There was David's ghost that haunted them all.

"Too bad we're not all made of stone," Molly thought.

She checked her blood sugar levels and administered a shot of insulin. Then she lay on the bed of her anonymous room and closed her eyes. It seemed so recent that she was growing up in Brighton, England before moving to small Killybegs in northwestern Ireland. How did so much time pass so quickly? Much had changed in both countries since her childhood, and now she was growing old in America with three grown American children, a dead stepchild, and two granddaughters. Molly had taken some expressive photographs and knew her life story could be a powerful cautionary tale, even a bit lyrical, but the book wasn't written, yet. A few photos did remain. Perhaps life was catching up to her. Like the original Molly Malone who died of a fever, death was not far behind.

When Molly awakened from a nap, the phone light blinked, and checking her messages, Molly saw Jenny had called. She called a number in London and her granddaughter answered.

"What's up, baby?"

"Thomas called. My mom came over and demanded we return immediately."

"We can't leave yet."

"She hit Tom. He's got a black eye."

Molly could see Kenya, eyes blazing with a sudden madness, swinging a big fist at Tom. She had once pushed her to the floor, as well.

"I'll call him. We'll be back soon."

"My father showed up," Jenny said. "Even *he's* worried."

"Let's hope he can help Tom with your sister."

"Grandma, what's wrong with Mom?"

"She's a sick person, Jenny. She needs help."

Just after her granddaughter hung up, Susan called.

"Molly, come over around 7:00 and we can have dinner."

"Sounds good," Molly said.

"You have a beautiful voice," Susan said. "It's really obvious on the phone. It has a distinctive husky rasp."

"I was born with it."

"I notice things like that working in theatre."

After a beat, Molly asked: "How are you doing?"

"I'm feeling a bit down…but I'm all right."

"You're still raw," Molly said.

"How are *you* doing?"

"Poorly. We can talk later."

They made plans and Molly hung up. Molly had known women like Susan Finegold, talented wealthy women, perhaps a bit insulated from the world of hard work and boring jobs, women used to cultivating the arts and following fashion, but always with a conscience. They would never lack for beautiful friends and handsome male escorts. Molly had never lost a beloved spouse, but she had lost lovers, friends and a stepson over the years. She understood the brutality of grief and compared it to Malaria that would return again and again. Thoughts of Kenya unsettled her mind. She knew it was only a matter of time before something violent happened. The angelic little girl she had rescued from a racist environment might one day break her neck.

When Molly arrived at the hotel, Susan waited, dressed in a stylish skirt and blouse combination with pearls. Molly wore a favorite flowing one-piece dress, her long white hair bright under the lights. Susan kissed her cheek and took her hands.

"Listen, I met a fellow at the bar close to my age who wants to join us at the restaurant."

"American?"

"Yes. He seemed a bit lonely. I hope you don't mind."

"I don't."

"Speaking of the bar, care for a drink?"

"Not for me, thanks."

Susan poured herself a martini from the room supplies and then glanced out the window.

"Bath is such a beautiful city."

"It is. I wonder why Jane Austen hated it?"

"She didn't say. Shall we?"

They took the elevator to the ground floor and walked toward the restaurant. Susan stumbled once, but seemed happy, holding Molly's arm in hers. Molly wondered how much alcohol she had consumed since Stonehenge.

"I've got some issues at home," Molly said. She explained her situation. "I just hope Tom can manage. Occasionally, Jenny's father shows up and it works for a while. Then he escapes when Kenya brings home a drug dealer or any other charming street person."

The restaurant was elegant and Susan followed the maître d' to their table where a stocky man with salt and pepper hair and beard waited. He had a cheerful-looking face, his smile genuine, his age possibly in the late fifties.

"Chris, this is my new girlfriend, Molly Malone."

"This is such a pleasure," Chris said. "I love to meet new people on the road."

"She has a statue in Dublin. Quite a buxom statue, too," Susan said. "I adore beautiful women, but don't worry, we're not lesbians." She motioned to the waiter. "Sir, we need drinks."

"I don't drink," Chris said.

"Well, that's too bad. Why not?"

"One drink and I become a madman."

"I'm afraid I also have to decline," Molly said.

"Suit yourself." Susan ordered a martini.

"So tell us about your travels, Chris," Molly said.

Delighted, Chris began his story. He had been traveling in Europe for ten years, with occasional visits to America. He had two sons, one a slacker who smoked dope and watched MTV all day, and the other an overachiever but with a cold heart. Chris had been married and divorced three times.

"I love traveling alone," Chris said. "The ultimate freedom to explore."

Susan saluted with her glass. "Tonight, you hit the jackpot. Two classy dames."

"Classy indeed," Chris said.

"Tomorrow, I leave for Cornwall. Don't you love England?"

"I do," Chris said.

Chris and Molly drank coffee while Susan sipped her martini.

"I always feel sad leaving fast friends behind," said Susan. "Like Molly, here."

"Boy, that's so true. I left a lovely Russian woman in Riga," Chris said. "Sad story. She wanted me to follow her to Rome, but I had to press on…in another direction. I had an old girlfriend from last year waiting in Berlin. To leave that beautiful Russian girl who I may never see again…to never know how it might have worked out. That's a sad story."

"Sad?" Molly could see the sudden anger in Susan's eyes. "My beautiful husband was crushed in an avalanche, last year. He was going to be a star but died young…horribly, I might add. *That's* sad!"

"That *is* sad. I'm sorry to hear about your husband."

"A beautiful man," Susan said.

"I must warn you, Chris, we're damaged goods." Chris looked nervously at Molly who glanced at her watch. "Susan, I need to call the States. I marked my menu. You can order for me."

"You bet!"

Chris stood up as Molly left the table. She found a public phone and took out her credit card. She knew Tom would be working on one of his self help books when she called. Their conversation was short.

"Kenya needs to be monitored, or even committed," Tom said. "I thought she was going to kill me. I've contacted the lawyer."

"Does she have Sonya?"

"Yes. She and her favorite drug dealer took her."

"Kenya won't come back until she needs something. We'll be in Berkeley next week."

"How is Jenny doing?"

"Beautiful to look at and beautiful to hear. She may be a concert violinist, someday." Molly paused. "Thomas? How are you feeling?"

"Hanging in there. Nice to hear that sexy voice, Molly."

"We'll see you soon. Love you."

When Molly returned to the table, Chris was holding forth while Susan ate. Molly picked at her food, thinking about her troubled daughter and her grandkids and home. They finished the meal, listening to Chris's narration about his life and travels. As they waited for dessert, Susan lit a cigarette.

"Didn't know you smoked," Molly said.

"Now and then."

"It's bad for you."

"I know. So what?"

"Do you drink more since you lost Brian?"

"Yeah, I do. People say Jews never become alcoholics, but they're wrong."

"Prove them right," Molly said.

"I don't need another Jewish mother," Susan said.

The waiter appeared with the dessert and Susan stubbed out her cigarette. Chris stared at her while she dipped her spoon into the chocolate covered vanilla ice cream. Susan returned his stare. "What?"

"You're so beautiful, I'd swear you were a Paris model."

Susan paused in mid bite. "What about Molly?"

"She's very…very elegant."

"Really?" Susan swallowed the ice cream. "What happened with this Russian girl?"

"Natasha?"

"Yeah. I'm curious."

Chris hesitated, watching her wet lips. The bitter light had left her eyes.

"Forget my little outburst. What happened?"

"Nothing. It was one of those painful Chekhovian moments on the road…strangers meet, are attracted to one another, then part, never to see each other again. Her face in the rain will haunt me for the rest of my life."

Molly wiped her lips. "Did you fuck her, at least?"

Chris looked at Molly, a bit startled. "Excuse me?"

Susan covered her mouth, stifling laughter.

"Sorry," Molly said. "I grow too bold."

"In fact, we didn't have sex."

"Why not?" Susan asked.

"The time for that came and went," Chris told them.

"What about the girl in Berlin?" Susan asked. "Did you bed her?"

They saw Chris was uncertain how to answer. "If you must know, we're just friends."

"Maybe that's good," Molly said. "Friends last longer."

"Friends? What's wrong, Chris? You have some problem getting it up?"

"That's none of your business."

Susan ran her fingers through her long brown hair and leaning forward, challenged him.

"You're right, Mr. Chris, it really *isn't* our business. You don't have a shot with us, anyway, so give us a little juicy gossip. Entertain us."

Molly reached over to restrain Susan. "Be nice."

"Nice? I am *always* nice. I hate to say this, Chris," Susan said, "but your bad luck with women will just have to continue. Waiter!"

Chris remained silent while Susan ordered another drink. Molly ordered coffee and Chris finally motioned for the same.

"To repeat, we're damaged goods," Molly said. "And I'm a married old broad."

"An elegant married old broad," Chris said.

"Thank you," Molly said. "Let's be friends."

Chris nodded in agreement and said, "I really just thought it would be nice to meet new people, have a little dinner, exchange stories."

"Stories, yes, we need stories!" Susan said. She gulped her martini.

"You weren't entertained?"

She glanced at the passive Chris. "I *was* entertained. You amuse me."

"Glad I'm amusing."

"You're not bad looking for your age."

"Neither are you."

"I'm not ready," she said. "I love men, even *older* men, but I am just not ready."

They sat at the table, a waiter hovering nearby.

"Don't flatter yourself," Chris told Susan. He dropped a 20 pound note on the table. "I have to get up early tomorrow. It's been a pleasure."

He stood up and left the table without a final word. After a pause, Molly said, "Ouch."

Susan showed a mock surprise. "Did I say something wrong?"

"Perhaps we were both a tad rude. He seems like a nice man."

"Too nice." Susan felt a brief shot of panic. "God, maybe he's right."

"Right about what?"

"Maybe I *am* flattering myself." Susan was slurring her words. "Who would want me?"

"A lot of people. Give it time. You are vulnerable…and I'm not very good company, myself."

Molly was surprised to see a sudden hardness in Susan's eyes. "You're *great* company." Susan finished her drink. Her expression changed. "I'm a little sick."

"Let's go for a walk."

They walked around the block, watching the fast traffic of Bath. Twilight had faded. The city of Bath looked like a glowing postcard after dark. They passed a pub but Molly kept Susan walking until they returned to the Pratt Hotel. In her room, Susan left for the bathroom. Molly sat in one of the ancient-looking chairs waiting until Susan emerged, wearing a bathrobe.

"You need coffee?"

"No. Maybe another drink."

"You should lie down."

The younger woman dropped her bathrobe and naked, turned toward the dresser photo of her late husband. Susan had a beautiful body, still slender and tight for a 45-year-old mother, and she now faced the smiling handsome man with his bright clear eyes and blond curly hair watching her from the other side. Touching her breasts, Susan spoke through tears.

"Oh God, Brian, where the hell are you? Your bride is waiting!"

Molly gently guided Susan to the bed where she slipped under the covers.

"Lie next to me," Susan said. "I need someone to hold me."

"Okay. First, lie on your stomach," Molly told her.

Susan turned over and Molly sat on the bed, gently rubbing Susan between her shoulders.

"Use the rubbing oil," Susan said. "And I want candle light."

Molly lit a candle by the bed and sprayed rubbing oil on her strong hands. She continued massaging Susan's long shapely back. Perhaps they would have been lovers in another world. Susan relaxed and went to sleep. Then Molly lay next to her, holding her slender body, kissing her gently on the neck.

In the morning, Susan awoke with a headache. Molly was gone. Susan saw the dead candle on the dresser and the bottle of scented rubbing lotion. She got up and took two aspirins with orange juice. Then she took a shower, feeling her body in the warm stream, trying to remember what had happened the night before. There was the American they met for dinner. Susan vaguely remembered the feel of Molly's strong hands. Did Molly watch her sleep after the rubdown? Did Molly squeeze out the candle flame and burn her fingers before leaving?

When Susan came out of the shower, there was a phone message. It was Alice stuck in traffic but she would soon arrive to take her to Polruan on the bay across from Fowey.

"We have to get you writing again," Alice said in her cultured English accent. "I say, I hope you're doing all right after what happened. Lovely man, Brian."

Susan dressed and packed, including the photo of her husband. Then Susan sat on the bed, badly wanting a drink and a cigarette. As her day at Stonehenge and night with Chris and Molly came back to her, Susan realized she and Molly had not exchanged personal information and numbers. Would they ever meet again? Then she noticed the photo lying on the dresser. Picking it up, she saw two attractive women, one middle-aged, one older, huddled together in front of the iconic Stonehenge.

I will find you, Susan said to herself. *Molly Malone, I will find you.*

At Gatwick Airport, Molly Malone relaxed on a plane waiting for takeoff to the United States. Rain fell on the tarmac. Her granddaughter, Jenny, had stashed her violin in the compartment above the seats. She had long straight hair and a handsome brown face.

"What did you do in Bath, Grandma?"

Molly remembered a naked woman in a hotel staring at a photo of her dead lover.

"Let's see. I saw the Jane Austen Center on Gay Street."

"Gay Street?"

"And the Pump Room, where Jane Austen's characters had tea and showed off their bonnets. I saw a lovely woman there who was in a lot of pain. We know pain, don't we? I saw the Roman Baths, *and*—I visited Stonehenge."

The plane began moving. The teenage girl regarded Molly.

"I heard of Stonehenge. A bunch of rocks, right?"

"Yes, but they're much more than that. When we are airborne, I'll tell you all about Stonehenge and the giants who brought those healing stones from Africa to Ireland, and Merlin the Magician who used his magic to bring them to Britain so King Arthur would have a place of worship and healing." Molly stopped. "I can't talk, now, we're moving."

Jenny, too old for those stories, looked out the window as the plane taxied onto the runway, preparing for takeoff.

The Day the World Blew Up
(After a story by Karen Lea Smith)

LEAH BROWN looked out the window at the dry
fountain in the garden. Their American flag was rippling hard
in the wind and Lester's pick-up was parked in the driveway.
His uneaten dinner sat on the table as Lester dialed a number
in his office. Unusually quiet, the kids waited in the living
room. Leah, wearing the pants she wore for school, wondered
if the children were more surprised than hurt that their father
hadn't taken his homemade presents.

Leah looked at the gleaming kitchen sink and
remembered irritants from the past that often set Lester off:
mail not on the table, the freezer door not quite sealed, or the
coffee pot still on. He never noticed anything unusual, not her
casual pants, or the house smelling of cleaning solvents, nor
the fresh flowers on the table with a meal of chilled wine,
lamb chops, vegetable casserole and scalloped potatoes. She
had showered and washed her hair, wanting to look good
when she asked him about teaching school rather than
cooking for his lambing crew.

Leah knew something was wrong when Lester walked
past Jared and Lucy and confronted her before she could even
ask the standard question: "How was your day?"

"Where the hell were you when world blew up?" he
yelled.

Leah looked into his round angry face. "What
happened?"

"What do you mean 'What happened'?"

After mimicking her tone, Lester entered his cluttered
office and quickly dialed, waiting for someone to pick up the
other phone.

Leah ran through the things that could have happened: Coyotes in the sheep? No, they were too close to the sheds. Machinery breaking down? But the new tractor wouldn't need parts for a while. How did "the world blow up"? For certain, Lester would talk on the phone, and Leah would postpone their conversation about continuing teaching. She would need again to talk with someone else. Someone finally picked up the other end of Lester's phone line. Lester's strong voice carried through the house.

"Soren, listen to me. Do we have wind damage insurance? The top of the granary was blown off, grain seed was blown right out of the field, and some rolling tumbleweed scattered the sheep. I don't know how many we can recover. It's bad out there. The wind twisted three wheel lines. One line is in the canal."

There was silence as Lester listened to their lawyer. Then Leah saw the children running into Lester's office. It was too late to stop them.

"Dad," Jared said, "can you glue my caboose? It came loose."

"I got 100's on all my papers," Lucy said.

Lester put down the phone and glared at them.

"Will you get out of my office? Just leave me alone. I have *real* problems to deal with now, okay? Go!"

The children backed out of the office, Lucy calm but Jared clearly hurt. Leah took the kids and guided them upstairs. Leah could feel her blood pressure spiking and would need to take her medication. She was also desperate for a cigarette.

"I'll talk to dad," she said. "It's not that serious. He's just had a bad day. Your parents aren't perfect, you know."

"If he doesn't glue my caboose, I won't give him no surprise," Jared said.

"I'll glue your train, Jared."

"We worked on those gifts all day," Lucy added.

"I know. Wait upstairs for now," Leah told them. "I know when you grow up, you'll be better people than your mom and dad. Maybe even better parents."

She could see the betrayal in Jared's eyes, and Lucy seemed resigned to another of her dad's tantrums. After the two children went to their room, Leah walked to the doorway and looked at her husband. He was listening to Soren and writing down figures. For the first time, she noticed how old Lester was getting. At forty, his hair was gone, he was getting paunchy with irregular meals and beer drinking during free time, and the bucolic scenes celebrated by poets had worn Lester's spirit. He slammed down the phone. Lester seemed calmer, staring at her.

"Well, maybe not all is lost."

"Lester," Leah began. "I'm sorry the wind did so much damage and upset you, but the kids and I didn't make it blow."

"I know, I know."

"We'll get through this. They've made surprises for you at school and I've made a special dinner. Please, dear, don't take it out on us."

He nodded in agreement. "I'm a horse's ass, you know that."

"The kids may not understand. Let me get them so they can give you your presents. Then let's eat. I need to talk to you about something."

"Honey, not now. I need to see Soren."

"You can see him tomorrow. I'll only be a moment."

"I need to take care of this. Jesus, Leah, I've had a rough day."

"You think mine has been easy?"

"No, but I have work to do."

"So do I."

Lester didn't respond, but wiped his moist brow. For a moment, he resembled a popular overweight comedian, only in overalls. Leah went upstairs to get Jared and Lucy but even as they walked back down the stairs, she heard Lester driving off in his pickup. He drove down the gravel road and turned onto the two lane highway.

"Is daddy going to the bar?"

At eleven, Lucy knew her father's patterns well.

"Well, Lucy, he's probably going to talk to Soren about insurance for the wind damage."

The younger brother, Jared, said nothing. Leah knew the local bar which faced a small manmade lake. She didn't want to drive there and confront Lester, particularly if he wasn't meeting their lawyer. Lester loved to drink and talk to his friends who would understand wind damage. A few women visited the bar to listen and occasionally talk, as well.

"I guess we'll spend a quiet night at home without dad," Leah said.

Leah ate by herself and cleaned off the table and washed the dishes. A neighbor child came over and the children left to play. The wind had dropped outside and it was a pleasant twilight. Leah looked at the empty table and imagined Cody Wolf sitting there. He taught chemistry at the local university and was a tall, ruggedly built man with a mild temperament and light brown hair. Cody Wolf was well named since he was passionate about wolves and tracked Idaho wolf packs on his web page. Leah knew Cody had a crush on her and had once even suggested they have an affair.

"I'm a married woman," Leah had told him.

"I'm married too," Cody said. "But my wife and I have an arrangement."

"Well, I don't, Cody. I am flattered, but sorry."

She knew Cody could not understand why she had married Lester.

"Leah. You should be in New York or L.A running some business firm. You're a professional business woman, not a common housewife or cook for a lambing crew."

"This is the life I chose," Leah said. "I like keeping a house and I have young children."

She didn't want to mention that she found Cody charming but a little dull, and it would be odd to have an affair with a man who loved the very wolves that preyed on their sheep. Of course, Cody could refute that.

"Wolves like live game that runs. Cows just stand there, too dumb to run, and sheep are too easy. Besides, wolves kill coyotes, the true predators of sheep. You should *like* the fact they're back in our state."

Leah didn't argue that one, but she had to point out something to Cody.

"Aren't you being a little disloyal? Lester saved your life, once."

Cody met her eyes and nodded. "True."

"Lester can be exasperating, at times, but he's great in a crisis."

"Leah, if I ever get lost in the desert or am snowed in on some mountain range, I want Lester looking for me. He's great at organizing search and rescue teams."

Leah remembered Lester's frantic activity when they heard the news. Cody had hiked into the wilderness to watch bears harvest moths just before they hibernated, but when he returned to his car, it was covered in early snow and the exit road to the main entrance—now marked closed—was blocked by deeper snow. His cell phone was useless in a dead zone, but Cody knew the rangers would see he hadn't returned.

It snowed for a week; Cody had a few rations and extra blankets. When Cody turned on the heater and car radio, he heard about a search and rescue operation to find him, but he also knew rangers would see the closed road and assume no one had traveled it. Then the cold killed his battery; Cody couldn't use the car heater or radio. He knew it was better to wait for rescue rather than risk getting lost in the deep snow. When the weather briefly cleared, Lester organized a fly over and spotted Cody's car and meager fire. Cody finally saw and met a search party. He survived, dehydrated, tired, a bit hungry, but alive. He could have perished on that blocked lonely road to nowhere.

"Lester is a good man," Cody had told her. "He deserves a hard working wife who can buck hay, but not someone so bright and attractive like you."

"Let's not discuss this again," Leah said. "And I can buck hay."

"Of course, but you're a special person."

"No I'm not."

Leah was a professional woman with a strong business education, but her secret goal was to be a journalist and not necessarily run a corporation. She could see herself covering a story in the Middle East. Having an affair seemed remote, something that only happened in movies. There would be no prince charming arriving on horseback. Leah also followed her church values and worried about her children's reaction. They needed some stability in their lives. Whether Lester was faithful might be a problem to confront, one day.

The house now seemed too quiet. After taking her blood pressure medicine and a pain pill, Leah felt her head ache subsiding. With the coming dark, she looked out the window at the gazebo and fixed herself a vodka and tonic. Then she went outside, turned on some garden lights, and sat on a bench, looking at the roses and the dry fountain. It was her favorite time, and though she knew Lester would come home late — probably drunk — ready to talk on the phone for hours, it didn't seem to matter now. She lit a cigarette, knowing the danger.

The drink relaxed her. She sat on a chair, watching the dying rays of the sun. There came a slight breeze blowing on her face. For the first time, she entertained the thought of a secret admirer. If she had a fantasy lover at this twilight hour, it would not be Cody Wolf. Leah thought back to her college days and Gordon, the handsome man one year ahead of her who was a promising ballet dancer, an unusual skill and occupation for someone from rural Idaho. They attended dances together, and Leah was flattered to have this gifted handsome man on her arm, so different from the others.

And then Gordon asked her to marry him. Thinking back on that day, it seemed like a dream from a remote past.

"I can't marry you, Gordon," she had said. "You're too perfect. You have a glamorous career ahead of you. I'm meant to work on a farm with some farmer and raise his children."

"You can follow other paths," Gordon had told her. "Besides, being married to you will prove I'm not gay."

Leah didn't mention that she often wondered if the too polite Gordon was gay. He had never touched her. How could such a beautiful man and ballet dancer *not* be gay?

Gordon left for Germany and Leah married Lester, at the time thin and crew-cut. He was always loud, boisterous and charming in his basic way, always dependable, and always a good worker. She followed Gordon's promising career in newspaper articles.

Gordon returned four years later stricken with leukemia; he died quickly. When Leah saw Gordon in a coffin at the viewing, the church filled with flowers and red drapes, she refused to believe that dead-looking, artificial husk was Gordon. She thought to herself, sitting alone in the church pew: *That can't be Gordon, who could leave the ground and sit in mid air. No, I refuse to accept that dead face as Gordon's.*

In the days that followed, Lester didn't notice Leah's grief but was annoyed that Leah wasn't responding to her usual commands and chores. Then a neighbor woman asked how Leah was doing.

"Fine. Why?"

"She's upset over losing her old boyfriend, Gordon."

"Boyfriend? Gordon? I doubt it."

"Maybe so, but Leah's sad Gordon died so young of that leukemia."

Lester looked his neighbor. "Are we sure it was leukemia?"

"What else could it be?"

Lester didn't answer. One afternoon, Lester saw Leah's grief.

"For God's sake, Leah, I liked Gordon all right, and it's too bad but—"

"I loved Gordon."

"Sure you did. Everyone liked Gordon, but he certainly didn't have any place in Idaho."

"Why not?"

"Why *not*?"

For once, Lester seemed unable to speak.

"Of course, it would be hard to find sponsors for a ballet company in rural Idaho. You know, Lester, Gordon asked me to marry him."

Lester had a way of making his face go stone-like and impassive when he was thinking of an appropriate response in a delicate situation.

"I know. Glad you didn't."

"Why?"

She waited for Lester to say he loved her and couldn't bear any rivals.

"We're starting a family, Leah."

"Gordon couldn't father children?"

Lester looked away for a moment.

"Do handsome male dancers make you nervous?"

"No—but Gordon was weird…I'm not saying he was a fruitcake or anything like that but—"

"Then what *are* you saying?"

Lester remained silent. "I got a sheep business to run," he finally said.

He left to visit the sheep and Leah left for her classes.

Now she sat in the latticed gazebo drinking her vodka tonic, and watching the dying light. She wondered if Gordon would appear. When she had visited him in the hospital, Gordon had slipped into a coma and looked very old. His once handsome face had a skull-like appearance. Closing her eyes, she now imagined him standing in the light-split darkness, the porch light catching highlights in his blond hair. She could hear Gordon's voice in her imagination.

"You would've *loved* Germany," he was telling her. "You love new cultures."

"But what would I *do* there, Gordon, while you were dancing?"

"Write. Pursue international journalism."

Leah suddenly laughed, sitting alone in the gazebo.

"I think Lester was very nervous when we saw your farewell performance in town. I caught him staring in disbelief at your rounded buns."

"I *did* make Lester nervous. He probably assumed I was queer."

"Were you?"

For a moment, Leah could hear Gordon's big laugh.

"I adore women, but why should I go through life with one hand tied behind my back?"

Leah opened her eyes and saw the night. The yard was empty. She got up and went inside and fixed herself a second drink, unusual for her. Leah walked toward the corral where Rocket, one of her old sway-back horses, walked slowly back and forth. She knew that soon they'd have to put Rocket down. Rocket had been her favorite horse when she was a teenager, and they rode all over the country together and appeared in parades. Leah sat on a chair by the corral and sipped her drink. She lit a cigarette, took a few puffs, then stepped on it.

"We're both getting old," she said to the horse. "Isn't that right, Rocket?"

She looked up at a sliver of moon and a sky filled with stars, and then unbuttoned her shirt, feeling the night breeze on her throat and breasts. She closed her eyes. A shudder of longing went through her body. Perhaps she fell asleep and dreamed because suddenly Rocket was staring at her with large equine eyes. Rocket seemed younger and she heard a voice: "You were my favorite rider, but I will have to leave you soon. One day, we will meet again and ride through green and golden fields." Rocket stared at the dead cigarette on the ground. "You'll meet me a lot sooner if you keep smoking."

Rocket placed his large hoof on the bent cigarette and turned it in the hard earth.

Leah suddenly sat up, feeling the cold; she opened her wet eyes on a black sky. Leah stood up and walked to the fence, peering at Rocket, quietly grazing in the low light. She couldn't see the details of his swayed back. Leah then heard sounds in the house, the voices of her returning children. Leah touched her throat and then buttoned her shirt. She found her glass and poured out the rest of the drink.

"I better go inside," she said.

The Wife and the Monk

LEAH had felt nothing after the initial headache, except a sense of drifting on a black sea, but she heard distant voices, some urgent and frightened, and a man asking when the harvest team would show. She heard another man sobbing and murmuring, "Please God." Leah tried to open her eyes and speak. Then the darkness parted and she saw a field washed in reddish-golden light, and in the distance, exotic animals: lions, tigers, zebras, and gazelle. She saw a lake and dolphins leap clear of the bright waters. Leah wanted to ask why dolphins were swimming in a fresh water lake, or in *any* inland lake. Then she saw her two favorite dogs running toward her.

"My God," Leah said. "Red Dog and Blue."

Leah knew something was wrong, for if this was a dream, it was intensely vivid. The two dogs had been dead for decades. Then she saw the large, gray, heavy-boned horse ambling toward her: Chuck was the name of the animal she had ridden as a little girl. Chuck would stand by a fence so Leah could mount him, and they would walk through open fields, often playing games with imaginary riders and horses.

Leah looked at the beautiful field. "I get it. So when do the dead relatives show up?"

Even as she spoke, Leah saw them: her parents, her favorite aunt and bow-legged uncle, and Gordon, her first boyfriend who died of a rare blood disease when she was in college.

Suddenly, the bright pale sky grew darker, the golden light faded, and other voices filled the air. They seemed unnaturally loud. Leah sat up and saw a nurse staring at her, the young face in shock. A round-faced heavy-set bald man in overalls was standing near the bed, sobbing.

"Praise Jesus," he said in a loud, grating voice.

"It's a miracle," the nurse said. She called for a doctor who came back into the bright intensive care room. Leah lay back and felt the thick tube sliding from her mouth but she couldn't speak.

"I don't understand this," the doctor said. "The aneurysm bled out and destroyed her brain stem. I have her brain scan. Her coma score was four. That means—"

"Maybe God intervened," the nurse said.

"The donor harvest team is here," he said, staring at Leah, an attractive young-looking sixty-year-old-female. "Good thing they're late."

The doctor studied Leah's pale smooth face. Her blue eyes were clear and alert. "Can you speak? What's your name? Where do you live?"

Leah wanted to tell them her name and that she lived in Idaho. She pressed her tongue against her front teeth and whispered, "Leah."

"I can't believe this." The doctor gazed at Leah. "Welcome back," he finally said.

Leah wanted to ask who the heavy-set man was but then she knew.

"*Something is wrong*," she thought to herself.

When Leah left the hospital the next day, the papers carried the article about her amazing recovery after being pronounced brain dead, and how she woke up moments before the donor team arrived to harvest her organs. The cerebral hemorrhage that nearly killed her had suddenly sealed itself. She was back with her husband and her two college-age children, Lucy and Jared, who had come home expecting a death. She vaguely remembered seeing another man, middle-aged, thin, standing in the hospital parking lot, a solitary man who seemed familiar, but then the waiting car took Leah back home. Her normal life resumed.

Learning to live again, she felt like a patient recovering from a stroke. The distant past was clear: her animals, her parents, her high school, her old boyfriends, but the recent past was like a misty twilight where figures appeared and then vanished. Sometimes she asked questions and received no answers but only averted looks. Her job as a loan officer in a bank came back to her. She quickly recognized the world of numbers and percents as old familiar friends. Lucy and Jared, both their early thirties, took her to lunch and told her about growing up in rural Idaho. Leah recognized them but remembered them better as younger children, not adults. They were certainly relieved but also slightly unnerved that she had survived.

"Maybe Jesus wasn't ready for you," Jared said.

"Or it was one of those strange medical occurrences that we can't explain," Lucy said.

"I wish I remembered recent events more clearly."

"I can catch you up on any details," her daughter said.

"But now you have to get used to familiar surroundings," Jared insisted. "Jog your memory of the home where you lived. You need stability."

Leah looked at Jared. "I remember my parents and their very poor farm. I remember the two of you sitting on a horse in front of me. You both were about two and five. I remember Lucy at about eight months walking around me, holding my little finger. But the months before I collapsed are a blur."

Her husband took her on a tour of the old house and the grounds, and he seemed like an old familiar friend. They made love but mechanically. She knew Lester was a well-meaning good person but sometimes took over conversations, talked loudly on the telephone when she was trying to sleep, and often ignored her suggestions about where to eat or what to do. Lester did not have any magic. Leah could not imagine marrying him, even when younger. There was also a phantom lover who appeared to her in dreams, tall, thin, face blurred, but with slender fingers and strong hands. At times she wanted to ask what had happened in the last five years that were lost. Was there a secret lover, somewhere? Or a public one? Her closest friend seemed to be a nun who received one of her loans, and Leah couldn't ask her about imagined past lovers. A next door neighbor, an elderly, partially blind woman named Mabel, would not have many answers.

One afternoon, Leah did laundry and found some men's underwear in the basket that didn't look like Lester's boxer shorts. Leah smelled them and suddenly had a vision of running naked with a naked man through a field of golden poppies. There was a river in the distance. She was still frolicking with her phantom lover when Lucy called her from England where she had just taken a new teaching job. After a bit of small talk, Leah got the nerve to ask if there was someone else in her life. Lucy didn't seem surprised.

"I often wondered if you had another man. I know dad can be a pain in the ass, sometimes. But I never had any proof. Did you?"

"I don't remember any," Leah said.

"Why do you ask?"

"I don't know. Why did you wonder if I had another man?"

"Just before your cerebral incident, you seemed so happy," Lucy said.

After a pause, Leah said, "Don't tell your brother."

"I won't."

Her miraculous recovery happened in September, and the fall was full of warm sun and cold night temperatures and bright fall colors. At Christmas time, Leah and Lester went to a convent that featured bread baked by nuns and wine sold by visiting Trappist monks from Utah. Though famous for their breweries, the monks were good wine makers, and even produced a local Riesling. One could also buy the best wines from California and even France. They paid a small sum and enjoyed an afternoon of wine tasting in the large but bland hall. The monks were dressed in dark robes and white hoods; a middle-aged but younger looking monk with unusually long hair served the customers. The monk stared at them as they walked the brightly lit room with other visitors. He seemed distracted but held up a bottle of white wine.

"Behold, the nectar of the gods." He looked at Leah. "You are an Idaho native, so you will relish our own Riesling," the monk said, regarding her with an intensity that made Leah uncomfortable. "This is made from sun-washed Idaho grapes. Nurtured in Idaho soil. Forget the homely potato, for here we have a noble wine."

Leah was surprised to hear so much speech from a monk dedicated to silence.

"I do like wine and I *am* a native of Idaho," Leah said. "Do I look like an Idaho native?"

"Idaho native, born and bred."

"True. And you?"

"California, originally. I prefer growing grapes and selling wine to raising the monastery's cattle. Ironic, since we're forced by the order to abstain from meat." The monk winked at Leah. "I love to drink and I'm a secret carnivore."

"The Trappists can drink?"

"Alcohol is not forbidden, praise Saint Benedict."

Leah smiled at the charming monk. At the end of the hall, Lester was entertaining other visitors with one of his over familiar stories about castrating sheep. Leah waved to one of the nuns she knew — Sister Mary — and then studied the cheerful talkative monk. He had a curved nose, close-set blue eyes, a small mouth and a slightly gaunt look. She would have said he had the face of a visionary painter they discussed in a humanities class. The face was familiar and unfamiliar, and he seemed to have an almost conspiratorial look.

"What wine would you suggest Mr. — ?"

"Brother Michaels. Leah, you will like this wine, but you also may want champagne for Christmas and Easter guests. We also have a cheaper Merlot that Lester can certainly guzzle…I mean, enjoy."

"You know my name. Do I know you?

The monk blushed. An older monk came over to the counter. He was a portly man with stern eyes. "Is there a problem here, Brother Michaels?"

"No problem, Brother John," the monk said. He looked at Leah. "*Everyone* knows you. You are Leah Brown and your husband is Lester Brown, the county commissioner."

"Yes, that's true. I know one of the nuns, here."

"Correct. Here are some suggestions."

Leah agreed to his suggestions and watched as Brother Michael left to get her bottles. Lester finished his story: "I mean, you have to get their minds off ass and onto grass."

The light inside the large hall was pleasant, and Leah wondered what the vineyards looked like. When Brother Michaels returned, she noticed that his expression carried a look of sadness…perhaps a nervous sadness.

"If you decide to visit us again, perhaps I can take you on a tour of the vineyards," he said. "I'm also growing a sculpted garden, modeled on the Kylemore Abbey garden in Ireland's Connemara County."

"Kylemore?"

"'Kylemore' means 'big wood.'"

"The garden sounds lovely," Leah said. "I love flowers."

"I know. I mean, I imagine you do," he added. "All the Kylemore nuns are growing old with no young ones to take their place. Do you think religious orders are dying?"

"I wouldn't know. My office gave a loan to the nuns to run this place, and they are elderly, but are religious orders actually dying? *You* joined."

"I did." He lowered his eyes. "I'm a novice monk in training. Three years before final vows. Then I have a life of obedience, prayer, silence, vegetables when not fasting, and dull men in robes." After a pause, he said, "A bargain is a bargain."

"We're Lutherans," Leah said.

"I remember."

"You *remember*?"

"I mean, I remember that Martin Luther had a point," the monk quickly said. "He had the *guts* to question the Catholic Church of his time."

Brother John suddenly appeared. "I can ring that up," he said. He made quick hand signals to Brother Michaels and pointed toward an elderly couple at the end of the counter.

"Of course," the monk said, his eyes lingering on Leah's face.

"It's been a delightful afternoon," Leah said, holding out her hand. Brother Michaels held it for a long time, meeting her eyes. Then he saw the pack of cigarettes in her shirt pocket.

"You *must* quit smoking," he said.

"Brother Michaels?" There was an angry tone in the older monk's voice. "The other customers?"

"Of course," Brother Michaels said. "Say hello to your children." He moved down the counter. Lester suddenly appeared at Leah's side. "You ready to go?"

Leah made a private note to read about the Trappists and was still watching Brother Michaels serving other customers, his face partially obscured by the hood, when Lester loudly informed her that he planned to see some friends on the way home.

"John and Alice bore you," Lester bellowed, "but I think we owe them a visit, and maybe we can have dinner. They may be getting a divorce, you know."

Leah looked at her husband's round, moist face. "I'm sorry," she finally said. "You said something?"

As they left the convent, they saw Brother Michaels in the parking lot with a tall man dressed in a suit. The man seemed to be admonishing Brother Michaels, who looked up and saw her. He gave her a little salute as she walked to the snow-covered car with Lester.

At work the following week, she questioned Sister Mary about the monks when she came in to pay on their convent loan.

"We're pretty much separate except for the Christmas and Easter holidays. The monks are lovely people, aren't they? Dedicated."

"What do you know about Brother Michaels?"

Sister Mary, her face wrinkled, was puzzled. "I don't know them well by name."

"He waited on me and seemed very friendly."

"Oh yes," Sister Mary said. "He's always joking. I heard that he plays guitar and sings when the other monks are maintaining verbal silence. Of course, singing isn't talking. They eventually discover if they have a true calling."

"Where is the vineyard?"

"Not far from the convent."

"And the garden?"

"I don't know about a garden," Sister Mary said.

Christmas was pleasant with her visiting children and Lester, though predictable, didn't annoy her with his loud voice and repeated stories. The weather was cold, the roads icy, but it was a season she loved with the lights and the tree, with the presents and the midnight church services she attended with her children. While sitting in the pew, she wondered briefly what prayers Brother Michaels was saying with his fellow monks. She remembered his youthful looking, sinewy hands. Who was the man in the suit? What "bargain" was Brother Michaels talking about? She had looked up the Trappist order on the internet, and also searched for photos of the Kylemore Abbey's artistically structured but functional garden. As the service concluded, Leah knew she would visit the convent in the spring.

During Easter week, Lester surprised Leah when he agreed to an afternoon of wine tasting, though they had enough wine at home. "I'd like to see how Alice is doing since their separation," he said. "I can drop you off at the nunnery."

"That would be fine," Leah said.

And then Leah stood in front of the convent and the large hall where the priests and nuns sold their wares to support themselves. Brother Michaels was not behind the counter. Leah wondered why she should care. She had a quick cigarette outside and then saw the distant vineyards, looking so symmetrical and beautiful in the soft April light. A monk passed.

"Excuse me, do you know where Brother Michaels is? He had some excellent suggestions for wine when we were here last Christmas."

The monk stopped. "Ah yes, Brother Michaels." He met her eyes and smiled. "He's taking a few tourists on a tour of the vineyards. He *does* know his plants and grapes."

"I guess every new member brings something to the table."

"Yes, they do."

The monk walked on. Leah finished her cigarette and walked toward the vineyards. She passed the tall man in a suit and remembered him from the parking lot.

This is ridiculous, Leah thought to herself. *Why do I need to see this cheerful, yet sad monk?*

But she felt a certain lift in the heart when she saw Brother Michaels, dressed in jeans and a white shirt with a Levi jacket. He was pointing to the vineyard. Something about him suggested a skilled actor giving a big speech. He stopped in midsentence when he saw her. The sun was bright on her blonde hair. Leah didn't think he would blush again, but he did.

"Welcome, Mrs. Brown. I was just explaining that monks' robes aren't conducive to the dirty work that needs to be done to protect and nurture flowers, plants, and rows of young grapes. You've been a farmer so you understand. I hope we have a hot summer." He looked at the small group. "Do robes make the monk?"

Everyone laughed and Leah joined them as they walked through the rows and listened to Brother Michaels's spiel. At one point, she took out a cigarette but when he glared at her, she put it away. "Young grapes are sensitive to poisonous nicotine," he lectured.

As they walked on, a young woman who worked at the winery took over. Brother Michaels addressed the group.

"Ms. Hawthorne knows more about the wine-making process than I do, but I'll meet you at the hall to help you select—after a taste, of course—the wine that's *begging* to be on your table."

Brother Michaels' strong but lyrical voice ceased. A gentle breeze stirred the leaves. Leah stood in the brown narrow path between the rows. She was uncertain whether or not to follow the group when Brother Michaels nodded to her.

"There's an irrigation canal near here that we use. Maybe you have an alternative suggestion in case there's a drought." He smiled. "Or maybe you want to join the others?"

Leah looked at the departing group and said, "I can walk with you."

"We have to be careful," Brother Michaels said with mock drama. "We may cause a scandal."

"I'm a grown-up," Leah told him.

At that moment, she imagined Lester sitting across from a sobbing Alice, having coffee and speaking to her in his softer voice. He would vow eternal friendship and hold her veined hand.

"It's nice to see you, again, Brother Michaels."

"Nice to see you."

They walked along the irrigation canal, but Leah could not make alternative suggestions.

"Moving pipe for irrigation wouldn't work well, here. This canal and steady rain are what you need. I'm sure Ms. Hawthorne knows that."

"I think she does."

They stopped at a bench and sat down. Leah took out a cigarette and lit it. "Sorry," she said. "I need a smoke."

"We all have addictions. It almost…it could kill you," he warned.

"I know." She looked at the water moving in the narrow channel. "I don't know why I'm here, but you *do* interest me. I know I interest you. Why?"

"You're an attractive woman."

"Thank you. I don't usually hear that from priests, pastors or Trappist wine-makers."

"I know. It's awkward."

"Tell me about yourself."

"It's a long story."

"Really? I have the time. You are unique," she said. "California, you say?"

He proceeded to tell her about his life in San Francisco and Los Angeles, about writing screenplays and plays, about working theatre in New York, and about teaching. Leah enjoyed the rhythms of his voice and the feel of sunlight on her face and shoulders.

"I think what I really am is a writer of fiction and nonfiction."

"A writer and not a monk?"

"I could do both, but I don't think I'm meant to be a Trappist."

"But you *joined* the order."

"Yes. I had to keep a promise."

"To whom?"

Leah could see the uncertainty in his face. "I'm not sure." He suddenly laughed. "I was something of an atheist. I guess the proper term is secular humanist. I still am, to some extent, but I made a bargain."

"With God?"

"Yes. A bargain with the Chief. If he, she, or it exists."

"I never thought I'd hear that from a monk."

"Neither did I." He looked at her and Leah felt a sudden warmth that disturbed her. The canal water made a comforting flowing sound. His eyes held hers for a long time. "You never have doubts, do you?"

"Sometimes. But I believe Jesus is my savior."

"I know. I find that charming, actually. I'm not convinced Jesus Christ meant to start a Christian church." He stood up. "We should head back. They'll be looking for me. I'm not supposed to get too friendly with the female customers. We *are* celibate, you know."

"I know. Lately, so am I."

Brother Michaels ignored her remark. They saw the group returning with Ms. Hawthorne.

"I can slip in with them." They walked on. "Tell me, what *was* the bargain?"

Brother Michaels sighed in a theatrical manner and Leah saw his expression go from sadness to resignation. "I was in love with a beautiful woman who had left her husband. After a wonderful time, together, she collapsed in a motel and I saw she was dying. At the hospital, I gave prayer a shot and told a God I didn't believe in that if she survived, I'd do anything, even become a monk living on bread and water for the rest of my life."

"And?"

"And it happened. She survived. A voice or maybe an angel told me she would live but I could never see her again or she would die, and then I was knocking on the door of the Utah Monastery. I picked the Trappists because I admired the work of Thomas Merton."

Leah stopped, staring at his face. "That's a touching...and amazing story. Why can't you see your beloved anymore?"

"Punishment for my non-belief," he said. "And yet I *do* see her and that makes it worse. Look, Leah, you better join the others. I'll meet you inside."

"I need to know more. What was her name?"

She could see a sudden panic in his eyes.

"No need to know that. It all happened in a parallel universe."

Brother Michaels consulted his watch and walked quickly across a bridge; after following him with her eyes, Leah joined the group walking toward the hall. She tried to process all the information. Was this monk a great story teller, did he have some divine connection, or was he living in a fantasy?

Inside the hall, the guests made selections. Leah said hello to Sister Mary and furtively watched as Brother Michaels, now in robes, waited on customers, his big theatrical voice filling the room. She waited, looking out the window for Lester whom she suspected would be late. Finally, she went to the counter and bought four bottles of Riesling.

"Excellent choice," Brother Michaels said.

As she took the box of wine, she looked into his face. "When will I see you again? Next Christmas?"

"That's a good time."

"Maybe I'll do a retreat at the monastery," Leah said.

"Excellent suggestion. Maybe I'll have a book done by then."

"I'll read it. Do you have an address for letters…besides the monastery?"

Another customer asked a question and Brother Michaels moved down the line. Occasionally, their eyes met. Leah finally walked outside and stood on the front steps. It began to rain heavily, and Lester was not in the parking lot. Blowing sheets of rain washed over the parked cars. Then Leah saw the man in the suit opening an umbrella. He stopped in front of the hall. "You're waiting for someone?"

"Yes. My husband." The tall man held the umbrella over her. "Are you a Trappist?"

"No, I'm a lay person, but I run the monastery in Utah until a new abbot arrives. Would you like to wait inside?"

"Yes."

Leah wanted to ask about Brother Michaels but didn't. "You have retreats for women?"

"Yes." He held out his hand. "Brett Anderson."

"Leah Brown."

The rain beat down on the parking lot as people ran for their cars. Inside the hall, customers had left and the monks were cleaning up. Leah could feel Brother Michaels watching her. She became aware of Brett Anderson speaking: "Many come to us to get away from the busy world, Mrs. Brown. A spiritual retreat is essential for mental health."

"Do some become monks?"

Brett Anderson laughed. "Well, now and then, someone decides they want to stay and cultivate a life of meditation in Christ." He looked into her eyes. "Is that what you want, Mrs. Brown? You might talk to the good sisters here."

"Just a thought, Mr. Anderson."

She dialed Alice's number on a cell phone and heard her high-pitched, somewhat whiny voice. "Yes? Who is it?"

"Alice, could you put my husband on, please? I need a ride and he's late."

"Oh, I'm sorry, Leah. Just a moment. Lester?"

Leah suddenly heard Lester's voice. "We forgot the time, honey. It's been so hard for Alice and all."

"I can imagine. Come get me — now."

After some off-phone murmuring, Lester came back on the line. "I'll be right there, dear."

Leah was startled when Brother Michaels took her cell phone, speaking in a disguised gruff voice: "Hey, big boy, you better come and get your woman or the nuns will get her."

"What? Who's this?"

"Or better yet, she may become the first female Trappist. Won't us monks love *that.*"

Stunned, Leah wasn't sure whether or laugh or be offended. She could hear Lester's shocked voice on the other end of the line as Brother Michaels began singing the Beatle song, "You're Gonna Lose that Girl." He had finished the first verse when Brett interrupted.

"Brother Michaels, I'm enjoying the concert but you need to help the others pack."

"At your service," the monk said. He winked at Leah and returned the dead cell phone. "Another time, perhaps. And tell Lester to start being punctual."

Brother Michaels joined another group of monks moving a table. Brett Anderson was professional, but Leah could see his slight annoyance at Brother Michaels' impulsive behavior. "Shall we wait outside, Mrs. Brown?"

"Sure. Was Brother Michaels a rock singer?"

"I wouldn't be surprised." Brett Anderson carried her box of wine bottles. As they stood outside, he offered information about the flamboyant monk. "Brother Michaels came to us one night after a personal tragedy. I guess he needed a place to heal and meditate. That's what we are here for. Of course, we don't provide therapy or sabbaticals. Then he asked to join the order. A novice can stay for a few months and then decide on a temporary three-year profession if the elders agree. After that three-year period, the monk can take final vows."

"Have the elders made that first agreement, yet?"

"No," Brett said. "But soon. Brother Michaels has brought some entertainment to the monastery…perhaps too much entertainment," Anderson added. "He needs to remember his vow of silence."

"I'd like to see his garden."

"He is creating a beautiful garden. Why are you so interested?"

"He's a charming man."

"A Trappist monk needs to be devoted to a life of silence, work and worship, not charm."

The rain had stopped by the time Lester arrived. Brett Anderson gave her the box and walked inside. Leah approached the pick-up and saw Lester's face in the window. "Who the hell was that clown on the phone?"

"My monk boyfriend. Why were you late? Holding Alice's scrawny hand?"

"No, I just forgot the time. I'm a horse's ass, you know that. And Alice has suffered a tragedy. She's never been alone, before."

"No, she hasn't."

Leah got into the truck. As they drove away, she looked through the streaked side window for Brother Michaels, but he had disappeared. She also realized she hadn't asked a vital question: what had happened to Brother Michaels' woman?

Then it was summer and extremely dry and hot. Leah went to the hospital for a check-up, and sat across from the doctor holding her chart. He looked at her brain scan and shook his head.

"Well, I guess if I was a religious man, I'd say it *was* a miracle. I was sure you were brain dead."

"What happened, exactly?"

The doctor explained how she had a hemorrhage between the brain and the skull and the pressure of the leaking blood created devastating pressure. Leah looked at the scan and though not a trained doctor, could see obstruction in the upper brain area.

"Then it seemed to heal itself. A subarachnoid hemorrhage can *sometimes* be contained, but in your case?" He shrugged. "Amazing. It does happen, occasionally, that some so-called medical miracle occurs. We don't know how it happens, however. Perhaps it's just the body's desperate drive to survive. I've seen one Alzheimer's patient essentially brain dead take a sniff of oxygen after a stroke and suddenly awake, wondering why she was in a hospital. She called her startled daughter but slipped back into a dead state before the daughter arrived. I've seen patients wake up after many years in a coma. We just can't explain everything," the doctor said.

"But you don't believe in divine miracles?"

"No," the doctor said. "I need empirical evidence." He looked at her and asked, "How is your memory?"

"I can remember everything going back to my childhood."

"How about your short term memory?"

"I've had lapses at work. It's coming back."

"And your husband?"

"He's fine. I may be back here if he talks me to death."

"He was quiet, that day, subdued, though I knew he was in deep shock. You failed all my tests and I called it. The harvest team was literally in the air when you woke up."

"And here I am."

"Here you are. How's the other fellow?"

"Other fellow?"

"Yes, your first husband. Lester, I believe?"

"Lester *is* my first and *only* husband."

"Really? I recall someone I thought to be your husband or maybe a significant other giving instructions to let Lester in."

Leah stared at the doctor. "Let Lester in? I don't understand."

"Only spouses and relatives are admitted into intensive care, unless they have permission. Lester *is* your husband? Then and now?"

"Of course."

The doctor reviewed the hospital report. "I guess you're right."

"What did this so-called 'other' husband look like?"

"He had a nice face, and was tall, relatively thin."

"My husband is Humpty Dumpty. He hasn't been thin in twenty years. Do you have a photo?"

"I'm afraid not."

Leah sat in the small office. "I don't understand."

"I hope you *do* understand this. You have high blood pressure so you're still at risk of this happening again...take your blood pressure medication and you *must* quit smoking," the doctor warned her. "Or you could be back here again, and with *no* miracles, this time."

"I'll try, Doctor. I guess I'm just a drug addict. Tell me—about this 'other' husband."

"Maybe I saw too many *Twilight Zones*."

"What was his name?"

"I don't remember. Look, I'm just confusing you with another case."

"How many brain aneurysms do you get?"

"Sadly, quite a few," the doctor said. "Usually it's from a trauma."

Leah got up and started toward the door. The doctor called out.

"I can review the original admissions report and let you know."

"Thanks." Before she left, Leah had one more question. "It happened on a weekend, right?

"Right. We got a 911 call for an ambulance. I don't think you were home."

"Who made the call?"

"I'll check."

When Leah arrived at home, she saw a note from Lester who had gone out to drink and play cards, so she ate dinner alone. It would soon become a pattern, eating alone and going to bed alone before Lester came home, often drunk.

"You need to spend more time at home," she said at breakfast.

He glared at her over cornflakes. "I know I'm a horse's ass, at times, but I need a little freedom, okay? We may have to sell the sheep. The New Zealand competition is kicking my ass. They don't got coyotes in New Zealand."

"We need to save our marriage," Leah said. "You're not a husband, you're a roommate."

"That's nuts," Lester said. "Besides, you need a familiar surrounding."

"How's Alice?"

"She's fine and she's got *nothin'* to do with this. In fact, she invited us to a diner party. I think we should go."

"Fine," Leah said.

Often, Leah found herself looking around the small house in this small town in a rural area of the state surrounded by farms. She tried to remember the house and it did seem familiar, but it also seemed dead and sterile, like created rooms in a museum. A tall old clock in the hall kept time. Perhaps she didn't belong here and Lester was meant to be a roommate. Perhaps Lester would soon leave.

But it was Leah who left first, leaving a note that summer on the kitchen table while Lester had the sheep on the open range. Mabel was in her front yard watering roses and waved to her as she drove toward the two-lane road. Leah drove across open country with distant mountains to the Trappist monastery in another state. Brett Anderson received her.

"What a pleasant surprise," he said. "The men and women live in separate bunkhouses but they come together for meals. You can join the monks for prayer in the big chapel, but we have many small private chapels for prayer and meditation. We ask that you help with chores, including the cattle, but you can have free time to meditate." He smiled warmly at her. "You need to escape from the world?"

"I need escape from a lot of things."

"Does your husband know you're here?"

"Yes."

"Why did you choose our monastery?"

"Is there another?"

"I guess not."

"Mr. Anderson?"

"Yes?"

"Could I work with Brother Michaels on his garden? I have a fondness for plants and even something of a green thumb."

Leah could feel the scrutiny as the monastery director observed her in silence.

"His garden is as big as a football field so we'll certainly have enough vegetables to sell. He doesn't use pesticides, either, so it's totally organic, the latest craze. You want to work with him, you say?"

"Yes. Is there a problem?"

"No, but it's hard work in the hot sun."

"I worked farms all my life."

"He's an interesting man," Brett said. "A few women who come here find him attractive. Maybe it's because monks are unavailable. You know—forbidden fruit. I don't have to add that this is a meditative environment. Romances are discouraged."

"Of course."

She hesitated. "What was his name before he came here?"

Brett Anderson leaned back in his chair. They could hear distant cattle and birds sang in the trees outside the office window. Leah was about to apologize for asking when he spoke: "Does it matter?"

"No."

"So far, we haven't got all his paperwork. We still need baptism and confirmation certificates, but they can easily disappear." There was a silence. "Bruce Michaels was the name he gave us when he came here. I think he's more comfortable with us, now," Brett said. He looked at her application. "It's not necessary and we have many faiths, even a few secularists here, but do you believe Jesus Christ is your lord and savior?"

"Of course."

"You don't consult crystal balls or astrology calendars?"

"God no."

"You're not coming here to research and write a novel?"

"No."

"Good." He stood up. "Let me show you around."

They walked the pleasant shaded grounds, looking at the cattle pens and the small rooms where each visitor slept. There were no televisions or radios. Brett Anderson pointed out a quiet grotto with a gazebo for visitors to sit quietly, and Leah felt a calm watching groups of monks and others on retreat. As they started walking toward the garden, Leah reached for a cigarette.

"You can't smoke here, Mrs. Brown."

"Of course." She put the cigarette away. "It will be tough."

"And we have only vegetarian meals, except for sick monks."

"I can handle that."

They stopped and looked at the massive garden built into a hill. Each quadrant was small but precisely laid out. It looked like a patchwork of many colors, and Leah knew the incline would help with irrigation. There were many colors: greens and reds and golds, the multi-colored roses and the leafy plants that the monks would soon harvest and sell. Workers stooped in the rows, weeding and moving soil. Then she saw Brother Michaels, wearing jeans, boots and a soiled shirt, preparing to run a waterline down a row. He looked thinner, and his face was tanned. He had grown a small beard, but the hair was shorter. Brett started to call out but Brother Michaels turned. He looked at Leah and nodded as Brett spoke:

"This is Leah Brown. She's going to join us for two weeks and work in the garden." Brett turned to her. "Lunch in an hour. We all believe in eating together, but in total silence."

"Okay. Thanks."

Brett glanced at Brother Michaels and walked away. Leah turned and saw the monk now walking toward her. Leah could feel her heart racing though the monk's expression remained neutral. She wanted to ask many questions and even embrace him. To Brother Michaels and the other workers, Leah was any new visitor volunteering for the garden crew. Brother Michaels walked past her to a parked van and came back with a spade, some gloves, and a hat.

"You'll need these, Mrs. Brown. I also have something for your arthritis, but don't overwork your hands." He directed her to a section of the garden. Brother Michaels addressed his crew. "Let the others attend to noisy, smelly cattle. Our purpose is more noble: the battle against the noxious weed."

It was good to hear that dramatic voice, again. They began working. Leah's hands started aching and she was glad when the bell for lunch sounded. There had been a strange moment when, trying to uncoil the long heavy hose, she felt Brother Michaels come up behind her and gently take the hose from her, their bodies close for a moment. She liked the feel of his arms, remembering the first time in high school she sat on a boy's lap and felt his sex and the warmth as his arms encircled her in a moving car. She smelled the sweat on the monk's headband and once again was running naked with a naked lover through a field of golden poppies.

Lunch was served in a hall and Leah sat with the other guests, the monks seated across from them. Brother Michaels faced her, either by coincidence or luck. She looked up from her vegetables and pea soup. She watched him spread mayonnaise on his asparagus and then lick it slowly before biting off the head. She slipped a juicy halved peach into her mouth and caught him watching. An old priest led them in a prayer, and with head bowed, Leah noticed Brother Michaels staring vacantly at the table. After the prayer, she wrote on a napkin: *I would like to talk to you.* He shook his head. Brett Anderson walked through the hall and nodded to her.

Back in the garden, Leah pulled more weeds until her hands ached. She suddenly felt dizzy. Brother Michaels gave her some water with a pill, and after their work was finished, Leah walked toward her dorm room, craving a cigarette. She stopped in the small chapel. Leah found the Catholic Mass dull compared to the lively Lutheran service, but the religion itself was more dramatic. They seemed to have more focus on the ceremony of the blood atonement and more martyred saints. Leah stared at Christ hanging on the cross, his gaping wounds still bleeding profusely. When she walked outside, she saw Brother Michaels sitting in the gazebo and walked toward the little grotto. With slow deliberation, she sat next to him.

"Brother Michaels, I presume?"

He pointed to his lips and shook his head.

"Still not talking?"

He nodded yes.

"Who is Bruce Michaels?"

The monk pointed to himself and winked. She saw no other change in Brother Michaels' face. Then he relaxed and shrugged.

"Are you glad to see me?"

He touched his heart like a mime. They heard crickets and the air was pleasantly warm. Leah started talking, explaining that soon she may divorce her husband. He had a choice, counseling which he would never accept, or a divorce, which didn't disturb her as it should have. "My kids will feel bad but they're grown." She looked at him. "I see you've gotten to like vegetables."

He nodded yes.

"Mr. Anderson warned me about romances while on retreat."

Brother Michaels whistled and wiped his brow in a theatrical manner. Leah laughed.

"I don't know why I'm here," she said. She faced him. "You tell me. Why am I here?"

He met her eyes but didn't speak. They heard the voice of Brett Anderson.

"Mrs. Brown, Brother Michaels has vespers. Why don't you come and look at our livestock? We have a few sheep, you know."

"Certainly," Leah said. She got up. Brother Michaels waved good-bye to her as she walked away with the director of the monastery. She walked past a pasture with Hereford beef cattle, and then Leah saw the small herd of sheep grazing on a hill.

"We use them for wool, but I guess we could start selling them."

"After lambing, that's what you're supposed to do, let them graze, fatten them up and sell them for meat."

"We also have a bee-keeping operation if you're interested." They leaned against a fence. Leah enjoyed the bucolic scene but sensed Brett Anderson was troubled. "Your husband called," he finally said. "He thinks you've been bewitched by some sick monk."

"Sick monk? I came here to get away from *Lester*. He comes home late and usually drunk. I think he's seeing another woman."

"Does he know Brother Michaels?"

"I doubt it."

"I don't want him coming down here disturbing our peaceful retreat."

"I don't either," Leah said. "Brother Michaels is a decent soul, a breath of fresh air."

Brett Anderson didn't respond. They started walking back. He didn't want to tell her that Brother Michaels' social security number was a fake, and that they had no proof of his age, a requirement for the monastery. The new abbot would demand an explanation. Occasionally, mentally disturbed people showed up at the monastery seeking some personal vision or salvation but not a true vocation.

"I do like the peaceful feeling, here," Leah said.

"The new abbot arrives tomorrow."

"I look forward to meeting him."

They walked toward the main hall and the large building where the guests slept. Leah wondered why she was here and if she would dream of Brother Michaels, that night. One past nightmare was disturbing: Leah was meeting the phantom lover in a motel, stripping off her clothes, waiting for his hot embrace and full lips, when a sharp pain hit her brain and she found herself in a vortex, swirling toward a black sea of oblivion. Voices were sounding all around her when she suddenly awoke, sweating and exhausted.

In the morning after bread and tea, she watched the monks finishing their early morning prayers. Brother Michaels knelt among them, and sitting in the pleasant chapel in an outdated building, she wondered why men would choose this cold sexless life of prayer and meditation. Were they worshipping God or denying life?

Her work detail at the garden revealed a problem. Brother Michaels pointed to a mound of dirt that looked like a small volcano. "Mole," he said, barely audible.

"Least it's not a gopher," said Leah. They're worse. They eat plants. Moles eat insects."

"But a mole can inadvertently damage the roots with his digging. Even in the garden of Eden comes this new snake."

He made hand signals to another assistant to who gave directions. "We're digging and preparing a new quadrant, people. This way."

Leah wanted to talk to Brother Michaels but followed the group of volunteers. She saw the monk staring at the molehill. In an hour, after using a rototiller, she felt an ache in her hands and the air was growing hotter, the morning dew gone. Then she heard a disturbing voice and turning, saw Lester glaring at her.

"What the hell are you doing? I got a crew back home that needs to be fed."

"So feed them. You know how to cook."

"Leah, be reasonable. You're not even a Catholic."

"It's peaceful, here."

"Peaceful? The kids are worried. You had some memory loss, you know. You're supposed to heal in a familiar environment."

"It's not my environment," Leah said. "It doesn't feel right."

"Look, we separated before it happened, but it's worth another shot."

"Separated? I knew it! Who did I run off with? Tell me that!"

"You ran off with no one. Please come home, Leah."

Lester stood in the bright morning light, holding a straw hat between his big hands. Leah saw Brett Anderson and an older priest walking toward them.

"You can't be here, Mr. Brown," Brett called out. "This is our abbot, Father Sheehan, and you need permission to stay here."

"This is…*was* my wife," Lester said. "She needs help."

"This is a place of meditation," the abbot said. "Surely you understand."

"Understand what? Where's that goofy sick monk bastard?"

"That's enough, Lester," Leah warned. "You need to leave."

As Brett Anderson and the abbot circled Lester, they saw Brother Michaels coming across the field carrying a shotgun. There was a burning unnatural light in his eyes.

"Jesus Christ," Lester said. "What new game is this?"

Leah felt a rush of fear. Perhaps there had been a moment when she fantasized loving this man outside the monastery. Brett Anderson and Father Sheehan pulled away from Lester who stood facing Brother Michaels as he walked by them lifting the shotgun; pointing at the molehill, he fired both barrels.

*　　*　　*

LEAH and Lester left the monastery in separate cars, Leah carrying a phone number of the mysterious monk who would explain everything if she chose to call. Leah drove down the highway, trying to put it all in perspective. Mabel and Alice had invited her to play cards and Lester would not be there. Did they have some secret to reveal? She also had a message to call her doctor. He would know who admitted her that day. Perhaps Leah would then call Brother Michaels, after talking to the doctor. At one point, feeling dizzy, she had to stop at a small town pharmacy. Leah found a blood pressure machine which confirmed her pressure had spiked. Leah knew she needed to get home and take her medication. She lived in fear of that sudden headache coming back, but lit a cigarette while driving home.

At the monastery, Brother Michaels stood in the small office and told Brett Anderson and the abbot that he had tried to keep his bargain with God, but either God had rejected his promise to serve or their celebrated deity didn't exist anymore than Jupiter or Zeus did.

"What bargain?" Brett Anderson finally asked, his voice subdued.

"I wanted Leah Brown to live. I promised to enter a monastery if God brought her back from a coma. She *did* come back and I came here."

"Her medical condition had nothing to do with any bargain," Brett said. "Maybe it was a coincidence. Maybe it's your fantasy. Maybe it's another elaborate lie. Mr. Brown is right—you need help."

"We don't recognize miracles as easily as you do."

"Well maybe I do, Father Sheehan. Or I did. I have kept my word."

"You don't have a true vocation, that's all," the abbot explained. "You are excused from all religious duties."

"I know I will never abandon the woman I love again…regardless of threats or promises."

"Speaking of promises, it's time for prayers," the abbot said.

Michaels couldn't leave without a parting shot from a favorite author, Albert Camus: "All your certainties aren't worth a single strand of a woman's hair."

"Three cheers for the French existentialists. Please go," Brett Anderson said. "We'll take care of your garden. It really is quite beautiful, you know," he added, not unkindly.

Brother Michaels appreciated the comment. He felt comfortable in jeans, a white shirt, and Levi jacket. "My work of art," he said. "Feed it, nurture it, enjoy its sparkling colors and partake of its fruit in remembrance of me."

"We'll retrieve your buckshot," said the abbot. "And deport the mole. Good bye and good luck, Mr. Michaels."

"Father Sheehan? My name is Brewer, Michael Brewer."

And then he was driving his old battered Chevy Nova through the open desert of Utah. Michael Brewer took some comfort that visitors in the future would marvel at his carefully sculpted garden, and that the gentle monks would benefit from the sale of its vegetables. Driving always allowed him the pleasure of thought and consideration. It was a form of meditation. He thought of the lovely Leah.

He remembered their chance meeting on good Friday and the days and nights of their secret liaison; he remembered Leah collapsing in his arms in a remote motel; he remembered kneeling at Leah's hospital bedside, her estranged husband waiting outside in the lobby demanding entrance; he remembered staring at Leah's still face with the animal-looking snout coming out of her mouth and the slow rise and fall of her chest with the respirator. Then he found himself kneeling by the bed, his hands touching her leg and shoulder, eyes wet with tears, his face pressed against her side, his lips moving in a desperate prayer: "Please, God." A bargain was made. Now the bargain was nullified. Despite the angel's warning, he would find Leah Brown and they would start again, two lovers committed to a life together, two lovers who had cheated death, earning a second chance.

Off the shotgun highway, he saw the familiar motel. A hitchhiker stood by the road. Michael Brewer's cell phone rang.

The Wedding

JAMES GREENE drove his wheelchair to the microphone and began speaking from a prepared manuscript. Though nearly bald, he had obviously been a handsome man in his youth. The audience of teachers, police and lawyers listened to his analysis of gun control and the Second Amendment. He had a strong conclusion.

"I've heard the joke about the fact we have a right to keep and bear arms, not artillery, but the Second Amendment is clear. What part of 'the right to keep and bear arms' do the gun control advocates not understand? Of course, we need to keep guns from felons, and I don't have a problem with gun registration, but as a former cop turned lawyer, I think the Constitution is clear. A gun's a gun, whether it's a pistol or an assault rifle, and Americans have a right to own them. Don't even think about mugging me. I've got mine under my coat."

The audience gave him scattered applause, and Greene turned the chair to ride off stage. He knew gun control advocates had a hard time getting angry with a man in a wheelchair, though his disability came from MS, not a gunshot wound. Off stage was Max Cochrane, the next speaker. He was a solidly built man with a pony tail and an expressive voice. He sat in a chair to be eye level with Greene, which Green recognized as good wheelchair etiquette. They shook hands.

"I don't own a gun but I guess you a have a point. What about bazookas and flame throwers?"

"They are *not* guns."

"Tell my scary neighbor that."

"Those weapons are illegal, anyway." He checked his watch. "Listen, I'd l like to hear your talk on Aristotle and court arguments," Greene said, "But I have a wedding to attend. I vowed to walk my daughter, Sandra, down the aisle."

"You will," Cochrane said. "As for my topic, all lawyers know the basic principles of argument, debate and persuasion. I'll just give them a few identifying labels like Aristotle's enthymemes for deductive reasoning. It should aid basic understanding."

"Definitions *do* aid understanding," Greene said. "Come to the reception, Mr. Cochrane. Loraine and I would love to have you. Let's hope I don't fall on my ass."

"You'll do fine, and I'll try to make it."

James Greene guided his chair out of the building and to his van which was built to accommodate wheelchairs. Once behind the wheel, he felt a sense of freedom. Many had remarked how lucky he was to still drive after 20 years of MS. Other MS victims had faced terrible paralysis and loss of speech. Greene hated the extreme valleys and mountains of MS. Any moment, his legs could go numb, or a bright light might flood his eyes, blinding him. He would never improve. At home, Greene had learned to navigate lurching from chair to table and from table to couch. He knew his gait was comic, but to walk Sandra down the aisle to wed another police officer would complete a dream he shared with his wife, Loraine.

At this moment in the dressing room, Loraine had finished her daughter's hair and now applied powder on her shoulder to hide a new double gun tattoo meant to honor "Mom and Dad." Loraine was celebrated by a .25 caliber and Greene a .45 caliber, the tattooed guns within double hearts. James Greene had never expected to see a tattoo on his daughter.

"That's what even professional women do, daddy," Sandra had explained. "They *all* get tattoos, these days. They aren't just for outlaw bikers and sailors. Times have changed."

"They certainly have," Greene had said. Then he kissed her.

James Greene arrived at the hall. After changing into a tux, he met his daughter in a separate room. Sandra had fine clear features framed by natural blonde hair, and a strong but shapely body. They had planned a secular wedding with a Justice of the Peace officiating.

"What do you think?" Sandra said. "The dress is traditional enough?"

Her playful expressive eyes always moved him deeply.

"It's lovely," Greene said, "and you're beautiful. John is a great guy. He'll be worthy of you."

"I'll train him well." She embraced him. "But I love you more than anyone, daddy."

"I love you, too, daughter. I hope I don't fall on my face. I could."

"Lean on me. If you fall, we'll fall together."

They heard the wedding march and when the doors opened, James Greene escorted his daughter down the aisle, walking one step at a time, his legs like lead weights. The young dark-haired groom fought tears as they slowly approached. James Greene got to the place to hand off his daughter and then, sweating heavily, sat down next to Loraine who was already dabbing her eyes. Years before, they had lost another daughter in a car crash, and moments like these helped to ease the pain of that terrible loss. The ceremony went quickly.

At the reception, James Greene led the guests in a toast.

"I made a vow that despite my MS, I would walk my daughter down the aisle at her wedding. I have kept my vow." He glanced at John. "And as to my new son-in-law, John, you take care of Sandra or I'll kick your ass."

John laughed. "You want a piece of me?" He raised his glass.

The guests could see the double gun tattoo showing through the powder on Sandra's shoulder. The hired band, Dexter Flanagan and the Backdoor Boys, covered songs by the Stones, Eagles and Johnny Cash. The lead singer, Dexter Flanagan, had an old fashioned hair style like Cash's, and a voice with a similar resonance. The dancers moved in time to the music.

As James Greene sat, watching his daughter turning on the dance floor with her new husband, he felt a hand on his shoulder. Looking up, it was Max Cochrane holding a glass of champagne in his other hand.

"Looks like a wonderful party," he said.

"You are welcome," James Greene said.

If I Had a Hammer

IT was oppressively hot in the university speech tutorial lab as one student stood up and another signed in, waiting for an available tutor. On the wall was Raphael's School of Athens and photos, including portraits of President John Kennedy and Martin Luther King, Jr. A headline on one computer screen mentioned job losses across the country. As tutors continued working, the department chairman walked into the lab. He was a small balding wiry man named David Cook and when he saw tutor number five, David motioned for him to follow, which number five did after removing his ID badge. Lisa behind the desk took it and smiled.

"Leaving so soon, Mr. Cochrane?"

"Dr. Cook needs to see me."

"Nothing serious, I'm sure," Lisa said.

"We'll see."

A few tutors watched Cook and the taller Cochrane leave. Lisa glanced at other instructors, her expression suddenly impassive. Cook's office across from the tutorial lab was large with a table for conferences near the open door and shelves with papers and books. His own desk sat by the far window. On the desk was a wedding photo of David Cook and his bride, Judy, an attractive blonde woman, her hard clear eyes confronting the camera. The two men took seats at the table. Cook held some papers and a file folder. Max Cochrane sat with his back to the hallway, and after a considerable silence, felt a need to speak.

"You got my dossier there, Dr. Cook?"

Cook smiled and said, "Max, I prefer to call it a personnel file."

"No major complaints, I hope?"

"Nothing major."

Cochrane squinted in the glare from the window as Cook studied his file.

"A bit hot for spring, wouldn't you say Dr. Cook?"

"It's very hot."

"Too hot for ice hockey?"

Cook said, "It is *never* too hot for ice hockey…which we play indoors anyway."

"I should probably exercise more," Cochrane said. "I'm getting heavy."

"Ice hockey can test your manhood, that's for sure. There's something about gliding fast across the ice pushing that puck to take a shot with some monster about to drive you into the wall. You can take the shot or you can flinch and miss the chance at a goal."

Cochrane thought to tell a story about one of his desperate lucky knockouts but decided to remain silent. There was a long pause, when Cook suddenly spoke. "I admit, I like to ambush bullies myself." Then he changed the subject. "I hear you're going to a Clarence Darrow symposium, this summer."

"In Boise. I'll read a paper on the law and persuasion."

"Sounds great. What about the rest of your summer?"

"A July class would've been nice."

"The administration canceled them because they claim summer classes lose money which isn't true, they make money." Cook closed the folder and regarded Cochrane. "It was sad about Joe's death."

"Lovely man. Good colleague, teacher and poet."

"You attended the memorial?"

"Of course. We each read one of his poems."

"I should read his work. Sally must be devastated."

"She is."

Cochrane could still hear Sally's voice as she celebrated the man she had lived with for 20 years, and he was touched, remembering how speechless he was at his sister's funeral. Cook's voice cut into his memory.

"You know, diabetes took my uncle. Terrible disease."

"It is," Cochrane said. "Why didn't you attend?"

Cook took a beat and said bluntly, "I didn't think I'd be welcome."

"But Joe liked you."

"I liked him…and his wife."

"Why would you be…unwelcome?"

"Max—have you been reading the papers?"

"I have. You're not at fault for this threatened job loss at the school."

"I feel responsible, all the same."

"I wonder how much of this is simple paranoia started by rumors." For a moment, Cochrane felt like he was back in court delivering an argument. "You've been fair, and so far, our department's done well. Enrollment is up, and we have many speech majors. That should help preserve jobs…right?"

"Yes. It should." Cook stared past him at another person passing in the hall. "But we are vulnerable to major changes."

"We are," Cochrane said.

He felt the heat in the room, despite air conditioning. Then Cook began to speak. He was a small man but had a loud, often grating voice, and Cochrane felt like he was hearing a speech in a play. The door was still open and Cochrane imagined students and faculty members listening outside as Cook's voice echoed off the walls.

"I carry a burden. We used to have an emergency fund to keep staff employed, even lesser teachers. At one time, I would have said this liberal arts university had a deserved reputation for being diverse, firm but fair, progressive but solid, and our department was exemplary for the state…maybe even the country. The last president was a scholar…and the perfect articulate gentleman." Cook put his hands to his temples in a dramatic fashion. "But now? President Luna can barely talk, and our emergency fund is gone. We have a new ruthless order in place, Mr. Cochrane, and they will take advantage of our national financial crisis." Cook met Cochrane's eyes. "This is *not* the university I originally joined. This is *not* the department I wanted to lead under these circumstances. These are *not* the conditions I envisioned."

"They may improve," Cochrane said.

"No."

"It will get worse?"

"It is getting worse." Cook leaned close to him, though his volume was still loud. "The president wants to transform our Wyoming teaching college into a research institution like MIT, which is absurd. We are *not* the Massachusetts Institute of Technology." Cook grinned, but Cochrane saw genuine sorrow in his eyes. Cook held up a letter. "This is from the administration. They ordered me to let people go…and *I* have to choose or they will choose for me. I am *forced* to make *awful* decisions. An era is ending. Destructive change has begun. I will watch my department being slowly dismantled while the administration gets rich and powerful."

Cochrane leaned back in his chair. Cook's penetrating gaze disturbed him, but his own voice was level when he finally said, "So the rumors are real?"

"The rumors are real."

"But we have record enrollment. You *need* teachers."

"Oh, we will keep the classes open—but as for teachers? Our nontenured professional lecturers have had a good ride: decent pay and benefits." Cook cleared his throat. "That brings me to the reason we're here, Max."

Cochrane nodded to himself. Perhaps he knew the truth before even sitting down. "Well, I knew my luck would run out eventually."

"Luck? This isn't a casino."

"But I am guaranteed one year's notice if you fire me."

"Few actually get fired. Lecturers with three consecutive years of service are guaranteed a year's notice," Cook said. "This month, letters will go out informing four nontenured instructors, including Sally, that their next contracts will be terminal. Two more *without* the year's notice will be let go this week." Cook took a deep breath. "That includes you. I'm sorry, Max."

"This week? David, I am in my third year!"

"But you haven't *completed* your third year."

Max felt his anger rising, and something else, a fear of some hidden motivation. His sense of comfort was ending. Max balled one fist and imagined facing a tangible opponent in the ring.

"I also teach political science. And what about my publishing credits?"

"Commendable but not compelling for the administration."

"What is this really about, David? Am I too liberal for this department?"

"Some students have complained about your liberal politics, which you shouldn't reveal…but certainly political speeches and rhetoric go together." Cook glanced at the file. "Actually, you're quite…quite popular."

"I am also 50 years old. It will be very difficult to get a comparable job with benefits in this tank town."

"I'm aware of that."

They sat facing each other. Max Cochrane wondered how many instructors were eavesdropping in the hall.

"I even bought a house, here."

"I know you did. What about a law practice? You could defend Abdul who is being fired for protesting too much. He has tenure."

"I won't go back to the law…unless I sue the university. You realize this is a breach of contract?"

"That's incorrect. You need three consecutive *complete* years, Max. That's the deal."

"Wait! When I started, it was *two* consecutive years."

"They moved the goal posts." Cook picked up his folder and papers.

"Who else is leaving, David?"

"I can't tell you, nor can I give reasons why."

"How convenient. Who will replace us?"

"Graduate students."

"Graduate students don't have the expertise of professional lecturers, some with years of experience."

"I agree. Eventually, the administration wants nothing but graduate students. If the departments are merged, I could lose my position."

Max Cochrane stood up. "I'll see you in court."

Cook walked him to the open door. "Max, I'm not at fault, here. This isn't the gunfight at the OK Corral."

"Maybe it is. I'll see the president myself."

"You'd be better off talking to Luna's dog. See Provost Davis instead, although I don't trust him. He's slick. His wife got an extension *and* a raise to coach women's basketball."

"They lost every game, last season."

"Of course. It's university logic. Oh — Mr. Cochrane?"

Cook was going to offer his private number and any possible help, but Max Cochrane was suddenly gone. Dr. Cook returned to his desk and filed Max Cochrane's folder. The wedding photo on the desk recalled happier days, and for a brief moment, he felt a bitter-sweet longing, staring at his wife's shining face. He murmured her name aloud: "Judy." Then he pulled open the drawer. A holstered .38 lay on an outdated calendar.

Walking down the hall, Cochrane met Sally, a short woman with grey hair.

"How's it going?" Cochrane motioned with a thumb down. "I'm next," Sally said.

That night, Cochrane lay in bed with Rita Johnson who chaired the English Department. She had a full body and dark silver-streaked curly hair, and liked to joke that she had been a sensuous plus size model in a parallel more realistic universe.

"Don't take it so hard," she said in the semi-darkness. "One door closes, another opens."

"Or all doors close. Rita, I really don't want to hear that passive Buddhist crap right now. My income will plummet."

"I had to let four people go, but we'll probably rehire them next year if massive enrollment continues in this bad economy."

"Rehire them…but without benefits?"

"That gravy train has derailed, I'm afraid…and I resent your comment about Buddhism. It's not a passive philosophy. It teaches that life is full of pain and how to deal with it. The first noble truth is suffering."

"I deal with pain by making my enemies suffer, so you can meditate in the garden while I kick some ass."

"You don't understand. Buddhists can protest, but not violently. Look what happened with the Buddhist monks in Burma. They protested, and many were killed or arrested."

"We have to fight back," Cochrane said. "If we had a union, we could go on strike."

"This is a right to work state. Unions can't do collective bargaining at the college level. Write an article refuting the Administration's policies. It might carry some weight."

"I doubt it."

They were silent for a few minutes.

"You know, Max, there *is* a genuine recession in the country. People are losing jobs everywhere. A lot of this bloodletting isn't the president's fault or the department chairman's fault."

"I know that," Cochrane said. "But something else is terribly wrong."

She kissed him gently on the cheek. "Why don't you make love to me, stay in the moment and forget David Cook?"

"Not tonight, Rita. Sorry."

He could feel her plump but sensuous body stir in the bed next to him. She rested her head on his shoulder, and then slid her hand down his chest and along his thigh. Rita kissed and licked his stomach.

"Maybe I can help you," she said. "My man needs to relax." He liked the sound of her rich contralto with its smoky edge. "Let me do all the work for my manly warrior."

A week later, Max Cochrane waited in the provost's office. The secretary didn't make eye contact. The president's office adjoined the provost's, and Cochrane wondered if President Luna was in. He found the president's regular addresses to the faculty surreal.

"Yes," he once said. "We can make this little college an 'MIT of the West,' a place to research, you know, make smart bombs. Boom!"

A professor asked an obvious question: "You really think this small Wyoming college can become comparable to MIT?"

"Sure. We just have to raise the bar. With dedicated enervation, teachers can….let's not forget…current teachers can…you know?" The voice trailed off. A reporter raised his hand.

"Current teachers can do what, exactly?"

"You tell me," the president said, his round joyful face moist in the lights, "I'm going to set an example and donate."

"Donate time?"

"My raise."

Another reporter called out: "In this economy with undergrad level teachers losing their jobs due to lack of funding, you're getting a *raise*?"

"Thirty-six big ones. It's called a president's 'market value.'"

"And you're donating it to saving a teacher's job?"

Luna grinned. "What I do or not do with my raise is my business."

There was a moment of silence. "Any final statement, Mr. President?"

"We live in uncanny times." There was a pause. "Go Cowboys," he said.

Cochrane was still thinking about that press conference when the secretary opened the door and motioned him inside. "Doctor Davis can see you, Mr. Cochrane."

"Thanks."

He entered the plush office. Provost Davis rose from behind his ornate desk and advanced to shake his hand. He was a well-dressed distinguished looking man with a handsome face, and grey hair at the temples. "Mr. Cochrane, let us have a seat."

Cochrane followed the provost to a separate couch. He felt a slight discomfort since the couch was small and they nearly touched thighs. He could smell cologne. A plate of cookies lay on a plate.

"Have a cookie?"

"No thanks," said Cochrane. The provost took one.

"Mr. Cochrane, you're in Speech and Rhetorical Studies?"

"Yes."

"Good old Aristotle. Don't you *love* the ancient Greeks?" The provost had a sweet resonance in his voice. "You've been a lawyer…and competed in the Golden Gloves, correct? You were good?"

"I coulda been a contender."

The provost laughed. "What can I do for you, Mr. Cochrane?"

"As provost, you're our faculty voice in court. We lecturers teach the required 101 courses needed to graduate. How can the university dismiss us without dropping them?"

"Required classes won't be dropped, Mr. Cochrane. We *will* find teachers, including some grad students or former teachers. Current instructors will teach extra classes without extra pay. It will be tough. You know yourself, the economy is *killing* us. Tax revenues are dropping."

"If I leave, next year, you'll have one fewer tax payer."

"That's sadly correct."

"And how can we become a research institution? This isn't Cambridge."

"Not yet." The provost held out his hand and made a fist. Cochrane saw the class ring and the image of a rodent. "Behold," he said.

"And that is?"

"The brass rat, the official image when I graduated from MIT."

"Congratulations," Cochrane said. "A rat."

"You can't fight a war or a disease without us. As to your question about turning this quaint little prairie college into what the president calls an 'MIT of the West,' it *will* take time."

"MIT started during the Civil War."

"Good history, there." The provost continued. "It will take grants, a new medical school, a strong emphasis on science and a gradual shift from liberal arts teaching to technology research."

"And if it doesn't succeed?"

"I don't know," Doctor Davis said. "Nothing is certain. It could all end, certainly at the undergrad level. Don't feel alone. I could be fired tomorrow."

"You believe that?"

The provost winked and touched his thigh. "Or I could move on. You don't really think I want to live and die *here* on the prairie?"

"Nor does the president?"

"I'm sure this is a stepping stone for him. He'd love to be a president of UC Berkeley, for instance. Their so-called radical days are over."

The provost removed his hand. He wet his fingers and picked up some cookie crumbs from the plate. Cochrane noticed a door leading to an adjoining office.

"Doctor Davis, is the president in?"

The provost licked his fingers. "I don't believe so."

"You know his office hours?"

He gave Cochrane a conspiratorial smile.

"I don't hear Barbra Streisand. That's his favorite singer. I don't know how many times I've heard that *awful* song, 'People.' She's not my favorite singer, I'm afraid."

"You don't like big show tunes?"

"In fact, President Luna also loves the musical, *Camelot*."

"He admires the Kennedys?"

"I'd say King Arthur."

"I don't see any round table here."

"You are again right on the money."

Max Cochrane noticed a wall photo of the provost with his arm around President Luna. There was a fleshy sensuality in Luna's face, not unlike the young Elvis, but a crew cut replaced the Presley pompadour.

"Did Dr. Luna go to MIT?"

"No."

"What is Luna's degree in?"

"Chicken Science."

"And what is—?"

Doctor Davis patted Cochrane's hand.

"My dear Mr. Cochrane, let's be frank, shall we? We are dependent on the cave people in the legislature for funding. Until the recession ends, there is *nothing* we can do. I will keep your situation in mind, however. Give me your resume. Who knows? Something may come up. I may even need a lawyer." The provost glanced at his watch. "I have another meeting."

Both men walked toward the door.

"Morale is low," Cochrane said. "There's anger and frustration."

The provost held his gaze and nodded. "I was afraid of that." He slapped him on the shoulder. "Don't give up hope, Mr. Cochrane."

"I won't. There's going to be a faculty meeting to discuss strategies. We'll even invite a union representative."

"I'll be there."

"You and President Luna may not like what you hear."

The provost folded his arms and gave him a slightly reproachful look. "I'm sure we won't, but it's a stressful time for *all* of us." Cochrane opened the door. The provost called out, his voice taking on a harder edge. "Mr. Cochrane, be careful and *do* remember you'll need good recommendations when you leave us."

"So will you," Cochrane said. He paused. "I knocked out a stronger opponent, once. Let him hit me until he got tired and dropped his guard. Then I decked his ass with a right cross."

"My, my," Doctor Davis said. "Clarence Darrow in boxing gloves."

When Max Cochrane left, the provost rapped gently on the president's door, and then walked into the large dark office. No music played. In a corner, the president was throwing darts at a well lighted dart board. He couldn't see the president's face.

"No 'people who need people', this afternoon?"

"The Jew girl from Brooklyn is beginning to bore me. Time to hear some Wagner." The provost suppressed a groan. "How did your meeting go, Bud?"

"All right. Another disgruntled employee."

"Another undergrad lecturer whining about losing his job?"

"Mr. Cochrane is not a whiner. He is someone to take seriously."

"Really?" The president threw a dart from the shadows. "He can take this seriously. It's progress, Bud, progress. Jobs are created and jobs are lost. That includes lecturers, deans and department chairs. The Lord giveth and the Lord taketh away." He threw another dart. "Join me?"

"I have work to do," the provost said. "Merging departments without chairmen takes effort."

For the first time, he saw the president's round face in the light.

"And I don't got no work? Making all these cuts takes effort." He threw another dart, a bull's eye. "Saving your wife's coaching job took *real* effort."

"Speaking of wives, where's yours?"

"At a health spa," Luna said. He laughed and picked up another dart." Any cookies left?"

Outside, Max Cochrane spotted Judy Cook standing near the office watching students on the quad. Her face, slender body and long blonde hair were striking, and she had a direct stare some found unsettling. Newspapers referred to her as a former model.

"It's getting pretty grim on campus these days," Cochrane said.

She saw him but didn't respond, quickly disappearing into the adjacent school museum. Moments later, Max Cochrane was walking across the campus when he saw two policemen escorting Abdul, a professor of engineering. Cochrane blocked the two officers.

"What is going on?" he demanded. "He's a professor, here."

"Please step aside, sir."

Abdul waved him away. "It's all right, Max. They are firing me but I'll sue."

"You have tenure! What's the charge?"

Abdul didn't answer.

"We need to escort him off campus, so step aside, sir."

The security guards marched Abdul off campus. Cochrane watched them go. That evening, he soaked in a hot tub in Rita's backyard. It was a cooler evening with a dark sky overhead full of stars and a low moon. Cochrane felt the relaxing rush of warm water. Rita lay back, gazing at the moon, water swirling around her breasts.

"Rita? What do they have on Abdul to fire him?"

"Nothing. A trumped up charge of hitting on female students. I don't believe it. Basically, he called for a no confidence vote on the president. That could be a career buster."

"Where will this end for us?"

"The president can only do so much," Rita said. "It's a fantasy to convert our university to a huge research institution like MIT. But he can do damage before he moves on. He could combine the colleges of arts and sciences…"

"Which means you lose your place as Department Chair?"

"That could happen. He could make some undergrad required classes no longer required. Or he could declare financial exigency and fire all of us, but that would be admitting the university is bankrupt. It won't look good on his resume. The bottom line is that it's a power grab and we have to resist these thugs."

"From you, that's strong." The pump stopped and he turned it back on; the warm water began swirling again. "Either way, I'm screwed. I'll have to find work out of the state."

"We will need instructors to teach classes filled to the rafters."

"Rugged devil that I am, I need medical insurance."

"You could have some of mine."

He watched her profile, feeling her hand clutching his thigh. Then she looked at him, the moonlight catching highlights in her thick curly hair.

"Your medical insurance? How so?"

Rita stood up, facing him, water running off her breasts and nipples.

"If you married me."

Cochrane suddenly felt something inside wither, withdraw; he no longer saw the sensuous middle-aged woman before him. They had made love in the tub many times, and it always took him out of his body with the warm nights and the hot swirling water and the feel of her rocking body, the touch of her hands and mouth.

"Jesus, Rita, you're lovely but are you going to take advantage of this crisis, too?"

Cochrane knew he had said the wrong thing, even as the last words escaped his lips. He watched her pull away, her eyes suddenly hard and focused, searching his face in disbelief. She lifted herself out of the tub and covered her naked body with a towel.

"Look," he said, "I know that sounded awful but…"

"You better leave right now," she said. "You son of a bitch. Get out."

Moments later, the door to her bedroom closed and he was alone. A cat walked along a support wall facing the foothills. Max Cochrane finally got out of the tub and pulled on a bathrobe. He gently opened the bedroom door. He could hear Rita crying, lying on the bed on her stomach, the towel across her buttocks.

"Jesus, I'm sorry, Rita."

After a moment, she rolled over on her side. "I understand. We're not partners, just friends with benefits. And you're right, for *real* benefits you'll need a job out of town. Well, go ahead. Why should a law scholar and teacher stay here? Maybe this should be our last night together." She sat up, lifting the towel, facing him. "You can leave. Adios."

"Rita?"

"You have a point, Max, why should you be trapped in marriage? Why make a *real* commitment? Go on, get lost!"

She had stopped crying. He was about to respond but he dropped the robe and settled on the sofa across from the bed, pulling on his jeans. Perhaps he wanted her to stop him but she stared at him in the partial darkness. His bulky outline in the mirror watched him.

"You got nothing to say?"

"No."

"Talk to me, Max."

"I'm sick of the situation at school, but I like what we have and I guess marriage is a little scary."

"I imagine for you it is. You better go. We can talk, tomorrow."

"I'll have something to say to Luna, that's for sure."

"I bet you will."

He dressed and quietly walked from the room. He wanted to kiss her good night but didn't. Rita lay back on the bed, staring at the ceiling. At the door, Max Cochrane stopped. It was raining outside and he saw lightning followed by thunder.

"*What the hell am I doing*?" he thought to himself.

"Max?"

He turned. Wearing a bathrobe, Rita stood in the front room. She walked toward him.

"Now is the time for love, not arguing. Come to bed."

"I think you're right," he said.

They lay next to each other and Cochrane had a strange dream. He was addressing the faculty, holding a smoking pistol in his left hand. He shouted, "From this very gun that I used to drill that traitorous school president, I have a bullet for myself." The faculty was screaming, "Live, Max, Live."

Cochrane woke up to find Rita on top of him. He entered her and they began to move together, the world rushing away into a stormy oblivion.

It was raining on the Rainbow Motel ten miles south of town when Judy Cook pulled into the parking lot. A few cars and two motorcycles were parked by the anonymous apartments. She stepped out of the car into the rain. In a lightning flash, her eyes reflected anxiety and anticipation. A clap of thunder rolled across the valley. She opened an umbrella and searched for number 9. She found it and knocked on the door. When it opened, a flood of tungsten light illuminated her youthful face and bright blonde hair beneath the dripping umbrella. She stepped inside.

After sex, her nipples still erect, Judy lay in bed hearing the storm which seemed louder than normal. The crack of thunder frightened her for a moment, and she wondered what she was doing in this small town, involved in a weekly tryst with a man who thought the word "Jew" was also a verb. Luna had turned off the bright lights and now played with the video playback. Judy stared at a wall painting of Indians on horseback hidden among quaking aspens and tried to recall when the fleshy but sensuous university president with bad grammar had seduced her. Perhaps it was that faculty party when he confronted her over the punch bowl, his unblinking eyes never leaving her face. She could see he was aroused. As expected, he was enthusiastic in bed, and Judy — still beautiful if aging — loved men with power. Judy sat up, the sheet falling from her small but firm breasts. Luna was kneeling by the television.

"Do we have to see the video now?"

"Why not? I'd like to watch you servicing Big Mickey."

"Big Mickey or Little Mickey?"

"It was big enough for you, baby. Come on, you mother, connect."

"Will this end up on the internet? It could ruin my reputation."

"Or make you famous," Luna said, squatting in the semi darkness. "Hell, this tape could get me in trouble if it goes public."

"They can see my face, not yours."

"They'll hear my voice cheering you on."

"You can erase the voice."

"You're right." Luna stood up and smiled at her. Naked, he looked like a paunchy version of the Greek God, Pan. All he needed was a goatee and a flute. "But your squirrely little hubby might recognize the famous Luna ass."

His laugh was throaty, like a young boy's. Luna slipped into the bed next to her. Judy did like his sensual if slightly crooked smile, but Luna's adolescent arrogance gave her pause. Was he, in fact, the God-awful crew-cut moronic shithead her husband claimed?

Suddenly an image appeared on the television screen, Judy's face topped with a wimple, an erect penis in her mouth. Though startling and gross, it thrilled her more than expected. They could hear Luna's hoarse breathy voice between occasional claps of thunder. When Luna came, Judy tore off the wimple, blonde hair spilling out, her lips wet as she faced the camera with an arrogant triumph. Seconds later, the screen turned to snow.

Luna nibbled her neck. "You play a beautiful skin flute."

"I was a music major in high school. Just ask the football team," Judy told him. "You know, that video could be used against me in divorce court."

"You're right," he said. "I'll delete it."

To her surprise, Luna was kissing her nipples again, and then mounting her with an animal surge. When they left the motel, the storm had stopped. Luna, looking less like a lover in his conservative suit, asked her a question: "Who is this Max Cochrane guy?"

Judy stared at him blankly. "A lecturer. Who cares?" Then her expression changed. "I can't believe I starred in an amateur porno film."

"Amateur? You're a pro." Hearing that, Judy felt excited and a little afraid.

"How many secret videos did you make? And you should not dismiss my husband."

"That little squirrel? He don't scare me."

"David's tougher than you think. I'm ready to tell him the truth. And just when will you divorce your mousy little wife so we can make it legal?"

Luna's grin always disarmed her. "Soon, baby, soon. Relax."

The confrontation between the faculty and the administration came at noon. President Luna was not in attendance. Cochrane had to dismiss his class early to attend. He heard Abdul's wife angrily denouncing the school president for suggesting her husband was not a good Muslim or a loyal American. Then Rita took the microphone and told them that she was no longer chair of the English Department, but now part of a combined English, Speech and Theatre Department.

"A Dr. Moth will run all three combined departments," Rita said.

Others shouted or waited for the microphone. Then David Cook addressed the crowd.

"I am Dr. David Cook, former chair of Speech and Rhetorical Studies. When you have a bully about to block your shot and throw you a dirty punch, you have no choice but to strike first head on, and then, if you're standing, pass or take the shot. Or you take the shot knowing the bully will take you out from the blind side, leaving your blood on the ice. So be it. President Luna and his administration of outsiders are destroying the small liberal arts college we once knew and respected. They are robbing us. They've had their shot. We have to take ours."

"And how do we do that?" Cochrane asked.

He could see the fury in Cook's eyes. "We can deliver a vote of no confidence, as Abdul suggested. That will embarrass President Luna before the legislature, the community, *and* future employers."

There was a general cheer. Max Cochrane grabbed the microphone. "We hold these truths to be self evident…that all undergrad lecturers are equal. I say we issue a vote of no confidence *and* walk off the job…an unofficial strike!"

People began shouting on both sides. The provost was standing in the back; he walked up on the small stage of the spacious room, raising his hands for silence.

"May I speak?"

Finally, the crowd grew silent. The provost paused, and Cochrane handed him the microphone.

"Thank you. I'm glad to see so much energy," Doctor Davis said. "Before you start singing 'We Shall Overcome' or "I'm Stickin' with the Union,' I suggest you hear from the president himself."

"He chose not to show," Rita said.

The provost gave the crowd a dazzling smile. "*Au contraire*," he said, "President Luna will speak."

"Where is he?"

"There, Mr. Cochrane."

The provost pointed to the screen that was suddenly activated. When someone hit the lights, President Luna appeared on a golf course. He stepped close to the camera so that his round wet face filled the screen. After a grin, he began speaking.

"My colleagues, fellow cowboys and faculty members, I have good news and sad news. The liberal arts 'Do Me' college as you know it is ending, but a new institute of technology will soon begin. That's the *good* news!" His lips moved but the words were unheard over booing. After the noise subsided, some words became audible. "Our state budget is showing deficits and a few jobs will be lost, but when the going gets tough, the tough get going. This is America. You get lemons, make lemonade. On my watch, we will *never* accept any federal aid or health program that smacks of Socialized Medicine."

Again, there was a loud uproar. Cochrane took Rita's hand and noticed that the provost had slipped out of the room. They watched the president take a playful swing and then the camera came in for another close-up.

"What is most important, however, is what I am about to say. With great sadness, I must announce my resignation." There were cheers but the crowd quickly suppressed its joy to hear the reasons for the president's departure. He rubbed his temple with the head of the golf club, and then continued. "I am taking a job as President of Bob Jones University. I feel it is time for a vile member of the scholastic academy to take up the battle against these atheistic Darwinians. It is time to bring intelligent design back into this phony evolution debate. I will lead that cause and refudicate those pseudo intellectuals." Then the president took out a handkerchief and wiped his eyes. "It's also time to bid you farewell. I never thought I could leave you at all…no, not in springtime, summer, winter or fall. But now and then, we all have to make that big drive."

The camera pulled back as President Luna turned and took a graceful swing, driving the ball down the course. Before the scene faded, they caught an image of a tall statuesque blonde woman pulling back beyond camera range. The screen went blank. The lights came on. The crowd stood quietly. Rita and Cochrane exchanged glances. "I need a drink," Cochrane said. When they left the auditorium, they found Doctor Davis leaning against the wall, smoking.

"Don't fret. It will all return back to normal," he said. "You'll get back your little cow college."

"But it will never be the same," Rita said. "And our vote of no confidence will come too late."

The provost nodded. "That's tragic, but the only constant is change."

"We have time to vote no confidence in you," Max Cochrane said. "You were supposed to defend us. Good luck getting a job elsewhere. Maybe your wife can find a job coaching."

For the first time, he saw a venomous fear in the provost's eyes, but Doctor Davis remained silent.

As they walked toward Rita's car, David Cook rushed past them, moving swiftly across the quad. They drove to a sports bar south of town that served food. Sally was leaving as they walked in. Cochrane took her hand.

"I lost my sister to ovarian cancer. I was psychotic with grief for months, but eventually, there are more good days than bad days. Joe was a wonderful man."

"Thanks." They could see a pain in her eyes, which Cochrane recognized as the stare of those who have crossed over a dark river into another country full of sadness and despair. "Joe's death wasn't unexpected," Sally said. "But I didn't think I would be concerned at my age about surviving until I get Medicare and Social Security. I refuse to wear an apron at Wal-Mart."

They embraced and Sally left. Rita and Max Cochrane took a table on the porch and looked across the vast prairie to a distant railroad. Tents were beginning to appear in the desert as more people lost jobs and homes.

"At least we still have houses to live in," Cochrane said. "Something should be done to help those people camping out."

"If it gets really bad, I got a big tent for us at home," Rita said. He could hear a strain in her voice. "Will you leave the state to seek employment?"

Cochrane sipped his beer and felt a slight breeze. Inside, silent television screens glowed with games and competing skate boarders no one watched.

"Well, maybe being a lawyer here won't be so bad. I should call Abdul. I could also help establish the teachers' union. Let's hope you get your department chairmanship back."

"It will take time to dislodge Dr. Moth."

"And just what *is* Bob Jones University?"

"An ultra conservative Christian university. They consider Catholics and Mormons to be part of a cult. They believe Noah took dinosaurs on the ark."

"Maybe that's a good place for Luna." He watched Rita's face. "Rita? Was that Cook's wife I observed on the golf course?"

"The blonde serpent, Judy Cook? I think it was. I have heard rumors of an affair."

"This is getting curiouser and curiouser," Cochrane said.

They finished a late lunch and Max Cochrane felt slightly tipsy as he and Rita left the sports bar. Suddenly, Rita grabbed his arm and pointed at one of the TV screens.

"Oh my God. Max, look!"

He looked. Police had taped off a crime scene at the golf course. A woman reporter was speaking into the microphone but they couldn't hear her words. Subtitles crawled across the screen: *Local speech professor, Dr. Cook, fatally shoots President Luna, and then takes his own life.* The camera found Mrs. Cook sobbing into her hands, long blonde hair hiding her face. That night, they watched local news and heard the audio from the film crew as the president, post broadcast, demanded to know what David Cook thought he was doing. They heard Cook's remarkably calm voice: "I'm here to exterminate a thieving parasitic bully. You think I'll let *you* destroy my department and take my wife as another trophy?" Cook's wife screamed, the president cried "No!" and three shots were fired. The terrified cameraman managed to get a quick if blurred shot of David Cook putting the gun to his head. The screen then went dark. Cook's last words, an obscenity screamed at his wife, and his suicide, were not aired.

After the local news ended, Max Cochrane and Rita Johnson turned off the television and remained silent. Finally, Rita spoke. "I don't know what to say, Max. What a sick day."

"Poor David." Cochrane stroked Rita's cheek and kissed her. "Let's go for a walk," he said. "Visit those so-called squatters."

"Were you serious about a vote of no confidence for the provost?"

"We got rid of the organ grinder, why not the monkey?"

"Max Cochrane, you are cruel."

The unusual heat wave was ending with the spring and soon the nights would be cool, the days gradually warming with the coming summer.

Studebaker Falls

Lyrics to "Coyotes" by Fred Anderson

THOUGH fitting, Dexter Flanagan knew he would resent the inevitable comment at Bill Ford's memorial service: "Bill Ford died doing what he loved best, kayaking on the river." It certainly was fitting, even poetic, that the "River Poet" drowned shooting some high rapids at the south fork of the Salmon River. It happened on the fourth of July, so fireworks illuminated the sky as they searched for the body. Friends rather than police found Bill Ford three days later. Dexter imagined those final moments of life, Bill torn loose from the Kayak as the rushing water took him, and then he was swimming toward shore in the furious current. Did he hit a rock? Did his lungs explode with the first swallow of water?

Dexter had a fear of drowning.

He turned onto the freeway heading west. "Love the river all you want," he said aloud, "no one wants to drown." He turned on his traveling blues music that always made the journey easier. It was a hundred miles to Twin Falls and he never particularly liked that stretch of highway. He heard his cell phone over Robert Johnson's slide guitar and felt a little lift to his heart when he saw the caller ID. "Hello, Stacey."

Dexter heard the familiar voice. "Where are you, Dexter?"

"Driving to the service, why?"

"I wonder if you could do me a favor."

"You can stay at my place anytime, Stacey," Dexter said. "I'm short a woman."

"Very funny," Stacey said. "Dexter Flanagan?"

"Oh boy, that sounds serious."

"I want you to pick up Lee Hunt. He needs a ride to Bill's service."

Dexter drove, holding the phone. "Do I have a sign that reads, 'Taxi Service'?"

"Dexter—Lee needs a ride."

"So what? Lee is a loud mouth bore, and a bad poet," Dexter added.

"He's *not* a bad poet. Look, I'm with John and we don't have room, and Lee can't drive for at least a month. He really needs to be at Bill's send-off."

Dexter was approaching a fertilizer factory on the city border and knew he had to decide whether to pick up Lee Hunt or continue down the highway. "Stacey?"

"What?"

"I saw your name on the caller ID and I said to myself, 'It's Stacey Flynn. She just realized she's sleeping with the wrong guitar player and coming back home—at last.'"

There was long pause.

"Knock it off, Dexter. You know I love you but it is different now and I am asking you as a friend. Lee *needs* to be there."

"Don't we all? Four hours in a closed car with Lee Hunt? Jesus. You owe me big time, Stacey."

"You're a prince, Dexter. Lee will be in front of his bookstore." There was another pause. "You know, Dexter, I really love your music. Take your songs to Nashville. You have a gift."

"So do you."

"Thanks, but I write poems, not songs. I think songs are harder."

His new song in A minor was about the cruelty of Mexican guides called Coyotes who often robbed and murdered the illegal immigrants they led across the desert to the promised land of America. He had lived in a sun-baked Mexican border town and witnessed the desperate migrant workers gathering in the town square, and he had seen the men with cruel eyes who would guide them. A few made it to work as laborers, but many were found dead by American border guards. "Coyotes" worked well in concert.

"Songs are hard, but teaching on the reservation, not music, pays the bills."

"Teaching English pays my bills," Stacey said. "Maybe someday the world will recognize our art."

"I sent a demo tape of songs to a producer in Memphis."

"Memphis? I stayed there once, even visited the Elvis mansion. I was moved, oddly enough, even though I wasn't into Elvis."

"Well, if they like my music, maybe we could visit Memphis together."

After a pause, Stacey said, "I gotta go, Dexter."

Dexter snapped the phone shut and took a turn-off, heading toward Lee Hunt's bookstore. The store had become a meeting place for writers and Lee had promoted many readings and writers' festivals. The books were not stacked alphabetically by author, but Lee had attempted, at least, to create some order by genre. Often he played his guitar while patrons hunted for books throughout the large store. Wearing a light jacket over a blue shirt, white shorts and sandals, Lee Hunt waited in front when Dexter arrived. Though 50, Lee was still handsome with thick black hair and dark glasses. He got into the car, strapped himself in and leaned back.

"Mr. Flanagan. Thanks, I appreciate this."

"No problem," said Dexter.

"Bill would want us there," Lee said.

Dexter drove toward the freeway and the two hour drive to Twin Falls.

"It was a shock," Lee said, "but Bill died doing what he loved."

"I imagine shooting the final rapids was an incredible rush, but he still died."

"Right, but he took a lot of extreme chances, man. I admire that. I might hike out to the lava rocks, but I won't be shooting dangerous rapids anytime soon."

"Nor I."

"Drowning is an awful way to die," Lee said.

"I imagine it is."

In another state, Dexter had seen a water skier pulled from the river after going over a falls, and he remembered a medic pushing on the man's chest and foaming water coming out of the victim's mouth.

"On the other hand," Lee said. "The average person leads such a dull life. Maybe the Flanagans of this world *should* take some chances, you know? Find a new key. An artist must never get *too* comfortable. We are always in the state of becoming, and Bill took risks."

"As a poet or as a kayaker?"

"As a kayaker, of course. I mean, I liked Bill but his small town poems are pretty conventional."

"Conventional? Every time a writer starts *anything,* that writer takes a risk. 'A step to the block,' as Eliot would say. His poems about the river are lovely," Dexter insisted.

"They *are* good," Lee said. "I don't want to be unfair."

As he drove, Dexter looked in the rear view mirror and expected Bill Ford to sit up and describe the surrounding area and the Indians who lived there centuries before. Ford had gone on an archeological dig and unearthed arrow heads thousands of years old. Dexter wondered who those ancient tribes were. He suddenly became aware of Lee watching him.

"I'm writing a novel, Flanagan. Poetry is too limiting."

"A novel? Good for you. It's not about bullfighting in Spain, is it?"

"Hell no. We've progressed beyond Hemingway."

"What's it about?"

"A great artist living in a small stifling town. Then he goes on the road."

"And the title?"

"*Horns*," Lee said.

"*Horns*? Would you buy a book called *Horns*?"

"It's a working title, that's all. What are you writing? A sweet love song, perhaps?"

"I'm writing nothing, at the moment."

"Writing isn't for everyone, and teaching is honorable. It's a steady job."

"Like the bookstore?"

"Yeah. The bookstore is steady… if risky." Lee took out a flask. "First drink of the morning," he said, taking a drink.

"I hope we don't get stopped by the cops."

"Don't be so paranoid. Want a snort?"

"I had to quit," Dexter said. "Alcohol is not my friend."

"Suit yourself." Lee slipped the flask into his wide, deep jacket pocket. "It's gonna be hot," he said. He produced a newspaper. "Bill got two columns in the obits," he said. "Not bad."

Dexter drove past a smoking factory and turned onto a long wide highway, driving with green potato fields on either side. Lee was quiet, leaning back, looking out the window. Dexter remembered Bill Ford's last reading, the dry wit, the quiet tenor voice, the sharp blue eyes and his connection with the audience. It was hard to accept Bill Ford dead. Dexter had played, that night, and it went well. It was one of those memorable nights when all the poems and songs worked and the audience felt privileged to attend. Even Stacey Flynn's recent erotic poems about her new lover impressed Dexter. She had never written anything that sensuous about him. Standing in the light, tall, wearing a cowboy hat, torn jeans and boots, reading with a slight eastern accent, Dexter was moved. Observing Stacey and John Jones with his long hair and pretty eyes and the way they touched each other convinced him: they were madly in love.

As he drove, Dexter saw Lee was asleep. When Lee awoke, Dexter was parking at a truck stop in Twin Falls.

"I need gas," he said. "Feel free to chip in."

Lee got out of the car. "I need a can of beer," he said.

"Flask empty?"

"Nearly — but I like a little variety."

After Dexter had filled the car and paid more than he ever thought possible for a tank of gas, Lee walked toward him laughing.

"They got a fake Garden of Eden in the truck stop, with tables for the bourgeoisie to eat fast food and get this — they have a fake snake in a fake tree. The snake has fake ruby eyes."

"No Adam and Eve?"

"No. Just the tree and snake. Elvis singing, 'I Can't Help Falling in Love with You.' So tacky. Only in America," Lee added.

"Only in America," Dexter agreed. "Could be a short story."

"I can't write about sad ugly people."

"Where's your beer?"

"They only sell those huge single cans, not the small ones I like."

"There'll be beer at the post memorial party. Can you hang on that long?"

Lee seemed puzzled. "Oh I bought the beer. I just drank it before getting in the car."

A half hour later, Dexter was parking by a dome-covered building on campus. He saw many people walking toward the hall. Lee stretched and got out of the car. The heat was oppressive and the sunlight blinding. They saw John Jones and Stacey Flynn. Her appearance always startled him: the tall statuesque female body, the fine features, the long flowing red hair.

"Glad you got here, Lee," she said.

He kissed her hand. "*Enchante.*"

"*Avec plaisir,*" she said. She smiled at Dexter. "Let's go inside."

They entered the building and signed the guest list, and then realized the reception room was packed and they would have to sit on the adjacent patio. Tables with umbrellas had been set up.

"I'm afraid we'll hear the ceremony but not see it," Dexter said.

"Not bad attendance," Lee said. "I guess Bill had a lot of relatives."

They sat with others on the bright patio and heard the voices of Bill Ford's son and daughter. Both of them broke during their eulogies and Dexter admired their courage for trying to speak at such a time. He glanced at a grinning Lee Hunt.

"Must be tough to get through the service without crying if you're the son or daughter," Dexter said.

"It's a Mormon thing," whispered Lee. "They *love* to sob at funerals."

"Bill was Mormon?"

"His wife is."

This fact struck Dexter since he remembered Bill Ford's irreverent new religion called the Church of the Willy Nilly. New members had to give testimony and read aloud the label of a Dickel whiskey bottle, then drink a shot. The Willy Nilly Church had no rules.

"I wonder if Bill's wife approved of his new church, since LDS people don't drink."

Lee didn't answer. Then a renowned elderly local poet named Gene Whiteleather spoke.

"Bill Ford was my brother," he said, "and a great poet. He had a line, 'So many dreams have drowned in this river.' Perhaps there is a river god who wants fresh victims each year, and he envied Bill's dreams. Now Bill Ford is drowned. Like my grandmother, Bill told great stories about Idaho in the old days." The voice paused. "When I get to your camp, let me know, Bill, because I miss you like I miss the sweet days of summer and the wet days of spring. Reach across the sky, Brother Bill, reach over and grab me and take me to grandma's house."

They could hear the voice breaking.

"Gene Whiteleather," Lee said. "Helluva poet."

The poet continued, reading a few of Bill's clean sinewy poems, many about kayaking and the beauty and dangers of white water. An editor followed. They listened to his disembodied voice:

"Bill once commented that he preferred rocks to flowers. When I praised the great cathedral, Notre Dame, Bill reminded me that birds didn't think much of the building except to shit on it. We talked the night before he died. Bill was eager to run the river, even when it was so high and fast and dangerous. It was always about the ultimate thrill. Bill, you know, had escaped death in a near fatal car accident that put him in the hospital for two months. After that, he vowed never to die in bed."

"I'd like to die in bed with a couple of hot hippy honeys," Lee said.

One of the mourners glared at Lee. Dexter turned and looked at Stacey. She caught his eye and nodded. John leaned forward listening. Lee sipped from the flask and lowered his head, eyes closed. An unseen third man stepped to the podium. "We're going to conclude this service with a video of Bill shooting the rapids," he said. "After all, he died doing what he loved best."

Dexter shook his head and looked at the concrete floor of the patio. They heard the tinny music but couldn't see the screen. Dexter felt the heat baking him where he sat, so he walked to the shade of a tree near the patio. Another colleague named Levine who had lost a leg to diabetes leaned against a tree, still holding his crutches. He wore a thick white beard and was sweating in the intense heat.

"I went to the wrong service at first," Levine said. "I should have known better. Here is this Rabbi extolling the virtues of the deceased, a great used furniture salesman. Of course, I somehow knew Bill Ford didn't sell used furniture and wasn't Jewish. I called Stacey and she gave us directions."

"Who drove you down here?"

"Harry."

"Harry, the custodian? I thought he was legally blind."

"He is but he has some peripheral vision, and he can recognize shapes. I have to say, his satellite guidance system is off. It almost directed his Volkswagen Bug into the Snake River."

"I hear they float."

"I don't want to test that claim. I just hope we can make it back."

Dexter remembered Harry's Volkswagen "Beetle" with its psychedelic paint job, a relic of the sixties.

"You can ride with me…or Stacey," Dexter said.

"Don't forget, Harry needs to get back, too."

"That's right."

"And his car."

"Why does Harry have a car in the first place?"

Levine didn't know. The service ended, people were leaving the building. Stacey came up to him and Dexter saw her tears. They embraced.

"I guess we can sit Shiva together," she said. "I can't believe Bill is gone."

"I can't either," said Dexter. He knew he would be feeling Bill's presence for weeks to come. "You going to the post memorial party in the park?"

"Yes," Stacey said. She wiped her eyes. "I'll see you there?"

"You will."

They were like two actors in a television soap. Dexter felt a strong personal connection to Stacey, a ghostly love that refused to stop haunting him, even though she loved another. He studied Stacey's tight female buttocks and long legs as she walked away.

Dexter found the park, taking Lee and Levine with him. Plates of food and ice chests full of drinks sat on tables and a few mourners sat in the shade of awnings, while others sat on chairs in the sun. A small stage was set up with a microphone for guests to discuss Bill Ford and his work. A slight breeze alleviated the day's heat. As Dexter was getting a soft drink, he saw Carole, Bill's widow. She was an attractive dark-haired, middle-aged woman, squarely built but with womanly curves. She wore dark glasses and had a slight smile.

"I'm so sorry," Dexter said.

"So am I," said Carole. "But I just had to laugh when I heard part of the news."

"What was that?"

"Bill's friends found him, and brought his body to the mortuary in a pick-up truck. Bill would have laughed his ass off."

"I agree," Dexter said. "That *is* funny. If you need to talk to someone."

"Of course," Carole said. "Thanks."

She walked toward her daughter and son, standing by the platform. Levine sat at a table, his empty pant leg draped over the edge, while Harry ate some fried chicken. For a brief moment, Dexter wondered how Harry got to the park. Lee Hunt sat in a chair in the sun, drinking a tall beer, his eyes hidden behind dark glasses. Near him sat Stacey and John, eating from paper plates. It was a nice bucolic scene.

"Why don't you play a song?"

He turned and saw Gene Whiteleather, his white bearded face and bald head looking older in the bright light. He wore a blue tank top tee-shirt.

"I need a guitar, Gene."

"One can be found, I'm sure."

Stacey appeared and hugged Whiteleather. "I loved what you said."

"Thank you. Grandma's house was a place to tell stories and remember the good things in life and lament the bad."

Someone on the stage was retelling the story of Bill's Church of the Willy Nilly. Many in the crowd laughed. A photo of Bill watched from a tree.

"The ranks are thinning," Whiteleather said. "We've lost too many poets."

He had a point. One writer had been swept away in a flash flood and another died from prostate cancer. A third had committed suicide.

"Too many," he said. Tears came to his eyes. "Jesus."

They heard Lee's loud laugher. He sat next to Levine who was telling him a story.

Moments later, a young musician approached Dexter. He carried an old Gibson.

"Go ahead, play a song. Get the ball rolling."

"Why not?" Dexter said. "For Bill."

He stepped on the small stage and played "He Was a Friend of Mine." The guitar and rich voice carried with the amplified sound, and a few people applauded. It felt good to sing and release some of the day's sadness. Dexter then played Stacey's favorite Dylan song, "Tambourine Man." He finished with "Coyotes" which ended with a strong chorus:

"Oh the coyotes never cry at night down south along the border

They glide amongst the cactus with the moonlight to their backs

Life is cheaper to them than the muddy Rio Grande Waters

And if the saints aren't with you, you just might lose your life."

The audience cheered. Stacey gave him a thumbs up sign. Suddenly, he heard Lee's voice.

"Gimme that instrument," Lee said. "Jesus, give protest a rest."

Dexter handed over the Gibson. "Go for it," he said.

Lee Hunt began to play some classical runs, melodic and impressive. Dexter walked toward Stacey and John, wondering how long Lee's bare fingers used to nylon strings would last on medium gauge steel. Then Lee began singing in an off- key voice. Dexter turned and saw Lee stagger slightly, blinking as he leaned into the microphone and continued singing, syllables lost in the harsh tones.

"Oh boy," John Jones said. He ran a hand through his long hair. "You might be able to play drunk, but it's hard to sing on key when you're loaded."

"It's a difficult day," Dexter said.

Stacey stood before him. "Thank you," she said. "That Dylan song is my fav, but I love yours, as well."

"Thanks."

After another song with slurred words, Bill's widow whispered in Lee's ear.

"I ain't finished, yet," he snapped.

She said something else and Lee nodded, stepping back from the microphone. Another friend gave testimony about Bill Ford, the man, the husband, the friend and the poet. Then John Jones took the guitar and played some covers and a few originals. Lee found another beer and sat on the stage. He pointed at someone in the audience and grinned.

"Let's walk," Stacey said. "We need to talk."

"Okay."

They walked into the park, John's voice and guitar fading. They came upon some Mexican picnickers and heard music in ¾ waltz time. They walked on and stopped in a grove of trees, sunlight shining through the branches.

"How are you, Dexter…really?"

"I'm good."

"I'm in love."

She waited for his response.

"I can see that. That's great."

Stacey's expression was intense, focused. "Really? You really mean that?"

"Yes. I want you to be happy."

Stacy gently touched his chest, facing him.

"Dexter, this isn't going to make you crazy is it? I mean, with the sauce. I remember what happened when we broke up."

Dexter remembered Stacey holding his hands and telling him they were finished as a couple and then he was crying, knowing it was over, and somehow they ended up in bed for one last bit of furious lovemaking, but after, he felt more alone and went to join friends at a local dive. At dawn, he woke up on a park bench and an officer was asking him if he was all right. Dexter remembered the headache and foggy thinking and the dry mouth and trembling hands. He had lost his love and now had to stop alcohol forever or lose his life.

"I'll be all right," Dexter told her.

"I *do* care for you." Stacey suddenly began crying and hugged him tightly. He knew then he wanted to make love to her to the background of Mexican music but only held her shaking body.

"It's rough for all of us, but Bill right now would want us to dance, be happy."

"Right," Stacey said. She looked into his face. "Even though sometimes you drove me crazy, I *wanted* to be in love with you. Maybe you generate more excitement than John, but that romantic rush just *never* happened."

"It *did* happen for me."

She stroked his face. "I know it did. I'm sorry."

"That's okay, I'll go home, sit by the radiator and cough blood into my handkerchief."

Her laugh was sudden and deep and he loved the sound of it.

"You always made me laugh," she said. The Mexican music stopped. Stacey undid his top shirt button. "You sure do have a golden speaking voice, Dexter. I *love* to hear it."

"Thank you. For five dollars, I'll say your name in my voice."

"It's a deal."

Dexter spoke aloud her name "Again," she said, eyes closed. He repeated her name and Stacey trembled. "Stop, you're turning me on."

"Maybe I *want* to turn you on," he said. "And for free."

Stacey shot him her best disapproving parent look. Then she relaxed.

"If we listen to the woods hard enough, I bet we'll hear Bill's voice."

"Okay. Let's try."

Dexter shut his eyes. He could hear a breeze rustling through the trees. Then he opened his eyes and looked at Stacey's sculpted face, her eyes closed. Quickly, he took her in his arms and kissed her. She responded, moving against him, and then Stacey pushed him away. Her voice was sharp and carried an edge. "Dexter, we *can't* do this."

"Of course," he said. "What was I thinking?"

"Let's walk back—now!"

"Let's." They walked toward the clearing. Soon, photos of the dead poet would appear on trees. "You know, John is your department chairman. Don't you think that will cause a problem?"

"No," Stacey said. She stopped and faced him. "That has *nothing* to do with it. We are colleagues. You and I are colleagues."

"Okay. I just thought some jealous rival in the future might accuse John of being unethical."

"I am *not* one of his cute young female students."

They saw the photograph of Bill Ford's face and then walked into the clearing. Another speaker was on the distant stage. Gene Whiteleather and Lee were in an animated conversation. Harry drank a beer while Levine slept on the grass, a hat over his eyes.

"You're a damn fine poet," Gene Whiteleather said. "I love your stuff."

"Of course you do," Lee said.

"But dead people don't write poems. I hated to lose Bill, but there's something poetic in the way he died. There's nothing poetic in drinking yourself to death. You ever see a drunk puking blood in the gutter?"

Lee lifted his dark glasses. A sudden hard focus came into his eyes.

"I am *not* a rummy," he said. "Whiskey fuels my genius."

"Bullshit," Whiteleather said. "It's killing you, like it killed Kerouac."

"I'm smarter than Kerouac. I'm from a hip younger generation."

"Younger generation? I'm 70 and you're 50."

"Technically, 50 *is* younger than 70," Stacey said.

"Fifty is the new thirty," Lee said. "No offense, Gene, but you're in the past. Old jive. What I do is new…and besides, I've abandoned poetry. Like Rimbaud, I need a new direction."

Gene Whiteleather looked into Lee's face. "New direction? Like the grave?"

"Go easy on him," Dexter said. "After all, he's writing a great novel called *Horns*."

They could see the anger in Lee's eyes.

"Go to hell, Dexter," he said. "People will be reading Lee Hunt when all of you are forgotten and turned to dust."

"There'll be nothing much to read if you keep drinking like this."

Lee Hunt glared at the old man. Then his expression softened.

"Okay, I promise to be nicer," he said. "I'll be a good boy."

He saluted with his flask, took a drink, and walked away. They watched him leave.

"Where did he get the refill?" Dexter asked.

"I hate to see a gifted writer destroy himself," Whiteleather said.

"You think Lee is *that* good?"

"Dexter, I know he is *potentially* that good."

"Better than all of us," Stacey said, "once he learns to rewrite."

Gene Whiteleather wiped his forehead and took a sudden deep breath. "I better sit down. I'm a little dizzy. And I could use a drink," he added, smiling.

"Let me talk to our local genius," Stacey said. She kissed Dexter on the cheek and walked toward Lee Hunt who had found some shade. John Jones caught up with her.

"You were gone awhile."

"We took a walk," she said. "Relax."

Dexter sat next to Whiteleather. "Nice turn out for Bill," he said.

"Yes," the older man said. It was very nice." He pinched his nose, the eyes closed. Then he said, "Dexter? I know it's hard to like Lee Hunt, but make sure he gets home all right. He's our next major poet, and you're our next major songwriter. Art is what we do."

"I'm not sure I'm so major, but I promise I will see he gets home."

As they sat, a young female reporter with a microphone and a cameraman appeared.

"You're the poet laureate, Gene Whiteleather?"

"I am Gene Whiteleather, but I am not a poet laureate. They are always *bad* poets."

"Well, Mr. Whiteleather, we're doing a spread on local writers. May I possibly ask you some questions?"

"You may, if they're about that great local poet, Bill Ford."

"Certainly. First, I have to ask if you knew Jack Kerouac."

"Of course. Another gifted soul who drank himself to death."

"Did you know Allen Ginsberg?"

Whiteleather turned up his face to meet her eyes. "Knew him? I blew him!"

The cameraman looked away smirking as the young woman lowered her microphone.

"I can't put that on the air, Mr. Whiteleather."

"Then don't ask obvious questions."

"Obvious?"

"You read about me, right? Then you must know that I ran with the Beats. I knew all of them."

"And what he said about Ginsberg is true," Dexter added.

"Sir, I can't do this interview if you're not quiet."

Dexter stood up. He bowed politely. "Pardon me," he said, waving good-bye.

Then it was late afternoon and a number of guests had left the small park. Dexter stood by Stacey's car, saying good-bye. They had agreed to take Levine back. Dexter would take Harry and Lee Hunt.

"I hope we can meet under better circumstances," Dexter said.

"We will," Stacey said. "Take care of Lee."

"I can invite him to attend AA meetings. Maybe that will help."

"We can all go." Stacey took his hands. "John's band is playing in Sun Valley, next weekend. Come with?"

"Maybe I could meet you there."

"Please do," John said. "I'd like to learn your coyote song."

"I'd be honored."

They shook hands, hugged and then Dexter watched them drive off. He felt a profound fatigue from sorrow and the hot sun. He also felt his old love for Stacey surging through him, and it was debilitating. *Stay awhile*, he thought. Dexter walked toward the parking lot, looking for Lee Hunt and Harry. Someone else would have to drive Harry's VW back. Dexter found his car but the lot was empty. He stood there for a moment and turning, he saw Carole walking with her daughter. The gaiety of the celebration was gone and Dexter recognized the sorrow that would haunt them in the months and years to come.

"Have you seen Lee Hunt? I'm supposed to drive him back."

"I saw him leave about five minutes ago. He was driving with someone else."

"Lee was driving?"

"Yes."

"Carole—Lee was drunk. Plowed."

"I saw that. He just grabbed that little man's keys and away they went in a hippy-colored Volkswagen."

"He's with Harry? God, I hope they make it home alive."

"So do I," Carole said.

He kissed her on the cheek. Then Dexter walked to his car and drove down the main street that led to the freeway. He approached the Perrine Bridge where Evel Knieval on a rocket motorcycle had tried to jump the deep wide gorge. As Dexter crossed the bridge, a jumper with a parachute left the railing 486 feet above the Snake River. Coming off the bridge, Dexter saw an ambulance and a police car coming toward him, sirens blasting, blue lights flashing. On an impulse, he turned and followed the distant fast moving ambulance and police car. They turned and drove along the river.

*   *   *

LEE Hunt took a wide turn at the Perrine Bridge. The little car handled well. Harry, wearing thick lenses, peered through the windshield. The satellite's mechanical voice ordered them back on the main highway. Lee turned off the guidance system.

"There was an explorer named Wilson Price Hunt who discovered Twin Falls," Lee said. "Around 1811. He came down the Snake River and lost a guy in the rapids. I wonder if there's a marker?"

"Indians were here 14,000 years ago," said Harry. "Long before Hunt. We should head home." He smiled nervously. "You have a lot of drinks, Lee?"

"A few."

Lee had a grin that might have been unsettling if Harry could see better. They drove toward the river. Lee took another hit from his flask.

"You know, our flashy paint job might attract a lot of cops."

"So what?" Lee said. "Today we're invincible."

"You might slow down."

"Relax."

A car honked at them and Lee pulled sharply back into his lane. He shouted an obscenity at the other driver. Then Lee continued down the two-lane highway. They passed some meadows and groves of trees and then finally saw the river.

"I think there's a gravel road and a wooden bridge over the river and near there is a plaque to Hunt."

"Who cares?" Harry said. "Let's go home."

"In a minute," Lee said. "You sound like my ex wife — always whining."

Lee stared at the black asphalt highway and then looked in the rear view mirror, watching the road unwind like a spool of black cloth; there was something romantic in it, those images of the open road that reminded him of Whitman and Kerouac and the traveling troubadours like Woody Guthrie, and even a line from his own poetry about boxcars and America seen through the car window. Lee relaxed, suddenly in the zone that produced his best writing. Meditating, he thought of a new line: "Smoke like blood, covering the city."

Though Harry only saw shapes and shadows, he knew something was wrong even before Lee felt the tires sliding on a soft shoulder. He turned sharply to get back on the road but they were now off it, sliding down the embankment toward the river. Lee cursed and floored the gas, the engine whining with a high pitch; Harry screamed as they slid backwards into the river shallows. Harry rolled down the window and crawled out. He touched the sides of the car and felt no damage. Lee had opened the roof hatch and was looking down the river, drinking.

"That was scary. For a second, I thought I lost my flask."

"Goddamn it, why can't you stay on the road? How are we gonna get my car back up on the highway?"

Lee began laughing. He had a cut on his forehead.

"We'll get a tow." He felt in his pockets. "I lost my mobile."

"You realize my Volkswagen was on the cover of the Beatles' *Abbey Road* album?"

"Don't give me that. I saw that bug in a German museum."

Harry put his hands up to his face in a theatrical gesture.

"I'll see if I can find someone to help us."

Panting, Harry climbed the steep hill and flagged a passing motorist. As he explained what had happened, the driver took out his cell phone.

"I'll call a tow truck. You got one of them old Volkswagen bugs, eh?"

"Yes."

"Let's check that sucker out."

Then they were looking down the hill and Harry could tell the car had vanished. The driver looked at him, shaking his head.

"I don't see the car. I guess it floated away. They *do* float, right?"

"Oh my God," Harry said. "My car."

"Your friend better abandon fast. There's a falls down stream."

"Oh my God," Harry repeated, frustration and fear in his face.

Framed in the sun roof, Lee took a swig from the flask and marveled at the way the car floated downstream like a raft, picking up speed in the current. He saw hikers on the bank and on various paths watching him in shock. They shouted and waved to him. Lee waved back. It seemed incredibly funny and Lee started to laugh. He even thought he saw Bill Ford in a kayak paddling alongside him.

"Get out now," the kayaker shouted. "It gets narrow about 100 yards ahead. Jump out and swim for it."

"My God," said Lee. He peered at the helmeted man. "Is that you, Bill Ford?"

"The falls," the man in the kayak shouted.

"Bill Falls?" Lee lifted his flask, finished the final swallow, and tossed it into the swiftly moving river. "I didn't mean to suggest your poems were commonplace," Lee shouted. "Forgive me. I know I'm a prick, sometimes. I can't help it."

He saw the river growing more narrow and faster but he hesitated jumping. It was dangerous to swim toward the shore in these rapids. Some people were running along the bank. One carried a line and a lifesaver. Lee even thought he saw Dexter. Then he felt water coming over his shoes on the seat. Evidently, there was a hole in the bottom of the Volkswagen. He heard the kayaker shout one more time: "Jump!"

Lee climbed through the hatch and stood unsteadily on the roof of the slowly sinking Volkswagen and held out his arms. He felt a numbing lassitude through his body. The breeze felt good and the running water created a melody of nature. Blood marked his forehead. He was now daring Icarus flying close to the sun. He never saw or heard the falls.

*   *   *

SITTING in the recording studio, Dexter listened to the playback of "Coyotes." The guitar had a rich but melancholy sound, and the deep voice sounded warm and expressive. The producer exited the booth.

"We can add some bass to that, and a lead guitar."

"Good," Dexter said. "Maybe some star will like it, Ramon."

"If not, I like it," Ramon said. "There is genuine art in the song. My father was robbed and killed by a coyote crossing the desert. I hate those greedy murderous bastards. It's a powerful song."

"Thank you."

"This is Memphis, however, and popular music is a commercial business. We'll need some love songs, maybe even a few songs with humor. Art's great, you know, but you need a commercial hook to move an album. Even Dylan is commercial."

"True." Dexter rested his arms on the old Martin and looked at the producer's handsome brown face. "I'm working on a love song about a woman I loved and lost."

"Sounds good," Ramon said. "Think 'Tequila Sunrise.'"

"And I have another unfinished song," Dexter said. "About a drowned writer. In fact, *two* drowned writers. The river god of death comes to claim them."

"Death is not commercial," Ramon said. "I hope it has a catchy melody and some nice guitar work."

"I hope so too. I have to shove off," Dexter told him. "See the sights."

"Check out Sun Studio where it all began."

Minutes later, he was walking down Beale Street, feeling the vibrations of artists dead and gone. He passed small clubs and heard live music within, knowing that even the local mailman had some great original songs. He knew he could walk into any bar and order a drink, but kept walking. Perhaps in his motel room, sober, he could shape a blues song celebrating his love for Stacey; it would be his masterpiece. Her last phone call stayed with him.

"How could this happen," she had said, "to lose both Bill *and* Lee?"

"Random tragedy," he said. After a pause, he asked, "Why are you really calling, Stacey?"

"I don't know. I guess I just had to hear your voice, Dexter."

"Why didn't you ever write sexy poems about me?"

"I don't know that either," she said. "Maybe it was an intellectual connection we had."

"Intellectual? I don't have 'hummingbird' kisses?"

Stacey laughed. "You don't. More like a golden retriever."

"Really? And you can't write a sonnet about *my* feet?"

After a pause, Stacey said, "I *could* write a sonnet about your hands."

"I bet you'd like to feel my hands right now."

"Dexter, we have to stop this. I appreciate your close reading of my poetry but—"

"And can you *really* say that mushrooms didn't spring up and circle the secret forest places where *we* made love?"

"Maybe toadstools."

"The only poem you wrote about me sounded like a math equation."

His voice had taken on an accusing edge, and he heard Stacey sighing melodramatically. "I'm sorry, Dexter. I *do* miss you. You've always been special to me. As friends, we'll know each other for life."

"That's some comfort," Dexter said. Then he heard himself saying words he had not intended to speak. "You still love John?"

There was a long silence on the other end. Then: "Yes. Enjoy Memphis and good luck."

"Stacey Flynn," he murmured.

"Oh my," she said. "I've got Golden Throat on the line."

He repeated her name, drawing out the final nasal. He imagined her in the small cluttered university office, clutching the phone to her ear. Perhaps her other hand had drifted to her throat, and then down to unbutton her blouse.

"I sure do love that thrilling sound," she finally said. "You could make the word 'mackerel' sound like a Keatsian poem." Dexter wanted to continue but Stacey's voice was sudden, sharp, a closing door. "I have to go, Dexter. Good-bye."

And the call was over.

I can write about Stacey, he thought. Expressing with lyrics Lee Hunt's fate would be more difficult. Dexter had asked himself: why should anyone care about Lee Hunt? He knew the answer. Dexter had not saved him, that day. He needed to write a song that would celebrate the artist Lee Hunt may have become. His working title was "Enchante," a deliberate attempt to make death alluring and deceptive, like a Typhoid Mary.

Walking, Dexter came upon a street festival. Antique cars lined the street. He saw many concession booths, and a four-piece band of senior citizens played "Folsom Prison Blues." They were good and Dexter watched the quick fingers of the lead guitarist, a man in his seventies. A toothless bald man in a pink and black jumpsuit carried an oxygen tank and danced to the music. Dexter suddenly felt moved by joy and appreciation. He saluted the obscure musicians. Dexter knew Bill Ford would approve, while Lee Hunt might have viewed the senior citizen band with a condescending smile.

"I'll join your band, one day," Dexter said to himself.

He turned and saw a statue of Elvis Presley holding a guitar.

Dexter was still thinking of Stacey when moments later, he caught a taxi to Graceland and bought a ticket to tour the famous white-columned mansion of the artist who combined black and white music, changing American pop culture forever. Though Dexter disliked the commercial exploitation of a dead celebrity, it was a trip he had to make. Perhaps at Elvis' grave, inspiration would inform his tribute to dead artists.

The Elvis mansion seemed remarkably small. Before one reached the resting place, tourists saw the jungle room, the music room and the media room in the basement. Dexter looked at the gold lame suit in the doorway of the trophy room, and examined the jumpsuits and the row of gold records on display. Dexter finally reached the Meditation Garden where the "King" lay buried with his family.

He stared at the plaque with dates and words about Elvis Aaron Presley, hearing the fountains in a circle above the grave. Dexter remembered the 1968 comeback concert with a thin handsome Elvis in leather singing with the old magic, and then the bloated drug-ridden older Elvis, the soaring voice attached to a dying body.

Dexter noticed an angel on the adjoining grave and recalled Stacey's aversion to angels in any form. He thought of Stacey standing on this spot and suddenly saw the river again and imagined Bill Ford preparing to shoot his last rapids. He saw Lee Hunt taking his final ride and recalled the bizarre photos in the newspaper of a man riding a brightly painted Volkswagen over a falls. Somewhere in a Memphis neighborhood, anonymous senior citizens were playing a musical soundtrack to his thoughts.

Suddenly, Dexter started to cry. It was unexpected and Dexter tried to control himself, moisture rolling down his cheeks. He felt a thick hand take his. Standing next to him wearing a muumuu and a bee-hive hair-do, a fat woman nodded and also began to weep. Somewhere down the line, he heard another woman's voice: "My God, that happens to all his true fans, don't it? We remember our king."

Voices Echo

SEAN DINEEN liked that nervous feeling just before appearing in a large auditorium to discuss his life as a political cartoonist and the successful film based on his work. Perhaps he had quit too soon since the current political race was a hot one, and his first novel had done poorly. There was also the nagging question of why he hadn't written a graphic novel, the new rage.

Sean Dineen's recent article attacking Andy Warhol and the pop art movement earned him enough notoriety to promote a college tour. The thin willowy Warhol had survived a gunshot wound from a crazed follower only to die after a botched routine operation. Made famous by his painting of a Campbell Soup can and the factory where he did experimental films, Warhol's image of the pop artist celebrity still lingered. Sean Dineen had dared to question Andy Warhol's artistic credentials.

Sean heard the introduction and when his name was called, he walked out onto the stage of this modest Idaho University. He heard applause and the spotlight caught the whiteness of his still thick curly hair. Sean Dineen had lost weight but was lifting weights for muscle tone. Some of his cartoons came up on a screen. He knew they had lost their punch with the passage of time, satires on candidates long out of office or forgotten. Sean was relieved when a few students laughed.

"I'm not a real artist," he said, "I just illustrate. Picasso was an artist. There is something anarchistic about a political cartoon, however. We can take great liberties and avoid law suits."

As he spoke, he noticed the students were quieter. A few held copies of Warhol's soup can. Sean waited for them to bring up the house lights so he could take questions, his favorite part of the college circuit. The audience was large and stared back at him, like a gigantic living painting. A young attractive woman with blonde hair fringed with purple watched him intensely.

"I realize my work is a bit dated," Sean said, "but aren't the political cartoons of Lincoln's time fascinating? Maybe a few of mine will have historical value. Any questions?"

A bearded professor he had met that afternoon raised his hand. He also had white hair but was short and portly.

"Yes?

"I am puzzled," he said, holding a copy of *The New Yorker*. "You tell us you're not an artist but you *are* a *pop* artist."

"I'm a pop artist?"

"You are, and here you attack the man who practically *created* pop art."

"I guess that's true."

"Of course it's true. In your article, you diminish Warhol's value as an artist."

"That's because I feel pop art has lower standards."

Sean could feel the students and faculty observing him. He wondered if Priscilla and Rachel were hovering somewhere, waiting for the confrontation.

"I think Warhol was more of a colorful personality. He created some new concepts, but admitted his art wasn't all that original or complex. Anyone can take a photo of Marilyn Monroe and make it into a silk screen."

"Warhol did it first," the professor insisted.

"Correct. He did it first. He created a commodity. Any good advertising illustrator could paint a realistic Campbell Soup can, but that doesn't mean it's an *artistic* interpretation, like Van Gogh's flowers, for instance. To me, even though maybe I'm a pop artist, I regard Warhol as a minor if influential blip on 20th century art. The Hammer and Sickle series is good, but neither Warhol nor Dineen will exhibit at the Louvre."

"*You* may not exhibit, but you might be wrong about Warhol."

"I might be, unfortunately."

"Unfortunately? So you only admire so-called 'High Art'?"

Sean was about to answer when a student raised his hand.

"I like your stuff and I disagree that pop art is minor…and I think Warhol was great."

Sean nodded and smiled. Then he shrugged.

"Look. I admire a lot of pop music. A few songwriters might even be great artists. Regarding painting and illustrations, I even like Andy Warhol as a cultural influence, but I just don't buy him as a *great* artist. A serious artist has a talent that is developed into a skill and expresses a *vision*. Picasso was a great *visionary* artist. I don't understand all of his Cubist stuff, but Guernica is devastating."

He could feel a tension running through the audience. The professor stared at him.

"I put Picasso as the foremost artist of the first half the 20th century, and Warhol" — he looked around the crowded auditorium — "Andy Warhol *owns* the *second* half."

The students and teachers applauded. Sean Dineen lowered his head. Then he looked at the professor.

"To me, that's the Mark Twain-Carrot Top comparison."

The air in the building seemed to contract as though the crowd suddenly drew in its collective breath.

"Hey," another student suddenly yelled. "I think you're full of shit."

The auditorium rang with laughter followed by applause. Sean stood alone on the stage. The professor was grinning, now.

"Have you seen *any* new work, Mr. Dineen?"

"Inside the museum, infinity goes up on trial," mumbled Sean, quoting a Dylan lyric.

"What was that?"

"Yes, I *have* seen modern work."

"And?"

"I've seen a basketball in a fish tank called art. I've seen a cow in formaldehyde called art. I've seen bronzed balloon dogs sell for millions. I've seen Mickey Mouse with fangs. Something is wrong with that picture, no pun intended," Sean insisted. "Art has become just another commercial market for commodities. For that, I blame Warhol."

"Artists have a right to make money," a third student shouted.

"True. Even a hack like me made a few bucks."

The professor looked at Sean with a smug but confident humor.

"You have made a few bucks off pop art and you *blame* Warhol?" The professor wiped his shiny forehead. "Sir, with due apologies, you are an embarrassment to the art world if you misunderstand or are so *blind* to current modern art. We've gone *beyond* Picasso and Rembrandt *and* Michelangelo. Modern art is creating new forms. Warhol started it all. He is our prince *and* yours!"

There were more cheers, then applause. For a moment, Sean wondered what would happen if he smacked the fat pompous professor. The woman with purple-fringed hair raised her hand.

"What about Jackson Pollock? Is he minor?"

"I don't understand Pollock but there is a method to his madness. Hey, what do I know? I'm a guy from New Jersey who got lucky." He glanced at the students grinning back at him. "If you don't have any questions, I have one. How far is it to Mexico?"

When he walked backstage, a tall young man with shaggy blonde hair and a bad complexion limply shook his hand.

"That was marvelous."

"It was? They hated me."

"But you got a discussion going. Half of them never heard of Andy Warhol."

The young man handed him a check. Sean stepped into the foyer and watched a few students exiting the building. He noticed an announcement for a talk on grief: "Declan Mulligan will discuss the loss of his wife and how writing a journal of grief saved his life."

Sean turned away.

What would he do had he the motive and the cue for passion that I have? Sean thought to himself, bagging a line from *Hamlet*. "I lost two women," he said aloud. "Two!"

He felt embarrassed to be speaking to no one. A passing young woman smiled at him and walked on. Sean Dineen swallowed his daily aspirin and walked outside the large grey Performing Arts Center. It was raining. Sean had a good walk to the parking lot across from the school. He actually liked the rain and sometimes saw Rachel's small but tight female figure walking toward him, her straight dark hair sun-streaked and shining, her eyes always merry in the handsome face much younger than her fifty years.

Boy, they nailed your ass, she might say, laughing. *But you're tough, Sean Dineen. Frankly, I'm not wild about Andy myself.*

But Rachel's ghost wasn't walking toward him through the rain. Not tonight. For a moment, watching rain blow across the lawn, he wondered what Priscilla would have thought of the evening. She had always been tougher than Sean, with a defiant edge. Their life together had been full of wild times and brutal arguments leading to a divorce, but as she bravely faced her death from ovarian cancer, peace and plans were made. They had enjoyed discussing their memories, like seeing their son, Carson, marry in Paraguay. When death came, it wasn't unexpected. Sean Dineen would continue to comfort her devastated husband.

Rachel's death was sudden, the result of a drunk driver with many priors. He had driven the wrong way down a freeway and Rachel had turned out to pass. The drunk survived the accident. After the shock had passed and the deep black grief set in, Sean had even considered committing a crime so he could find the drunk in prison and slip a shiv between his ribs. Carson had saved him from that sick fantasy.

Sean, without an umbrella, began walking quickly toward his car.

"Mr. Dineen, wait!"

He turned, feeling the heavier rain now soaking through his light coat. The young woman with purple-fringed hair was running toward him. She wore striped pants and carried an umbrella.

"Let me walk you to your car," she said.

"Okay."

They walked, the rain spattering on the open umbrella.

"I liked what you said, tonight. I also like Warhol, but we all have to move on."

"You're a painter?"

"Yes. My name is Samantha, but people call me Sami. Don't mind Professor Heckler. He's a pompous ass."

"I don't mind pompous asses. I've known a few hecklers in my time." They came to the small rental car. "Thanks," he said.

"I like your work," Sami said. "Why don't we talk some more? There's a local boy who made good in Memphis and he's playing at the brewpub on First Street."

The rain was lighter and Sean looked at her handsome face in the street light. He could see a spider tattoo on her neck. She had high cheekbones, a strong jaw, and in profile, her face suggested a bird-like appearance.

"I'm old enough to be your father," he said.

Sami reacted, clearly surprised. Then her eyes narrowed. "I am *not* a groupie. I am an artist and like to learn everything I can from other artists, particularly pros."

"Thanks for calling me a pro."

She wrote directions to the pub. "Show up if you feel like a beer and some live music."

"Okay."

"You're wrong about Warhol. He's still important, but you may be right about commercialism taking over art."

The rain stopped. He watched her walk quickly away closing the umbrella. She had long legs and prominent breasts and Sean wondered how he might have acted twenty years earlier. He called out. Sami stopped and turned. "What?"

"What do you paint? Portraits? Soup cans?"

Sami laughed. "I paint landscapes, but they're not realistic nor are they surreal or abstract. Frankly, I don't know what I paint."

"Good," Sean said. "Promising."

Following her scribbled directions, he drove through the university town, finding a dark street in the warehouse district and a small brewpub with blues music coming through the partially open window. The street was bathed in the yellow light from the pub. A blue neon sign read "Open." He could see the band from the back and people sitting at tables, and beyond, a distant bar. When Sean walked up stairs and inside, the music was suddenly louder with a stocky black female singer belting out a raunchy number: "I'm in the blues bidnez, and bidnez is good."

Huge tanks for the homemade brew were visible through a window, and the red brick walls had signatures of musicians. Sean walked past a tall lean older man wearing jeans and a Levi jacket; the man was pressed against the wall and watching the band. He wore round spectacles like John Lennon, and had brown hair streaked with grey. Like Sean, he carried a slight paunch with the advancing years.

Sean looked around the tavern and saw Sami sitting at a table with friends. They were young, and Sean knew he would soon feel out of place, but he made his way toward the table through the dancers and spectators. Overhead bulbs caught highlights in the blonde-purple border of Sami's hair.

"This is Sean Dineen," Sami said. "He spoke at the school."

The others nodded and briefly shook his hand. The blues band broke into another lively number and the music swept over the patrons sitting and eating pizza, drinking beer or just listening. Conversation became impossible. Then a rugged looking man in his mid-thirties stepped to the mic and sang a song about the Mexican guides called "coyotes" who often led immigrants to their death in the desert. He had a deep voice, and the song had a country flavor. The female singer now played saxophone. When the song ended, Sean was impressed.

"He's good," he said.

"That's Dexter Flanagan. He'll be big songwriter, someday. Glad someone from this tank town has a shot. I sometimes I think I'll die here."

"No matter where you are, all artists are vulnerable," Sean said. "I gambled everything away. I lost my wife and even my child for a while. Then after a reconciliation, my ex died."

He saw Sami watching him, her blouse cut low, her eyes focused. She knew how to flirt and yet keep a distance. "I know," she said. "I checked your biography. I'm sorry."

Flanagan began a twelve bar Jimmy Reed blues, playing guitar under a high-pitched wailing harmonica. It was the kind of primitive blues that could resonant with a person's inner needs and desires. They didn't talk over the music, and Sean Dineen wondered if Sami also read about Rachel, a woman he met at the zoo who gave him a second chance at love and died tragically. He imagined Rachel sitting next to him, leaning against his shoulder, moving with the music. Flanagan then sang a poignant love song about two lovers who were doomed by conditions beyond their control. It reminded Sean of "Angie" by the Rolling Stones. A striking-looking woman with auburn hair stood up and applauded, wiping away tears.

The tall man in Levis watched the band intently, and Sean suspected he was a musician. Though he didn't smile, he obviously understood and felt the vibrant music. Occasionally, he glanced at the crowd. Sean saw something in the eyes that disturbed him. Their table was now surrounded by patrons. People had trouble walking to the back of the brewpub with its narrow bottleneck corridor by the bar.

Suddenly, Sami was holding his hands. The others ignored him, watching the band. One young woman got up to dance.

"Tell me," said Sami. "Do you have an agent?"

"Yes. He's a pain in the ass but knows his stuff."

"Do I need one?"

"Everyone usually needs one," said Sean. "But I don't know I can help you find one," he quickly added.

Sami released his hands and sipped her beer.

"Maybe I should leave town."

"Get a showing," Sean said. "Then get a showing in a bigger place like Sun Valley. Then apply at a school like Yale or Harvard. They are giving away scholarships and tuition if you're poor."

Sami shrugged. "Yale? I wish. But I *am* poor."

"After Yale, hitchhike to New York and paint a Campbell Soup can."

He liked the sound of Sami's laughter. "It's been done," she said.

"I'm thinking of a Warhol experiment," Sean said. "I'm going to photograph dogs' asses and turn the dog butts into silkscreen images. After following the master, my fame will be assured." He lifted his glass of beer in a salute.

"You may have something, there," Sami said.

"Then I will start on my portraits of kitty asses."

Sami laughed again. After a soft ballad, the woman singer took over for another suggestive blues, Dexter Flanagan playing lead guitar. She held the microphone and began to wail with a Janis Joplin abandon. Dancers crowded the small space before the band. A short older woman suddenly grabbed the tall man in Levi's and pulled him toward the dance floor. He shook his head and pulled way. The woman swayed once and tugged at him again. Suddenly, the stranger pushed her away and bolted down the stairs and out into the street. Sean watched the scene and Sami said, "That's Declan Mulligan. He now teaches communication. He also lost a wife some years ago."

"I'm sorry to hear that."

"He won't dance with me, either."

Without replying, Sean forced his way past the spectators and dancers and headed toward the exit. He saw Declan walking down the street and called out to him. The man turned and took a step toward him in the yellow light. "Do I know you?"

"No, you don't. Listen, I've been there. I couldn't dance for a long time, either."

"Dance?"

"I saw you back away from the woman who wanted to dance with you. I understand, Mr. Mulligan. Dancing was a kind of phobia for me until my son said, 'Dad, get over it.'"

Declan Mulligan advanced another step. "You know me. Who the hell are you?"

"A friend. I saw you bolt from the joint and —"

 "Bolt? Maybe it was just time to go."

"Maybe. But I saw something in your eyes that I've seen in mine."

"Really?" The two men stood, regarding each other. "You always study and confront strangers?"

"No."

"You got a name?"

"Sean Dineen. Listen, I lost an ex wife *and* a lover." For a moment, Declan Mulligan's expression softened. Sean continued: "You talked about grief tonight, right?"

"Yeah, I did. And you discussed cartoons. Now go back inside and have a ball."

Declan began walking down the street. Sean called out again: "Tomorrow, I'll be having breakfast at the Holiday Inn. Join me."

Sean turned and saw Sami swaying in the doorway, smoking and holding a beer. Sami shouted:

"Don't leave us, Mulligan. We're gonna boogie, tonight!"

Declan paused and turned and walked back toward the tavern. The music had picked up with a fast blues. Sean could see lines in Declan's face and the eyes were clear and penetrating behind the circular glasses. Declan regarded Sami, who slipped and caught herself.

"One too many beers," she said.

Declan gave a mock salute and said, "See you at the art gallery." He walked away without looking back.

"Say hello to the Duck Lady!" Sami screamed. Sean caught her as she stumbled again.

"Sami? Maybe we should go inside and sit down."

"Sure. Maybe *you'd* like to dance."

"Good idea."

Sean looked down the dark street but Declan Mulligan had disappeared. The band paused for a break and Sean followed Sami to their table.

"I guess you've spent time with Mr. Mulligan?"

"He was a kind of mentor."

"Who's the Duck Lady? She owns ducks?"

"She owns ducks, she breeds ducks, and she *looks* like a duck."

"I like ducks," Sean said.

Sami put her fingers under his chin and held his eyes.

"Maybe Mr. Mulligan can't dance, but he has no problem with other things, if you catch my drift."

"This is a bit delicate, but isn't Mr. Mulligan a tad old for you?"

Sami looked away. "I like older men," she said, "particularly *artistic* older men."

"Really?"

Sami turned to study his face and then suddenly laughed, slapping his shoulder. "Don't worry, I won't hit on you."

"Is that good or bad?"

"It's good."

"You know, I'm not sure I approve of teachers sleeping with students."

"Who says Mulligan was my teacher or that we were sleeping, together?"

A young man at the table was watching Sami and she returned his stare. "I wanna boogie, tonight," she said. "Let's get drunk and boogie! Bring your girlfriend."

The band started playing and Sami joined the others in a slam dance. Sean sipped his wine. He knew the festive bar scene would soon begin to depress him. It still happened with large crowds, a feeling of isolation amid cheer and talking heads. Of course, the blues band was good and he could easily lose himself in good blues. A little wine always helped with depression, but too much alcohol brought back demons and with the demons, nightmares. He had been told by a therapist that falling in love with another woman would ease his grief, but that hadn't happened since, and he knew he wasn't ready for that to happen.

Sean got up and walked through the crowd to the back dining room. He stepped out onto a porch and saw the distant train tracks and a train pulling out, heading west. Sean thought about the depression days and traveling troubadours like Woody Guthrie. Would those hungry days come back? A few patrons sat on the porch or leaned on the railing smoking and drinking. Sean was glad no one smoked inside the brewpub. Then he saw Mr. Heckler, holding a beer.

"Mr. Dineen, I admire your work. Good political satire, a fine movie about modern love, and I liked your novel."

"No one else did," Sean said. "But thanks."

"I am sorry I was so rough on you, but the students loved it. I admit Warhol isn't the only great pop artist, but they may pay more attention to Warhol's work, now."

"Good."

The professor smiled, his teeth bright against the beard. "I liked the lead actress in your film. She's good."

"Lovely person," Sean said.

"You ever score with her?"

"No." Sean noticed some steps leading to an alley. "Where does that alley lead?"

"It leads to the side street. You can exit without anyone seeing you if you like."

"I could use a walk," Sean said.

"See you in the funny papers," the professor said.

Sean left his drink and walked down the stairs and out toward the street. The band had broken into a faster blues-jazz number. Sean walked by the window and saw the silhouetted backs of the musicians as they played to the dancing joyful crowd. He continued walking to his rental car and drove to the Holiday Inn. It would be nice to relax in his quiet L-shaped room, resting in silence with no distractions. First, he stopped in the Inn bar but it was smoky so he bought a small bottle of wine and went to his room. On the dresser was a picture of him and Rachel on a Mexican beach. It showed a laughing couple in love. It was one of those happy moments captured on film, a tribute and a mocking reminder of paradise lost.

He poured a drink of white wine and 7 Up. He drank, sitting on the bed, looking at the western-themed art on the wall that resembled so many pictures on walls in motels and hotels across the country. Oddly enough, he took comfort in the uniform sameness of motel and hotel rooms. Of course, Rachel would not be sleeping with him, tonight, and he would not hear her hair dryer in the morning.

You still have your son and great memories of Rachel and feisty old Priscilla, and you have a book out, he thought. *And a movie about the tragedy of romantic love.*

"What a laugh," he said aloud. "What do I know about romantic love?"

Sean wasn't sure what to make of Sami. She was the kind of woman he would have pursued twenty years before, but now she seemed part of another world, and there was something dangerous and sad about her. Perhaps if Declan Mulligan showed up for breakfast, he would ask him about her. And he would buy and read his book. Declan Mulligan knew grief and Sean Dineen knew grief and there was nothing to completely cure it except death.

But if there's no grief, then it wasn't worth much to start with, he thought.

He drank another glass of wine and then went to sleep. Sometime in the early morning, he woke up. It had happened often and then he had the choice of simply lying there in the bed or watching the early morning news shows at three AM. He turned on the television. Congress had finally passed a bill to rescue the nation's credit after bad loans had ruined Wall Street. At one time, Sean Dineen the revolutionary would have rejoiced at the death of Capitalism. Now he worried about his retirement funds.

He thought of pouring another drink but decided not to.

Just lie down in bed and wait until first light, he thought.

Then he heard a tapping on the front door. Perhaps security felt his TV was too loud. Sean pulled on his pants and went to the front door and peered through the view finder; Sami's face suddenly came into focus, her eyes blinking. He opened the door.

"What the hell happened to you?" she demanded. "When did you sneak away?"

She was swaying on her feet.

"I just felt uncomfortable so I left. Come in."

She followed him into the spacious front room. "I need another drink," she said.

"You need some coffee," Sean insisted.

"Then you'll have a wide awake drunk." She flopped on the sofa.

"What are you doing here, Sami? You realize what time it is?"

"I knew you'd be up." She took out a cigarette and then put it away. "My heart is broken, Sean Dineen, and I hate Idaho."

Sean sat next to her. "There'll be others," he said.

Sami saw the wine bottle and took a swig. There was little left.

"I need to blow this town," she said. "And why didn't you tell me you were leaving?"

"You were having fun. I didn't want to be a wet blanket."

She looked into his face. "And just why *are* you up so late?"

"I get insomnia," he said.

"I'm sure you do. Look, I need to talk to someone who knows art."

"I don't know art."

"Bullshit." Sami shook her head. "You are a cartoonist, and their art is *just* as important as the stuff hanging in Paris galleries. *And* I need personal guidance."

"Personal guidance from me? You need to get some sleep."

He looked at the young woman's face, slack and bleary eyed, the blonde hair still bright under the light. Sami grinned at him.

"I'll sleep when I'm dead." She touched his face. He saw something appear in her eyes, a lascivious glance suggesting hidden desire. "You want to sleep with me, professor?"

"I'm an old dog."

"So what? You have that 'haven't been laid in six months' look."

"A lot longer than that."

"Poor baby." Sami saw the photo on the table. She picked it up and studied it. "What a beautiful woman. This is the one who was killed?"

"Yes."

She put the photo back on the table. "I'm so sorry." After a moment, she said, "You can't dwell on the past."

"I try not to."

Sami lay back on the sofa and gently rubbed his thigh. "Maybe you need some loving."

"Maybe you need some sober time alone."

"Alone?" She sat up. "Are you rejecting me too, Mr. Dineen? Huh?"

She stretched and Sean saw she wasn't wearing a bra as her blouse opened.

"Lie down. I'll get you a blanket," he said.

"I don't want a blanket. I want another drink."

"I am out of liquor," he told her. He went to the closet to find an extra blanket. "Who rejected you? You're very attractive and I'm sure talented, so who would reject you? A student? A professor?"

He could hear her voice in the other room. "What difference does it make? Hey, maybe you could sketch me."

"Maybe I could."

Sean Dineen went to his large bag by the side of the bed and found his sketch pad. Perhaps it was a good idea to sketch this lost soul for a future cartoon or story. He had often thought of creating a book of sketches of people he had met on the road. He also wondered what it would be like to sleep with this young vibrant woman, even if she was drunk. It had been a long time and he felt the need for sex even if he still feared intimacy. Sean came into the room and saw Sami had removed her blouse. She followed his gaze and cupped her breasts.

"Maybe you could sketch me nude, old timer."

Sami winked at him and started cackling.

"Maybe I don't do nudes," he said.

He tossed her the blanker which she pulled up, lying back on the sofa. Sean could feel an unexplained anger.

"I don't mean to be rude." Sean heard a deep theatrical sigh. "Mr. Dineen. Why am I so messed up?"

"It could be self-pity."

"No, it *isn't* self-pity. You talk like that and you won't get laid."

"Neither will you."

Sami laughed, and then she peered at him over the blanket. "I got enough men in my life."

"I bet you do."

"Get me some water — please?"

"Sure."

Sean walked to the bathroom sink just beyond the queen size bed.

"Maybe you need to relax, Sami," he said. "Dry out, find some nice little country retreat, and just paint. Don't worry about great art. You could also use a good counselor. I still see a therapist."

He didn't hear a response. When Sean returned, Sami had fallen asleep. Her face was beautiful in repose. He pulled up the blanket to her chin and sketched her face quickly. Then he turned off the light and went to bed to lie there in the semi darkness, waiting for sleep. Sometime later, he woke up and saw Sami walking toward the bathroom, wearing only panties, her breasts and lovely curving hips visible in the light from the parking lot. He could hear her gagging behind the closed door, and then she came out and walked by his bed. Eyes closed, he felt her watching his face. Would she slip under the covers and violently make love to him, releasing all the tension of his two year sexual drought? Later in the dead of night, perhaps her boyfriend would show up and pull a gun demanding money; Sean would realize the whole scene was a ploy to rob him, but he would disarm the punk and break his jaw while Sami sat up, watching with shock and even a little sexual arousal.

It was a nice fantasy but Sami groaned and walked to the couch, a fleeting apparition. Sean closed his eyes again and waited for sleep or dawn, whichever came first. When he woke in the morning, he noticed that Sami had pulled the blanket over her face and body. Sean wondered if Sami was faking sleep but then he heard her deep breathing. It was the breathing of exhaustion. Sean closed the door, brushed his teeth, showered and dressed. Sean then examined his sketch, signed it and placed it on a chair near the sofa. He left the room to have coffee and breakfast downstairs. When he came back, it would take little time to pack and they could talk then, if she was awake. For the first time, Sean wondered what her art looked like.

The dining room of the Holiday Inn had that uniform sameness he had grown to expect. The first cup of coffee was wonderful, and after ordering breakfast, he studied some of the other dining patrons. A few were families traveling through, and others were dressed like rodeo cowboys. He had not seen any notice of a rodeo, however. As he finished breakfast, he looked up to see if Sami had come down looking for him. Instead, he saw the tall intense spectator from the night before approaching his table. Declan Mulligan was close to his age, the hair veined with gray, the face and eyes behind round glasses reflecting the pain of one who suffered some hidden loss.

Declan sat down and ordered coffee. Then he regarded Sean. "So how long has it been?"

"Nearly three years since I lost my beloved Rachel, and six months since I lost my ex-wife, Priscilla, the mother of my son. And you?"

"I lost Kate, my wife, three years ago. It was sudden. As you know, grief goes in cycles, it's not linear. We have no choice but to endure as each cycle comes around. Grief can't be cured."

They began to talk about a subject they knew well. Others watching them at the table might think they were brothers meeting after a reunion. Sean told Declan about Rachel and Priscilla and Declan listened carefully. Declan then spoke in detail about the day he suddenly lost Kate. Both men enjoyed remembering their lost loves.

"Dante's description of hell is quite vivid," Declan said, "but hell doesn't come in such a dramatic fashion. It happens on a nice Indian Summer morning in September when you get a phone call that changes your life."

"Or a young smooth-cheeked cop knocks on your door in late afternoon, around dinner time."

"It seems to happen on routine days." Declan looked around the restaurant. "Kate and I had a cat we loved. It liked blues harmonica and I used to play guitar with the mouth harp in a neck holder, and the cat would go crazy. Then Missy died in my arms and we finally got a new cat. Kate loved her and named her Karma as in 'good karma.' Karma managed to help us forget the wonderful cat named Missy." Sean could hear a catch in Declan's voice. "The second cat outlived Kate."

"You still have Karma?"

"Yes. A great cat, but she doesn't like blues harmonica."

"Can't have everything," Sean said.

"Kate played solitaire in the morning," Declan said. "The cards from her last game are still laid out on the table. I guess I'm waiting for her to come back and finish the game. Life is hard, buddy. Grief is hard. We have to simply keep on keepin' on."

Sean looked across the table at Declan. "You are a depressing son of a bitch, you know that?"

"I am," Declan said, smiling for the first time. "We both have dark Celtic genes." He finished his coffee. "Have you sold your house?"

"No. Why would I do that?"

"I found the house I shared with Kate to be a comfort, at first, but now it occasionally feels like a museum. Still, I won't sell it and move to a different place."

"Make the house more your house. I'm fine where I am," insisted Sean.

The waitress poured more coffee.

"Speaking of museums, I hear Professor Heckler and some students attacked your attack on Warhol."

"I've met people like Heckler before," Sean said. "He's a showboat. Are you a Warhol fan?"

"It's all subjective. I either like a painting or I don't. I do know the Impressionists move me. The postmodern movement has some artists I like, but others leave me cold and I can't say why."

"What does that mean, 'postmodern'?"

"I guess it's a combination of high and low art."

"I'm a cartoonist," said Sean. "Therefore, I represent low art?"

"Perhaps. But don't discount popular art. Mozart and Shakespeare were popular. I don't study Warhol, but I find his work innovative…and even dead, he still makes millions off jeans, shoes and perfume."

"Good for him. Business…the new art."

Declan seemed amused, but a moment later, he turned serious.

"Warhol is gone and we're talking about him. Who will talk about us after we get our fifteen minutes of fame?"

"Who cares?"

"Maybe you should care. Why not start another comic strip?"

"I've thought of it."

For a moment, both men were silent. "You fly out today?"

"Yes."

"Travel can help treat grief. Or work. Prescription drugs can blunt it. Alcohol can smother it for a while, but then it gets worse and you can't work. Another treatment is to fall in love again," Declan said. "I know a few who have."

"It hasn't happened for me. Maybe it has for you?"

"No."

"Not the Duck Lady?"

Declan laughed. "You've been talking to that sad but talented drunk, Sami."

"I have."

"The Duck Lady is a 'friend with benefits.' I tolerate her ducks but we're not in love."

Sean finished his coffee and slipped his credit card in with the bill.

"You've never slept with Sami?"

Declan seemed surprised and annoyed. "She's talented and lovely but needs a therapist, not another lecherous old man. I think Sami needs to sober up, live in Paris to just paint and find compassionate lovers—preferably Irish."

It was Sean's turn to laugh. They walked to the cash register where Sean signed the statement and retrieved his card. A few guests had gathered in the lobby, including a visiting Amish family.

"Sami is upstairs in my room," Sean said. "She knocked on my door, last night, quite drunk."

Declan didn't seem surprised, this time. "Did you sleep with her?"

"She has a beautiful young body…but no."

"I see. You're a man of honor."

"Not quite."

"She has much baggage," Declan said. He handed Sean a book. It was his journal of sorrow called *The Grief That Does Not Speak*. It was signed.

"Thank you, Declan. I will need this, I'm sure."

"I hope it's a source of comfort and a tribute to Kate. There *is* light between the cycles. Say hello to Sami. I'll try to watch out for her. And contact me if you drive back through. We're very much alike." Declan shook his hand. "Some days are better than others. You have your son, at least. Kate's children bring me comfort."

"I *will* stay in touch," said Sean, suddenly feeling a hollowness inside. "It still hurts for you?"

"Every day. But we have to carry on. Kate would want that for me. Rachel and Priscilla would want that for you. We are at that age when we'll start losing friends. Take care of yourself and good luck."

"Good luck to you."

They embraced. Declan nodded and walked through the lobby. Then Sean walked to the elevator and took it to the second floor and his room. When he opened the door, his sketch and Sami were gone. She had left a note on a post card.

"I'm so sorry for breaking in on you. Don't think too badly of me. And thanks for the flattering sketch. I will send a painting to you. Please stay in touch. This *can't* be the ending. We *must* meet again on the avenue, tangled up in blue. Love, Sami."

Sami had added her e mail. Sean turned over the post card. It was a photo of Andy Warhol's soup can. He stared at the familiar image, waiting for it to move.

DEXTER FLANGAN found the only way he could keep his Bannock Shoshone Indian students together and calm was to play some blues at the end of each day. His Fort Hall twelfth graders would rock back and forth, eyes closed, following the predictable but poignant rhythms of twelve bar blues. They smiled at chauvinistic songs about men beating their "wimmins," getting drunk, or destroying rivals by taking care of "bidnez." Lost love, depression, hell hounds, devils, and the inevitable trains rolling down the midnight tracks added color to the songs. It was the only time they heard their English instructor deliberately use double negatives.

Dexter finished the song, "Crossroads" by Robert Johnson, a bottleneck piece using a slide over the taut strings. Once again, the spirit of the legendary bluesman tried to flag a ride at the crossroads. The students sat in unusual silence. Dexter felt drained from a week of teaching.

"We are off for Easter, next week," Dexter said. "Enjoy your time off."

The class filed out. Many of the young students were overweight, suffering from diabetes and other ailments, including T.B. They often watched him with a detached curiosity as he discussed English poets, viewing him the way they might a barking reservation dog. A heavy-set youth stopped and addressed him: "Hey, Teacher Man, you play good."

Dexter closed his guitar case. "Thank you."

Lance Bronco observed Dexter, something secret lurking in the dark opaque eyes. His teeth were capped with silver, and Lance rarely spoke in class, ignoring Dexter with a profound indifference. He wore baggy clothes and a stocking cap hid his shaved scalp. For a moment, Dexter wondered why Lance bothered to speak to him. His smile was unsettling.

"You should play more. We don't need to learn no white man's English."

"But if you learn the white man's language, you can write about your people."

"I write a language you never heard of."

"Is that so?"

After a silence, Lance said, "Hal Hayball likes to play blues, too."

"That's right. He's getting better than I am."

"My little Injun Homie *loves* that white music."

"Blacks created the blues."

"A lot of white people play it."

"Why not? It's great music."

"I like Chicano rap." Lance's shirt was open and Dexter saw the skull tattoo on one side of his chest, and a black hand on the other. "If black Crips and bloods come here" — Lance made a gun out of his fingers — "They dead."

"What's with the black hand tattoo, Mr. Bronco?" Lance didn't reply. They could hear a passing car outside. "Is there something you need?" Dexter finally asked.

"You ain't got nothin' I need. Maybe I got something for you."

"What's that?"

The young man, large for his age, stared at him with a sudden malevolence in his bulging eyes. Then he shrugged. "I got a warning."

"Warning?"

"Check outside."

"Lance?" The Indian boy stopped, avoiding eye contact. "Where *is* Hal? He's absent, today."

"Why don't you ask him?"

Then Lance was gone. When Dexter walked from the small building used for class, he saw the graffiti on the wall and recognized the markings of a Latino LA gang that had invaded the Fort Hall Reservation. There was a huge S 13 with an X sitting in the lower half circle of the S. They called themselves SUR 13 for *Sureños* or "Southerners." An hour later, Dexter walked to the tribal police station and used the outside phone, waiting for the buzzer to open the door. Dexter then sat in the small dark office of Teton, the police chief. He was a giant, with broad shoulders, thick black hair and a round, often tragic face. Photos from his days as a bull rider and film actor sat on his desk.

"The graffiti sends a message," Chief Teton said in a resonant voice.

"What message is that?"

"They're warning the gangs from Blackfoot this is their turf."

"Gangs? This isn't LA."

"No, but they're starting here. Blame *La Eme*."

"*La Eme*?"

"*Eme* is the Spanish word for the letter "M" which is the thirteenth letter in the alphabet."

"But *La Eme* is the Mexican Mafia. Why would Bannock Shoshone kids imitate them? They're Native American."

"It's a kind of family where they can carry guns and get respect. They can sell drugs and make serious money. They don't care about the old traditional Indian ways. They see the so-called gangsta lifestyle as a way out and it's sad." Teton picked up a newspaper. "In New Mexico, tribal police found graffiti on some ancient Indian petroglyphs. Indian taggers were arrested."

Dexter looked at Teton's face, broad and striking like an old Indian carving.

"They didn't realize they were defacing the work of their ancestors?"

"I guess not. I'm putting together a gang task force, but that's not all we need. We need more education."

Dexter got up to leave. "One of my promising students failed to show today. Hal Hayball." For a moment, Teton averted his eyes. "He's got the potential to be a great blues guitarist," Dexter said.

"That skill won't help him here."

Dexter opened the door.

"Mr. Flanagan?"

"Yes?"

"I'll talk to Hal. You be careful."

"Of what?"

"That graffiti could have been a warning to you. *Sureño* 13 doesn't want white influence on their members."

"Thanks for the tip."

Dexter left the police station and drove through Fort Hall. Gleaming trucks were parked in front of the casino and trading post. He saw the empty fairgrounds where all the tribes met every August to celebrate Indian dancing and rodeo skills. Near the small town, Sheepskin Road led deep into the bottoms land. It was still beautiful open country with meadows, streams, and rolling grass-covered prairie for stray and wild horses and the Indian buffalo herds. Dexter saw graffiti on a few buildings and walls, though none of the many trailers were marked. He knew that whites paid good money to hunt and fish on the reservation, but rarely did he see Bannock-Shoshone members hunting or fishing.

What would LA gangs want here, he thought, *except to sell drugs and destroy the Indian population even more? And why did Lance Bronco call Hal his "Homie"?*

Dexter Flanagan drove toward his home in Pocatello.

"Perhaps my teaching days are over," Dexter muttered to himself.

His album had done reasonably well with two popular singles downloaded from the Internet. After the semester ended, he had a gig at Bucknell College, warming up for a group that would tour Pennsylvania, Washington DC and New York. In the summer, Dexter would play at a club in Galway, Ireland. Then he remembered how difficult it was to make a consistent living as a musician. He volunteered at a local soup kitchen, but that didn't pay the mortgage.

Coming up his street, he saw black gang signs across his recently painted yellow garage doors. Dexter carried a camera in his car and snapped a photo of the graffiti. He then headed for the freeway and soon was racing across reservation farm land, driving toward the river bottoms. He passed the bullet-riddled sign warning trespassers and continued down a narrow dusty road, leaving behind potato fields for open prairie. Dexter drove until he saw Hal's shack just off the road.

He stopped in front of the weathered cabin. Hal's grandmother, a wrinkled old Indian woman with a pipe and a tin cup, sat in a rocking chair staring out at the unpaved road and grasslands. She flashed her single-toothed grin and nodded to herself. Dexter saw the bottle of Yukon Jack liqueur on the porch. He walked past the old woman into the small shack where Hal stood, waiting for him. Hal wore a white tee-shirt, size fifty baggy jeans and a red bandana. Hal offered him no greeting, and he saw the defiance in his eyes. A beat-up guitar case leaned against the wall. An old severed buffalo head sat facing up on a corner chair. There was no glass in some of the windows.

"You weren't in class, today," Dexter said.

"You are razor sharp, Homes. Razor."

"My name is Dexter Flanagan… it isn't 'Homes.'"

"Okay. You are razor sharp, Mr. Flanagan…and you better leave."

"Why weren't you in class, today?" Hal didn't answer. "You practice those runs I showed you?"

"I played a few chords."

"My guitar's in the trunk."

For a few moments, Dexter was uncertain that Hal even knew he was in the room. They heard the woman cackling on the porch. Somewhere, a dog was barking a warning. Hal finally motioned to the single table with two chairs.

"Sit down."

They sat. Dexter glanced at the shaggy horned bison head.

"Who shot the buffalo?"

"My great grandfather…a hunter from the old days."

"Why don't you break out that old Gibson and let's play a few songs?"

"Blues music is nice, but it's obsolete. I'm into something else."

"Like gangs?"

"They ain't gangs. My homies are part of a crew." Hal met his eyes. "I can't come to class, no more."

"Why? You're close to graduation. And since when do you use double negatives?"

"It's the language of my people."

Dexter was shocked. "*Your* people? That woman out there is *your* people. What about her?"

"What about her? *Look* at my grandmother. Her mind's gone. My grandfather, father and mother are dead."

"But she represents your true people."

Hal's intense focus made Dexter look away.

"True people? You think I'm gonna dance this summer at the Indian pow wow, dressed in feathers? You know why I'm so smart as you like to brag? Because my mother carried me in jail and couldn't drink until after I was born." Hal took a deep breath. "Go home. You are pissing me off and you ain't safe, here."

"Is that right?" Dexter listened to the woman mumbling outside. "Hal? What happened to you?"

"I found something."

"What can you possibly get from a punk like Lance?"

"Respect."

Suddenly, Dexter pulled apart Hal's shirt. His chest was free of tattoos. "When do you get your black hand?"

"Next week. Then there's no turning back. You don't leave SUR 13 except when you die."

Dexter took out his camera and brought up the last image.

"You see this? Who the fuck did this to my garage door?"

Hal examined the photo. "It wasn't my people. That's the Maravilla gang. We'll take care of it."

"Who is 'We'? Your punk-ass crew?"

Hal's voice was quiet. "That's right. We take care of business. And if my homies catch you here, you'll be at the bottom of the Snake River."

"Jesus, that sounds like bad movie dialogue."

Dexter never saw the gun. Suddenly, the twenty-two revolver was under his chin. Hal's eyes had a fierce urgency, and he saw moisture on his face.

"This ain't a movie prop, Flanagan."

Dexter could feel tightness in his voice as he spoke: "Hal, Hal." He gently pushed the gun away. "You pull a gun on me?"

"Get out of here—now!"

Then they heard the cars outside, and when Dexter stepped to the door, he saw the young Indian boys dressed like LA gang bangers in bandannas and baggy pants. Gangsta rap music played loudly. Approaching the cabin, they did not look at him but he felt their passive malice even as they made him invisible.

"This is my English teacher," Hal said. The gang members began to laugh. "He was just leaving."

Dexter smiled at the young men. "Why haven't I seen you gentlemen at school?"

The young men laughed again.

Dexter walked to his car. He turned as Hal herded his crew into the shack past the smiling old woman who saluted Dexter with her cup. Hal stood on the porch and called out to him. "You keep writing your pretty love songs and stay away from me."

Dexter yelled back: "I play this weekend. Come sit in."

Then Dexter was driving down the narrow road toward the small town and the freeway heading back to Pocatello. He passed Lance Bronco coming the other way and the men exchanged glances, Bronco's eyes hard and cold, the silver-capped teeth set in a grin. For the first time, Dexter felt fear, and wondered if Hal's warning was accurate. Moments later, Teton pulled him over in an unmarked car and repeated Hal's warning. "Keep a distance."

"Why should I stay away from a gifted Indian student, a potential blues great and Harvard student?"

"Maybe he's lost, right now," the sheriff said. "You can't help him and I don't want you hurt. Besides, you need a permit to be out on the reservation."

"Hal's packing a gun."

"I'll take care of it. That's my job."

"Then do it."

Dexter hit the gas and drove toward Fort Hall's small town and trailer park. He stopped in a local store and bought some yellow paint. As he paid, he asked the tall Indian youth behind the counter if there was a gang problem at Fort Hall. The handsome young man lifted his eyes to the ceiling. "It's exaggerated," he said, sounding more like an educated white man. "I mean, really, they're all gangster wannabes. And those *awful* baggy pants."

Dexter drove to Pocatello. The next morning as Dexter painted over the graffiti markings, he noticed how intricate they were. Why didn't Indian youth spend as much time learning to read and write English?

"What if they return and do it again?"

Dexter turned and saw his neighbor, a retired Viet Nam vet who led a POW-MIA organization. He wore jeans, boots, a vest and beret. His face was lined and covered with a white beard.

"I don't know, Scott," Dexter said.

"I didn't fight a war to come back to this. I'll blow those assholes away."

"It's a Latino gang called The Maravillas."

"They'll be a dead gang if they come back."

"The police could arrest you if you shoot a tagger," Dexter said.

Scott turned and walked back into his house. From the neighbor's flagpole, a black POW-MIA flag flew beneath an American flag. Needing some release, Dexter went into his house and played guitar, singing for two hours. One of the songs celebrated Ira Hayes, the Pima Indian who helped raise the flag over Iwo Jima and came home to drink himself to death. Maybe Hal was right: certain folk songs were obsolete. What new scope was Hal into?

That night, Dexter went to a brewpub to hear two acoustic guitarists and drink a root beer. Posters on the wall advertised upcoming groups: Elvis Has Left the Building, Steelhead Redd and someone named Montana Mike, King of the Blues Ukulele. He noticed Sami, a local female artist, sitting at the end of the bar and drinking a pint.

"You gonna play tonight?"

"It's not my night," Dexter said.

"That's too bad," Sami said. "You're good. I like your love song about the girl who ran off with another musician. Was she real?"

"I'm afraid so. She broke my heart."

"All you get from a broken heart is a love song," Sami said.

She smiled at him. He liked her face and the bleached blonde hair with a star-shaped patch of dark hair marking the back of her head. Dexter also admired her body, but Sami loved to drink and Dexter could not get close to someone who might lure him to drink. He listened to the two musicians playing blues and folk music, and when asked to sit in, Dexter played a borrowed guitar. Maybe Hal would walk in and add some bottleneck guitar, fueling the music of the old black blues singers with some Indian soul. After a set, he waved goodbye to Sami and left. Driving toward the cul-de-sac where he lived, Dexter saw the police car lights and an ambulance pulling out of his driveway. The police were questioning Scott on his lawn. Dexter parked in his driveway and got out.

"What's going on?" he asked.

An officer told him. Scott shook his head. "I didn't shoot the tagger," he said. "It was a drive-by. I heard them fire and drive off."

"Will he live?"

"He was shot in the hip," the officer said. "He could be paralyzed. I guess he didn't appreciate you painting over his art work." The young officer stepped close to Dexter and asked, "Why your house, Mr. Flanagan?"

"I teach Indian kids. Maybe that's why."

"They'll be tagging other houses," Scott insisted. "And businesses. They're like dogs pissing on trees to mark their turf."

The next morning, Dexter drove out to the Fort Hall Reservation. With school out for Easter, the reservation was deserted. He wanted to visit Hal but drove to the police station where he saw officers running to parked cars and driving away. He stopped a young patrolman.

"What happened?"

The Indian officer had a neutral expression. "Nothing we can't handle."

Dexter knew no one would tell him why officers were suddenly driving out quickly, as though an emergency had sounded. Then he saw a news van and Dexter stopped a female reporter.

"Why all the excitement?"

"Someone shot up the police chief's house," the woman said.

She got into her news van and drove away. Dexter didn't know if Teton was hurt or dead. Lance Bronco watched the departing police cars, and shuffled over to confront Dexter. "What are you doing here, teacher? You got a weekend class?"

"Maybe I like the reservation."

"I believe that. Whites like to see the buffalo herds. Think of the old days. Maybe I can take you on a little tour of the river bottoms."

"I'll pass for now."

Smiling to himself, Lance Bronco walked away. Dexter got into his car and drove to Teton's house. Police were gathered on the front lawn, and Dexter could see the bullet holes along the front of the house, two windows shattered. Teton stood in front, putting on a flak jacket and talking to officers. The Pocatello Swat Team arrived, and Dexter saw another man in a suit talking on a radio.

"Teton!"

The sheriff ignored Dexter. "I can't talk, now, Flanagan."

The officers and Swat Team drove off.

That night, as Dexter played solo at the brewpub, Hal entered. He wore a workman's shirt, jeans and boots and didn't resemble a gangbanger. He also carried his guitar. At the break, they talked.

"Dexter? I'm sorry I pulled a gun on you."

"Forget it."

"You better stay off the reservation for a while. There was a big raid, today."

"You know anything about it?"

"What would I know?" Hal glanced toward the door. "Let's play."

They played a strong set with the audience whistling, cheering and clapping, Hal's bottleneck slide guitar in open G tuning screaming over Dexter's full chords and plaintive rich voice. They conjured Robert Johnson's ghost and revived the music of black blues singers long dead: Blind Lemon Jefferson, Lightning Hopkins, Mississippi Fred McDowell, and Mississippi John Hurt. They ended the set with Hal singing "Tumblin' Dice" by the Stones, always a crowd pleaser. After the final chord, Hal grinned back at the cheering crowd. No Indians were in the tavern. Then they sat at the bar drinking soft drinks and Hal displayed his bottleneck, cut and prepared from an old wine bottle. The glass had a bluish tinge.

"You can buy readymade chrome bottlenecks at the music store," Dexter told him. "They have a sharper sound."

"Maybe, but I got this from an old bluesman in New Orleans. It's authentic."

"I understand. It's good luck when one musician passes on something to another."

"I'd like to find Robert Johnson's bottleneck," Hal said.

They discussed old blues legends the way others discussed great athletes, past and present, and then Dexter toasted with his glass. "Nice playing with you again."

"Blues is healing music," Hal said. "It's a way to play all the sorrow out."

"Forgive me, but did you get your gang tattoo yet?"

Hal placed his palms over the top of the upright guitar case. "No."

"I'm glad to hear that," Dexter said. "What happened with the raid? Are they after you?"

"Which 'They' do you mean?"

"Any 'They.'"

"I'll be all right. Don't you fret your set." Beads of sweat formed on his forehead, and Hal again glanced at the front door. "I need to disappear, Mr. Flanagan. Nice jamming with you. Our friendship has meant a lot to me." Carrying his guitar, Hal walked toward the back door. Dexter wanted to follow him, but Hal only gave him a short wave and was gone. Dexter wondered if they would ever meet again. Then he heard a female voice.

"That was some great blues."

He turned and saw Sami sitting beside him, drinking a soft drink.

"Thanks," Dexter said. She was pale and he noticed her hands were trembling. "Are you all right?"

"I quit drinking yesterday and I'm a bit shaky."

"Perhaps I can help," Dexter said. "One day at a time."

The next morning, the papers carried the news of the massive raid with over 50 gang members arrested. Hal Hayball had not been arrested but was missing. Some gang members were bailed out and when Dexter returned to finish the semester, Hal had dropped out of his class. Occasionally, Lance showed, not to work but to sit and stare out the window or to watch Dexter quietly as he moved about the class. Lance had not been charged with a crime.

Then Dexter was on the road, playing on the East coast and one month in Galway, Ireland, opening for Irish and English rock groups at a Celtic club named after a mythical black rose. It had a large stage and a wide dance floor.

"Play popular covers the customers know," the Irish club owner insisted. "And include your song. A few here know it."

"No blues?"

"Oh, the Irish love the blues," the owner said.

Dexter played the club, sometimes joined by other band members, and he enjoyed the Galway buskers playing on the corners; he drank coffee in the many pubs, listening to traditional Irish music. On occasion, he played on the ancient cobble stone streets, running through his favorites for tourists visiting the shops, restaurants and pubs. He imagined Hal playing on these same streets and building a reputation. Dexter's guitar case filled with Euros. He visited and jammed with Irish, Australian and American buskers, listening to their stories of life on the road playing for food and drink money.

"We do well," a young red-haired Irish busker named Jamie said. "Times are harder, but we're still well fed and watered, don't you think?"

"I think you do well." Dexter hated to leave the city by the famous Galway Bay. Sami kept in touch through e mail. Back home, a trial was beginning.

"Damn, I wish I was in Galway...but with all those flowing pints, I may not stay sober," Sami wrote. "Please come back. I miss you." To his question about Hal, the answer was the same: "He vanished and no one has seen him."

Dexter returned to Idaho in time for the trial. He and Sami sat in the crowded court room. On the third day, Hal Hayball wearing a suit entered with two guards and took the stand. The Indian defendants appeared stoic and indifferent, but Dexter felt their toxic hatred. Hal didn't make eye contact with Dexter or Lance who also sat in the courtroom.

"Please tell the court who you are and who you work for," the prosecuting attorney said.

"My name is Hal Hayball. I was a senior recently at Fort Hall and I just graduated from Highland High School."

"But you took classes off campus?"

"Yes."

"Why is that?"

"For my protection."

"Protection? But you're a student, Mr. Hayball."

"That's right. I am also a musician."

"I see. You are a student and a musician. So what else that demanded protection?"

Hal took a beat. "I worked as an informant for State and Federal Police."

A gasp went through the courtroom, but the Indian defendants were quiet, watching Hayball.

"And what did you discover working as an informant, Mr. Hayball?"

"That there was a significant gang presence on the reservation and a lot of drug traffic, mostly meth. The Mexican Mafia known as *La Eme* was directing and profiting from the drug traffic, recruiting and using Native American gangs."

"Are any of these gang members in the courtroom, today?"

"Yes," Hal said. He pointed. "Those chicken shit injuns sitting there." Then he pointed at Lance. "And him. Fatboy."

"Mr. Bronco isn't on trial," the prosecutor said.

"He should be. He takes orders from the devil. He is a traitor to his people."

The Indian defendants stood up and began shouting. A few made gang signs. Hal sat quietly but Teton stood up, ready to defend the witness.

"You're dead," one of the young men said to Hal before the bailiff took him from the room. "You are fucking dead!"

"You died a long time ago," Hal shouted back.

The testimony continued as Hal Hayball detailed all the gang activity, what he observed and what he did, including buys. The court heard recordings from a device Hal had hidden in a buffalo head. Then two officers escorted Hal from the courtroom. For a minute, he and Dexter exchanged glances. Dexter nodded. Lance sat staring ahead, not smiling. The jury left to deliberate and returned after two hours with a guilty verdict for all the gang members. They would go to prison for a long time.

"Maybe the reservation can get back to the old ways," the judge said, "free from gangs, meth, graffiti and intimidation."

When Dexter visited Teton, he would not say where authorities had taken Hal or if he was in the Witness Protection Program.

"He will contact you if he has to," Teton said. "He's still in danger. *La Eme* knows about his testimony and they'll track him."

"How long does he have to hide?"

"Maybe not long. Maybe for life. Just be checking out the charts for a new Indian blues singer."

That August, the Indian rodeo and pow wow was a big success. Dexter liked to walk the fairgrounds and visit the various booths and watch the dancing and bareback relay horse races. When the fall coolness arrived, Dexter knew he was finished teaching. He had enough offers from his album sales to tour the college circuit, and being a busker troubadour, should be playing on the road. Dexter still asked after Hal and was told not to ask too many questions, so he played local clubs and listened and waited for his favorite student and guitarist to walk in the door. Lance remained at large and one day appeared in the music store where Dexter bought new strings. Lance grinned, showing his silver-capped teeth.

"How come you don't teach no more? Whitey left the reservation for good?"

Dexter met Lance's dark malignant eyes. "Why do you care?"

"Maybe you miss your little bitch Injun. If I find him, I'll let you know."

Dexter didn't answer. He left the music store and saw an idling car parked with four men inside, their faces concealed. The men wore suits. Lance walked past the car as they pulled out and drove away. Dexter bought the morning paper which carried stories of new graffiti in neighboring Blackfoot. The local gang rivalries were starting again. Dexter then walked across the street to check Mr. Dee's local pawnshop for any old guitars.

Inside the pawnshop, the wall was hung with many rifles, but Dexter saw no guitars. There were racks of second-hand clothes and shelves of books, items left behind or hocked by desperate people. Dexter nodded once to Mr. Dee, an older heavy-set man who carried a holstered .38 on his hip. Two men played chess at a table by the window. The car with the four men suddenly parked in front of the pawnshop and a short handsome Mexican man in a suit entered. He was wiry and didn't look at Dexter but admired the guns in cases and the rifles on the wall.

"I can't believe it. You got an AK 47, an M 16, and so many semi autos. You even got a sniper rifle," the short man said. "Look at that long barrel."

"You can bring down a target from a mile away," Mr. Dee said.

"In Mexico, guns aren't legal, so all the bad guys have them. Here in America, we citizens can get protection, you know? Thank God I became an American."

"Not many of us left," Mr. Dee said.

"My name is Robbie Ruiz. I'll buy all you got…especially the AK 47 and the M 16."

"I'll need an ID, Mr. Ruiz, and they'll do a police check."

"No problem," Ruiz said. "I'm a gun dealer."

Ruiz reached in his wallet and took out his driver's license and firearms permit. Mr. Dee asked a question: "These here weapons won't ship to Mexico, will they?"

The two chess players looked up. Ruiz smiled. "I hope not. It's gettin' bad, down there. Federales and drug cartels shooting it out. A lot of people getting killed, man."

Dexter started toward the door. Ruiz suddenly blocked his way, and Dexter saw a sharp glint in the black rubbery eyes. Ruiz didn't move.

"Excuse me," Dexter said.

"Wait. Don't I know you?"

"I doubt it."

"Maybe you sold little girls in Tijuana?"

"I don't think so."

"Maybe you like little Indian boys?"

Dexter felt something nauseating inside when Ruiz suddenly laughed.

"Maybe not, *Señor*. Relax." Ruiz turned away and admired again the many guns on display. "Thank God for the NRA," he said. "No gun control in Idaho."

"Oh, we got gun control," Mr. Dee told them. He took out his pistol and held it in both hands, pointing at an imaginary target and making vocal gun sounds. "Two hands is gun control."

Ruiz and the chess players enjoyed the joke. Dexter Flanagan quickly left the pawnshop. The three men in the car outside stared at him as he crossed the street.

One Saturday night while playing the brewpub, Dexter saw Teton in the audience. The police chief nursed a soft drink and seemed to appreciate the music, only now, Dexter had a band that also played blues-rock and popular covers. During the break, Teton sat next to him.

"You're good. Too bad Hal can't join you."

"Do you know where he is?"

"I don't know, and I wouldn't tell you if I did."

"Then why *are* you here, Teton?"

Teton shrugged his broad shoulders. "Just to listen to your music. I *like* rock and blues. Better than that Indian racket with the drums." Teton sipped his drink. "Have *you* seen Hal?"

"Of course not."

Dexter knew Teton would not speak until he was ready. When the break ended, Sami who worked the bar nodded to Dexter. He got up; Teton reached out and took his wrist. "Word has it some gang activity has been starting, recently."

"I heard."

"*La Eme* thugs might be in town. Just no good."

Dexter sat back down. "How do you know?"

"I just know."

"Can you arrest them?"

"On what charge?"

"Why are they here?"

"Maybe to recruit new people. Hal put quite a few away for some years, but they can communicate with gang members outside the joint."

Dexter remembered driving through a gang shootout in Los Angeles.

"Is Hal safe?"

The band on the small stage waited for Dexter.

"There is Nicaraguan justice," Teton said.

Dexter didn't understand the reference, and while they played Dexter's song about Mexican guides or "coyotes," Teton left through the back door. Occasionally, Dexter observed the audience searching for Hal's face. He also expected the gargoyle face of Lance, always smiling at some secret joke. Dexter briefly imagined gunmen one night entering the narrow brewpub to shoot him on stage. The band ripped into a Dylan favorite, "Where Are You Tonight, Sweet Marie?"

*****

DEXTER woke up. Sami slept quietly by his side and Dexter glanced at the illuminated hands of the clock; why did he awake at 4:00 AM? The nights he played, Dexter always got to bed late and would sleep until late morning, though sometimes the sunlight on the shade or outside noise stirred him. He sat up in bed and listened to the house, but it was quiet. There was no wind outside. Dexter felt an unexplained anxiety. He lay in bed for a half hour and then decided to get up and drink a glass of milk. He walked into the kitchen and opened the refrigerator. The bottle of milk and a carton of orange juice sat on a shelf. Dexter drank a glass of milk and walked into the dark front room, looking out the window at the quiet street, visible in the moonlight. There were no pedestrians. Scott's flags hung limply. Then he walked toward the kitchen glass door which faced a garden with roses and a green lawn. The porch was empty except for a table and a few overturned lawn chairs. Dexter rubbed his eyes.

When he opened them, Hal Hayball stood on the porch.

The moonlight was soft on his bare chest and face, the eyes large and luminous. Dexter felt a cold wave seize his body; he waited for Hal to speak when a wind blew and the overturned chairs slid a few inches. The railing glowed with a strange light. Then a soundless burst of lightning illuminated the face and body of the young Indian boy. For a moment, Dexter saw a 19th century warrior dressed in feathers and buckskin, the image like that of a washed-out negative, and then the vision shattered when a sudden wave splashed against the glass. Dexter cried out: "Hal!"

Dexter gripped the heavy glass door when he heard Sami's voice.

"Why are you up?" She wore a blue bathrobe.

"I think I saw Hal."

"Hal?"

He slid back the door and they walked onto the porch. It was a warm night and the lawn and rose bushes were pale in the late September moon. The glass door was dry, the night air still.

"Are you all right?"

Dexter saw the concern in Sami's eyes. "Something has happened to Hal," he said. "Did you see any lightning?"

"No."

That night, lying next to Sami, Dexter listened for voices in the darkness, thinking about ghosts and wondering if Hal had indeed contacted him from the other side, though he didn't believe in such hallucinations. In the morning as he prepared to leave, he heard Sami scream downstairs. Dexter rushed toward the garage and the laundry room where Sami held some dirty clothes in a basket. She pointed toward the garage door. Inside the garage on Dexter's car sat the severed buffalo head.

That afternoon, Dexter sat in Teton's office.

"The buffalo head was a warning from Sur 13. The visitation? Maybe Hal was communicating from the other side."

"He's dead?"

"They fished a headless body with no hands out of the Snake river, this morning. It will be hard to identify him because I don't think Hal's DNA is on record. The body fits Hal's size."

Dexter sat, feeling sick but saying nothing. He wanted to track down and kill Lance. Teton took out a studio portrait and slid it across the desk. "Have you seen this man?"

It was the handsome face of the Mexican man in the pawnshop.

"Yes. He was buying handguns and assault rifles at Mr. Dee's."

"The FBI says Mr. Robbie Ruiz supplies guns and cash for *La Eme*. He immigrated here as a child, fought in Iraq, became an American citizen, and evidently has a clean record. That means his gun business is legal."

"He stopped me at the pawnshop and gave me the willies."

"He should. Ruiz is a dangerous, egotistical sociopath. He travels with his lawyer and two body guards."

"Are we gonna have a shootout here?"

"They're distributors, and won't risk a gun battle with police." Teton took back the photo. "Tonight, these four gentlemen are flying a small private plane loaded with weapons to Salt Lake before flying to San Diego on a private jet." There was a pause. "I'm a pilot. Did I ever tell you that?"

"No."

"Maybe they need to check their little airplane. Too much weight can be a problem." Teton pushed back his chair. "I shouldn't tell you this, but Hal considered you a friend. After I arrest Lance Bronco, I'm meeting a federal plane at eight, tonight."

"Why?"

Teton did not reply.

That evening, Dexter drove to the small airport outside of town. The lobby was empty. A stocky Latino police officer with a crew cut sat inside his office with a canine unit outside. Then Dexter saw Teton pulling a handcuffed Lance Bronco out of his police car. He turned Lance around and forced him toward the door. As they were walking toward the airport lobby, Dexter saw a van drive up and Ruiz and his men get out. They were wearing new sport suits. Two of the men unloaded guns in their cases and put them on a luggage carrier. Ruiz and a tall white man began walking toward the airport police office when they saw Teton with his prisoner.

"You can't deport me," Lance screamed. "I'm a Bannock Shoshone. I'm American!"

"Then how come you got a Nicaraguan passport?"

"It's not mine, it's a fake."

"It's authentic. *You're* a fake." Teton barked at the two men blocking the doorway. "Excuse me, gentleman. I got a prisoner."

Robbie Ruiz called out to Lance, asking in Spanish if he was Nicaraguan.

"You know I don't speak no damn Spanish, Homes."

"Homes?" Teton gestured toward Ruiz. "Is he one of your crew, Lance?"

Lance didn't answer. Ruiz regarded Teton with the same fixed stare Dexter saw in the pawnshop. Teton suddenly found himself in a confrontation. From a distance it resembled a comedy act, a very short man facing down a very tall one. Though the voice was soft and polite, Dexter could hear the threat.

"Ain't none of my business, Chief, but he's right. He don't speak no Spanish I ever heard. He looks like an Indian to me. You of all people should know that…badge or no badge."

"And I bet you know him real well, don't you?"

Ruiz glared at Teton. "What's that supposed to mean?"

"Take the cuffs off," Lance cried in outrage. "You can't do this."

"Yes I can," Teton said. "And I will."

"Let's go," the tall man said. He was thin and wore dark glasses. "We got other business." After a pause, Ruiz finally agreed and started to leave when Teton patted his jacket.

"You packin', sir?"

Ruiz didn't back away. His gaze was steady, calm. Teton's deputy got out of the tribal police car while Dexter stood silently. The airport police officer came out of his office.

"What's it to you?" Ruiz finally said.

"Taking guns on an airplane?"

"We are licensed to carry guns and it's a private plane."

"A Pilatus PC-12. A nice plane," Teton said. "And only one engine. I like two for heavy lifting."

"I only need one, Chief."

"Good. No drug cargo on board?"

Ruiz seemed amused. "Listen to him," he said. "I have only guns and they are legal."

"I represent Mr. Ruiz," the tall man said. "Unless you have some official business, I suggest you don't interfere with us." He leaned down and whispered to his client. The two assistants pushed another load of guns toward the waiting plane as Ruiz and his lawyer turned to go. Lance suddenly tried to pull away from the tribal deputy.

"If this is about Hal, I had nothin' to do with it. I don't know where he is!" Lance glared at the men as they walked way. "Mr. Ruiz! You tell him."

For a moment, it could have been a silent tableau from a movie. The short man finally looked at Lance.

"Tell me what?" Teton said. "Mr. Ruiz—you know anything about Hal Hayball?"

"Hold on," the lawyer said.

Ruiz grinned, the eyes black and venomous. He finally spoke: "I never met Mr. Hayball, Chief."

"My name isn't 'Chief,' it's Teton…like the mountain."

The lawyer pulled Robbie Ruiz back as the airport officer approached. "*Buenas Dias*. Is there a problem here?"

Dexter felt a moment of relief as the tension was broken.

"There *is* a problem," Teton said. "These men are armed and work for *La Eme*, better known as the Mexican Mafia."

"That's slander," the lawyer said.

"I'm out of time." Teton pushed Lance toward the lobby doors. "This punk *is* a Nicaraguan National soon to be deported. A federal plane is picking him up."

Teton and his deputy escorted Lance into the lobby. The airport officer studied Ruiz and his lawyer. "I am Captain Maldonado. Did he say you're Mexican Mafia?" The officer then repeated the question in Spanish.

"No, we're the Russian Mafia," Ruiz said, in Spanish and English. "I don't deal in drugs. My cousin, though, he's got a whole plane load of illegal bananas."

After a pause, Ruiz and his lawyer began to laugh, showing white teeth. The officer also laughed.

"You have objections if my drug dog checks your plane?"

"None," Ruiz said.

The other two men joined them and watched the security officer with open mouths and dull eyes. They had an unhealthy pallor to their skin.

"I have to ask: are you gentleman armed?"

"Yes, officer," said Ruiz. "We are."

"I need to see gun permits, IDs, your flight plan and cargo listing."

Officer Maldonado took their documents. He had a cheerful presence. At times their exchange slipped into Spanish, though the two body guards said nothing.

"Your Spanish has that Castilian lisp. You from Spain?"

"I spent two years there on a mission, Mr. Ruiz."

"Church or Military?"

"Church."

"I like missionaries," Ruiz said. "Any converts?"

"Maybe a few."

"Listen, the boy that Indian cop arrested isn't from Nicaragua. You test his Spanish yourself."

"I don't mix in tribal affairs," Maldonado said. He handed back the papers to Ruiz and his lawyer. "Everything checks out. I personally believe in gun ownership. It's our right as American citizens."

"Amen to that," Ruiz said. "The second amendment."

"After I check your plane with my dog, you have a safe trip."

As they walked onto the tarmac toward their waiting single prop plane, they began to speak in Spanish. "Robbie? Why are they deporting Bronco?"

"Who cares?" Robbie Ruiz said in English. "Some tribal shit."

"But that fat punk knows a lot."

"I'll take care of it. First, I'd like to blow that injun *cabron* away. No one talks to me like that."

After Officer Maldonado left the plane with his dog, a beagle with a police ID sweater, they boarded. On another part of the tarmac, Lance began crying out for help and Teton gagged him as they waited for the federal plan to land. Teton had some final instructions:

"You know, Lance, when you arrive, Customs will see their mistake and cut you loose but you better get to a parlor that removes gang tattoos because when the Nicaraguan soldiers see *any* tattoo that's gang related, like a black hand, it's prison for life. They don't mess around, them Nicaraguan federales. When you *do* get your gang tats removed, get to the American embassy real quick and they can send you back…when we confirm your tribal membership. It won't take long. Maybe a few months. Maybe a few years."

Lance cursed through his gag and the tribal policeman jabbed him with his club. Teton glared at Lance and seized him by the collar. "I understand you and your crew shooting up my home, this is a war, but you're gonna pay for Hal."

The government plane came in for a landing. Lance furiously shook his head and Dexter saw fear in his eyes. Teton spoke in a quiet voice. "You got something to tell us, Lance, before we depot your sorry ass?"

Teton removed the gag. Lance started talking.

"I don't know what happened to Hal. All I did is point Ruiz and his boys in the right direction so they could talk to him."

"*Talk* to him? They're killers."

"How would I know that? I don't kill nobody, I just recruit."

"Is Hal alive?"

"Maybe. They didn't have no picture. Hal was good at disappearing."

"Then who was fished out of the river?"

"I don't know."

"I think you're lying. Enjoy Nicaragua."

Teton replaced the gag. Federal agents got out of the plane and approached. "Another illegal drug thug, huh?"

"Yeah. And he's good. Fake accent, fake papers, fake everything. He even looks like one of our tribe. We're sending him back to Managua."

"We got a plane load of foreign criminals," the federal officer said. "It's an epidemic. They send us gang bangers, meth and heroin and we send them cash and guns."

"Keep him gagged for awhile," Teton said. "He's a live wire."

"Will do."

The agent took Teton's papers and escorted Lance Bronco toward the jet, a second agent holding Lance's arms. When the government plane took off, the Pilatus idled onto the runway. There was a gentle breeze on the tarmac.

"What the hell just happened?" Dexter said.

"I got a contact in LA to get a fake Nicaraguan passport."

"So Lance was right. You really think he killed Hal?"

"Only *La Eme* beheads people, but Lance admitted he set him up."

"But can you deport Lance to another country and get away with it?"

"He's not going to another country. The Feds will pick him up in Denver for further questioning."

"My God, lies and counterfeit passports."

"What of it? Did Mr. Ruiz make you a little nervous?"

"Ruiz made me *very* nervous."

"Let's hope our tiny gangster knows how to fly."

As Dexter drove out of the airport parking, he saw a fireball over the Indian cemetery just beyond the airport. He heard sirens and knew a small plane had gone down shortly after takeoff. He wanted to investigate but decided to drive home. The morning newspaper would carry the story of a light aircraft crashing with four men aboard, and people putting flowers on graves would talk about the single engine stalling and then the plane veering into a nose dive. It would be ruled engine failure due to a cargo overload. Mr. Dee would lament all those beautiful assault rifles and handguns destroyed.

The headless body fished from the river was buried after viable body parts were donated. Occasionally, some of the old people on the reservation insisted they had seen Hal by the Snake River, and that *La Eme* had killed the wrong boy. Others argued it was Hal's ghost. The Bronco family sued Chief Teton when the Feds deported Lance Bronco to Nicaragua by mistake.

"I hate it when the Feds do that," he told Dexter.

"Did you sabotage the Ruiz plane?"

"And risk injuries to people on the ground? Of course not. They needed a bigger plane."

One day, Dexter substituted at the Fort Hall School and when finished, drove out to Hal's dilapidated shack. It was empty and leaning badly in the overcast wet afternoon, a lonely image on the open prairie. For a moment, he wondered what had happened to Hal's grandmother and Hal's old Gibson guitar. Would it turn up in a pawn shop somewhere? He parked by the Snake River and meditated on the bright flowing surface, suddenly hearing a mournful crying sound. Perhaps it was the ghostly lament of dead Indian children tribal elders claimed lived beneath the waters. They could kill and take human shape. Turning to leave, Dexter saw three Indian Students walking on the gravel road. They stopped.

"Hello, Mr. Flanagan."

"Hello. How are you boys doing?"

They looked at one another and quickly walked on. He thought he saw fear.

When Dexter arrived home, Sami was painting an impressionistic outdoor scene for a scheduled showing.

"I found something on the doorstep," she said. "I think it's your bottleneck, but it's from an actual bottle. Looks old."

"I use a chrome tube," Dexter said. He followed the pattern of color on Sami's canvas. "Hal used a real bottleneck. Where is it?"

"It's on the table."

Dexter went to the table and picked up the bottleneck that had been cut from an old wine bottle for use as a blues slide. For a long time, he held the blue tinged bottleneck in his hand.

Never Again

THE old man double-parked in front of the Holocaust Museum. The fact such a big lie could have a museum perpetuating itself disturbed him profoundly. He reached in the back of the car and seized his century old .22 rifle. John Wayne playing the fatally ill gunslinger in *The Shootist* would demand a better weapon, but the old gun was still lethal. The elderly man held the rifle against his side and walked toward the entrance. He remembered his best painting, Jesus and Hitler standing together. He heard a roaring in his ears louder than the DC traffic as a black security officer rushed to open the door for him. *Perfect*, he thought, *a nigger policeman guarding a museum dedicated to a Jewish lie.* The old man noticed the metal detector beyond the door and had to act fast. There was surprise and then fear in the black face when the officer saw the rifle. The old man pointed at the guard's chest and pulled the trigger.

*   *   *

CLAUSTROPHOBIA might be the appropriate word, Sean Dineen thought, as he took the elevator to the fourth floor of the Holocaust Museum after his son dropped him off. With his pass, Sean carried an ID card showing a photo of Wladyslaw Tadeusz Surmacki, a Polish Catholic shot by the Nazis in 1942. The very building with its opaque windows, distorted skylight, bridges over open spaces and moving walkways inspired a feeling of paranoia and discomfort. There were no signs in the museum, but soon he began walking through the exhibits that continued down to the third and second floors. It was a descent into hell.

He passed a history of the holocaust and viewed hundreds of Jewish faces on a massive wall. He confronted *Kristallnacht*, or "Night of the Broken Glass," an anti-Jewish pogrom in 1938. Angry German voices echoed down the corridor. Sean stopped at a window that faced the Washington Monument, but the window was opaque. Sean felt the presence of unseen people moving around him; then he saw the boxcar.

Sean paused for a moment and finally walked through the train car that seemed remarkably small for the large number of Jews transported to the camps. As he came out the other side, Sean felt a wave of nausea. He had not expected it, but the image of people crammed together in railroad cars heading for the extermination camps poisoned his consciousness, as though he were among them, dying of malnutrition, thirst, packed in the heat and body waste.

He had become Mr. Surmacki, and Sean leaned against a wall, his mouth open. "Jesus Christ," he whispered to himself. No wonder his son, Carson, had declined to see the exhibits again. Sean heard gagging. An elegant older woman in a long dress stood in front of the women's bathroom holding her throat. She was short and stout but elegant, with long silver-white hair. As he walked toward her, the woman recovered.

"My God," the woman said.

"That boxcar is disturbing, isn't it?" he said.

"Yes, it is," she answered in a distinctive husky voice.

Sean examined his ID card. "I'm Mr. Surmaki, who are you?"

The woman glanced at her ID card. "I am Josephine Kohn Dermer, killed in a death camp in the fall of 1942."

"Looks like we both died that year."

"Josephine also lost a son," the woman told him. "I normally have more control. As disturbing as these exhibits are, I'll bring my granddaughter here tomorrow. Being racially mixed, she has to see this."

They walked under a replica of the famous concentration camp sign: *Arbeit Macht Frie* or "Work makes you free."

"Free from what?" the woman asked. She looked at him. "I'm Molly Malone."

"Sean Dineen," he replied. "What's your granddaughter's name?"

"Jenny. She's studying the violin. I want her to learn as much as possible before those hormones kick in."

"That's a good idea."

As they walked, they viewed continuous films of the Allies liberating the concentration camps. General Eisenhower stared in shock at the Jewish prisoners and dead bodies. They heard spoken testimony from victims. They remembered a bin full of shoes discarded by Jews on the way to the gas chambers. Once again, Sean felt a little sick.

Finally, they entered a large six-sided room called the Hall of Remembrance, and Sean liked the sudden expanse of polished floor and walls. The room felt like a church. A black marble coffin structure sat with an eternal flame on top. Dirt from concentration camps filled the black block. Light flooded the hall and glowed in a six-sided skylight. For a few minutes, they were quiet. Sean and Molly lit candles. Then they moved on, walking in silence. The tour would soon end.

"There's an exhibit about the holocaust seen from the viewpoint of a little boy called Daniel," Molly finally said. "I think I'll see if it's appropriate for Jenny."

"I planned to see the museum's play about Ann Frank, but I think I've had enough for one day," Sean said. "I saw a play by Arthur Miler where a man touring the death camps says, 'My brothers died here . . . but my brothers built this place.' That is hard to digest."

"It is, isn't it?"

"I don't understand the people who deny the Holocaust happened. The Nazis kept great records, and the Americans shot film in the camps. We have tattooed survivors."

"I bet neo Nazis are secretly proud of what happened." Molly stopped and shook his hand. "I enjoyed your company, Sean."

"Molly, I enjoyed yours. I think it's better to share this experience, even with a stranger."

"The Irish suffered over the centuries, but nothing like this." Molly paused, peering at his face. "You look familiar."

"I did some political cartoons, and wrote a book that became a film."

"Of course. I've seen you on TV."

They faced each other, locked in the moment. He liked her face and clear blue eyes and imagined them as a couple in some remote time.

"I'll look for your book and film," Molly said.

"Maybe I'll see Jenny at Carnegie Hall."

"I hope so."

Then they parted. Their brief journey was over.

Sean looked around for an exit. He needed to see his son and recover from the unsettling images. As he walked, Sean realized he was lost. Suddenly he heard a single shot, and then shouts. Sean moved toward the main entrance, running through crowds of people who were also suddenly running. Sean stopped. A guard lay on the floor of the main entrance. An old man was holding a rifle, his wrinkled white face full of hate and a wild joy; more shots were fired and the gunman suddenly fell.

*   *   *

AS they ascended the steps of the Lincoln Memorial, the Emancipator's massive figure appeared sitting in a giant chair. Then Sean and Carson walked into the enclosure and read the carved words of the Gettysburg Address and the Second Inaugural. Sean felt his breathing slowing, and some of the disturbing images receded. A light rain was falling on the Capitol Mall.

"It's a brutal exhibit at the Holocaust Museum," his son said. "But necessary. I thought the Lincoln Memorial would be a good antidote."

"You thought right," Sean said.

"There's another exhibit downstairs," Carson said.

"Let's go," Sean said.

Incident at Gettysburg

EARLY that morning, Declan sat in a Gettysburg restaurant. The waitress was fat with a bland face and a piercing nasal tone. He gave her his order.

"Two eggs over medium and wheat toast is fine."

"I got it, Hon. No meat or nothin'?"

"No, just wheat toast and two eggs."

Before leaving, the waitress turned to another customer.

"Don't you forget, Fergie. The dog needs washed."

"I won't forget, Wilma."

Declan couldn't resist a comment on her use of language.

"Excuse me, don't you mean, 'The dog needs *to be* washed'?"

The dull eyes regarded him. "That's what I said, Darlin'. Dog needs fed, too."

"Well good, Wilma," Declan said. "I need eat."

Wilma left with his order. Declan looked across the table at the empty seat and imagined Kate anxious to visit another historic site. He then looked out at the busy Gettysburg street. Some of the old buildings had small imbedded cannon balls. Pennsylvania was a different country, almost, with a different accent and a different culture. At a flea market, he watched an Amish man buying a shotgun. Evidently their philosophy of nonviolence allowed them to own guns. Out in the country, Declan liked the way the long narrow roads cut through fields of crops, and signs warned of horse and buggy crossings.

A tall copper-haired woman wearing a tank top and white skirt walked past the restaurant window, and Declan suddenly realized how long it had been since he was intimate with a woman he loved beyond desire. An old longing swept over him as he watched her walk out of view. Then the woman returned and stared at him through the window, though he didn't believe she actually saw him. Up close, she looked older, perhaps middle aged, but still attractive with a voluptuous body. Then she quickly disappeared.

In another universe, he thought to himself, *we would've been passionate lovers. Farewell, my sweet, fare thee well.*

Declan took a taxi to the Gettysburg battlefield to meet a guide named Thomas hired to drive him to battlefield locations. At one point, they stopped near an area that had a personal connection to Declan. Thomas held up two puppets to dramatize a tragic incident from the long ago battle. One puppet represented General Kilpatrick, the commanding officer, and the other, General Elon Farnsworth. As Declan Mulligan watched, Thomas did the voices for dramatic if limited effect.

"You make that charge or I will," the Kilpatrick puppet said. "I will do it," replied the Farnsworth puppet. The guide put down the puppets.

"Elon Farnsworth knew the attack would be disastrous."

"I know the story on a personal level," Declan said.

"How so?"

For Declan Mulligan, it would always be twilight of that third day at Gettysburg when his great great grandfather, Michael Mulligan, followed General Elon John Farnsworth on his fatal cavalry charge into Confederate guns. Riding through trees and over ditches and rocky ground, the slow-moving horses and their riders offered Confederate marksmen prime targets. Shot five times, the dying Farnsworth lay on a hill, firing his pistol at advancing Rebs. Many horses and men fell. The woods ran with blood. Thrown from his dying horse, Michael Mulligan suffered a concussion and woke up in a hospital tent for wounded Federals and Confederates.

"My great great grandfather, Michael Mulligan, had his horse shot from under him riding behind Farnsworth," Declan told him.

Thomas was impressed.

"Then you know Kilpatrick's order was a tragic blunder. The charge was unnecessary, and you can't maneuver horses in a forest. It was a bloody end to a bloody day."

Walking along a path near the same woods, Declan saw a monument beneath a Celtic cross honoring the Union Irish Brigade. An Irish wolf hound lay at the base of the cross, waiting for a master who would never return. There were Irish Brigades on both sides, each carrying a green flag, so it touched him that an Irish Confederate soldier had sculpted the monument. Looking now at the Celtic cross in the soft greenish light, Declan knew Michael Mulligan was at Gettysburg in 1888 for the dedication ceremony.

"The name Michael Mulligan does sound familiar," Thomas said. "At the center, I think there's a photo of him standing next to General Farnsworth."

"I know. I've come to see it."

"This ground must be even more sacred for you."

"Oh, it is. I've had some tragedy in my life, and I visit these places to put it all into perspective."

Thomas seemed to understand.

Declan Mulligan then walked along a wide open field and imagined Pickett's Charge moving toward the Union forces on Cemetery Ridge. In terrible heat, they walked into blistering fire: rifle, canister, and canon. The open field once strewn with corpses now seemed unnaturally quiet on this sunny day. The Wheat Field where the Irish Brigade was caught in a cross-fire also seemed too peaceful. Declan looked around at the many statues and monuments.

"Sometimes I wonder if my great great grandfather wanted to die in the Civil War."

"Why is that?"

"To end his grief. He worked as a horse groom on an Irish plantation run by a tyrannical Anglo-Irish landlord named Burke. As revenge, he stole Burke's wife and fled to America. Her name was Maria. She was beautiful but died of ship fever on Grosse Isle near Quebec."

"This was during the famine?"

"Yes. Michael Mulligan mourned her for the rest of his life."

"You have a fascinating family history, Mr. Mulligan. Quite romantic."

Observing the battlefield, Declan could easily imagine the actual carnage and thick smoke and screams of dying men. Declan saw Michael Mulligan's horse falling to a bullet, his Irish ancestor suddenly airborne. Declan winced. When Declan again looked over the vista, he felt something, a presence. He turned to see if anyone was watching him. A grounds crew was cutting down new trees to make the battlefield look like it did those three bloody days in July of 1863. A few tourists were taking pictures, and nothing seemed unusual.

An hour later at the visitor center, Declan Mulligan stared at a sepia-toned photograph; a tall ruggedly built man with hard light-colored eyes stood next to a handsome cavalry general sporting a fashionable mustache, a beautiful white horse looking over their shoulders. They stared into light from another century. Looking at the photo of his long dead ancestor, Declan waited to hear an inner voice. What would Michael Mulligan say to him from that afternoon just before one of America's most bloody battles? Did Michael Mulligan fight for the American union, to free the slaves, or to forget his heartbreak over losing a woman he loved enough to abandon his country?

Tourists walked through the center, examining the photos and artifacts from the battle. Declan noticed horse trainer Mulligan was "unidentified." Thomas appeared by his side.

"I can add his name," Thomas assured him, as they stared at the old photo.

"He couldn't go back to Ireland for a long time. Not only did the Burke family want him dead, but he abandoned a band of Irish assassins called the Whiteboys. Working with Irish Gypsies called Tinkers, they killed tyrannical landlords. The Whiteboys wanted his head."

Without warning, the same woman Declan had seen through the restaurant window suddenly appeared.

"Hello, Thomas."

She looked at Declan and was about to speak when Thomas took her arm.

"Excuse us," he said and they walked off, arguing.

Declan left the center and returned to his motel to check the bus schedule. Early in the morning, his plane left from Harrisburg, some distance away. There would be a brief stop in Washington, D.C., and then the flight to Idaho. Declan thought later he might walk around the town, find a nice restaurant or tavern, and possibly talk to the locals.

Declan took a short nap and had a brief dream. He saw an ante bellum styled mansion painted white and yellow. A Union cavalry officer was approaching on horseback. Declan woke up, the motel room lit with late afternoon light. Who was inside the mansion?

At dusk, Declan found a small Irish pub. A Celtic band played modern and traditional Irish songs. Declan ordered a familiar dish of corned beef and cabbage with a beer and sat at a table. He liked the lively music, including a ballad by U2. After finishing the meal, he saw a young woman who resembled his late wife, Kate, now working behind the bar. Declan looked at her handsome face and suddenly felt a slight wave of fear. He got up and walked outside to the back alley. A few men stood smoking. Declan leaned against the back wall of the tavern and listened to the muted music. Then he saw her, the woman with long red hair peering at his face.

"Hello again," she said.

"Hello," Declan said.

"Minnesota is a lovely state but so humid in the summer."

"This is Pennsylvania."

"I know, but I come from Minnesota. You?"

"I was born in San Francisco. I now live in Idaho."

"You have potatoes, we have acres of corn. You work in Idaho?"

"Retired."

"Oh." After a pause, the woman said, "I saw you at the battlefield and the Gettysburg Visitor Center with my old boyfriend, Thomas."

"I remember. Tell Thomas to lose those dumb puppets."

"I will. You didn't look like a tourist. You looked more like a ghost returning to the battlefield."

"It's a moving place."

The woman nodded. "Incredible vibes," she told him. "What's your name?"

"Declan Mulligan. Yours?"

"Guinevere."

"People call you Jenny?"

"Yes, but I prefer Jenny Rose. Very southern."

"Rose is your last name?"

"Chaney is my last name." Jenny Rose watched his face and finally said, "Relax, Declan, the war is over."

"I know. I left the bar for another reason." When she said nothing, he continued. "I am a widower. Her name was Kate."

"And the barmaid reminded you of her. It happens. How long ago?"

"Over four years now. Almost five," Declan said. He regarded her face. She was in her mid-forties, her face handsome, the eyes a dark brown, the streetlight catching highlights in her flowing red hair. He noticed her full lips and a body firm, he suspected, from working out. She might be aggressive sexually which disturbed rather than excited him. "You always talk to strangers?"

"No, but you stood out. I could feel your pain at 50 yards."

The men finished smoking and went inside. The red-haired woman was still watching him, but Declan felt more relaxed.

"You have a Lancelot in your life, Guinevere?"

"No. Not for a while, Declan."

"Why not?"

"Sometimes it happens, and sometimes it doesn't. You?"

"I'm single."

"Sounds familiar. Any kids?"

"Two step kids. You?"

"That's a sad story."

Declan liked the pattern of red hair over her shoulders and for a brief moment, wanted to touch her. "You want a drink?"

Jenny Rose didn't move but finally spoke.

"It is 241 1942."

"I beg your pardon?"

"My cell is: 241 1942. Area code, 507. Can you remember that number?"

Declan felt a sudden attraction but hesitated. "I can, but there's a problem."

"You're leaving tomorrow?"

"Yes."

"And this is happening too fast?"

"Maybe it is, yes."

After a pause, Jenny Rose agreed to have a drink. Inside the Irish pub, the band was playing an overwrought version of "Danny Boy." The barmaid who resembled a young Kate was laughing and talking with customers. Declan ordered a second beer and Jenny Rose ordered a beer with a shot of Jamison Irish Whiskey. They faced each other across a smooth table.

"It is interesting that even only six months after I lost my wife, men would tell me to get a new woman or a dog. Women commiserated with me, and often took me places: dinner or a show. I was alone, but not always *completely* alone."

"Women are more sensitive than men," Jenny Rose said.

He leaned forward. "You think like a man."

"Really?"

"I suspect you think I need laid."

"Need laid?" For a moment, she seemed puzzled, and then began laughing, coughing through the laugh. "You've got the Pennsylvania lingo down. We drop the infinitive."

"I noticed. So am I right? You think sex will cure my grief?"

"Of course not. But intimate touching is good."

She sipped her drink. Declan stared at the dark depth of the whiskey and thought how nice it would be to order a shot for himself. He did not want to drink many shots.

"You need to step outside and have a smoke?"

"How do you know I smoke?"

"By your cough. Kate was a smoker," he told her.

"I'll wait on the cigarette, Declan."

"Thank you."

"It's been awhile since I've been intimate with anyone. I broke up with Thomas two years ago. He's nice but a bit dull."

"I saw your argument. An attractive woman like you should have a lot of dates."

Jenny Rose pushed back a thickness of hair and said, "Yes, but I just wasn't ready. I needed something more than physical attraction."

"I guess I should be flattered since we just met."

Jenny Rose had a direct stare that seemed to penetrate him. "You *should* be flattered. I like your energy, though I can feel the darkness and pain." She lowered her eyes. "I lost my only son to a drug overdose at 21."

"I'm very sorry to hear that."

"He had recovered and then a terrible car accident forced him to take pain medication. It built up in his system. One morning, he didn't wake up." She stared past him into a void Declan could understand. "The only solace is to do what you can to end suffering and remember that there is a world elsewhere…and that world is inside."

He took her hands in his. "I guess you keep busy to forget?"

"I'm a professional psychic."

"That's a profession?"

She saw the surprise in his face.

"Yes. I work for the police department. They take me *very* seriously. I can visit a murder scene and feel the vibes and see the murderer's face. I can vision the place where the killer is hiding. I feel human energy."

The lead singer began a plaintive ballad about the Irish brigades facing each other at Fredericksburg. How the Irish soldiers wept to kill their own. Declan listened and became aware of Jenny Rose watching him.

"You have a photo of Kate?"

Declan showed her a card with Kate's photo. Jenny Rose examined the well groomed hair and smiling face. "She was very beautiful. I understand your loss, Declan. Did she like dinner parties with friends and beautiful old houses and lovely gardens and animals?"

"Yes, but who doesn't?"

"Did she play cards?"

"Solitaire every morning. I used to wake up to the sound of slapping cards. The cards are still on the table where she left them."

"Kate is not coming back, Declan. Give up the shrine."

"I'll decide that."

"Maybe she's happy, now, and it's time for *you* to be happy."

"No one is happy dead."

"Let me see your hand."

"Give me a break," Declan said. "I don't believe in that hippy-dippy stuff."

"I know. Give me your hand."

Jenny Rose studied his left hand. "There's a battlefield, here, but things will improve. You *can* fall in love, again. Maybe not with me."

"I don't know you!"

"No, but can't you read people and make instant connections?"

"To a point."

"Supposing you saw John Keats or James Dean or Greta Garbo at a party before they became famous. Wouldn't you feel they were somehow special?"

"I'm not so sure. Michelangelo looked like a hangman. He might scare me." Declan smiled at her. "So who are *you*? Joan of Arc?"

"Not hardly." Jenny Rose released his hand. "You have a lot of ghosts, Declan. When I close my eyes, I see a beautiful woman with red hair and green eyes."

"Like you?"

"My eyes are brown, and this woman is dressed in mid-19th century style: corset, hoop skirt, puffy sleeves, and bonnet."

"Don't know who that is."

"You don't? No matter. Soon her man will free her from all those layers of clothing."

Jenny Rose leaned back in the chair, laughing. Declan didn't join her.

"Okay. Let's enjoy the evening, Declan."

They drank and listened to the music. He bought Jenny Rose another beer with a shot and switched to ginger ale for himself. They occasionally tried to speak over the amped music and singing. Briefly Jenny Rose touched his arm, and he liked the feel of her tightening fingers. Near closing time, Declan stood up. "Jenny Rose, this has been fun, but I have an early airport bus to catch. It's been a pleasure."

She was tipsy and looked at him through wisps of parted hair. He looked down the open blouse at her curving cleavage, and imagined them in bed, passionate and furiously rocking before parting forever.

"You remember my number?"

"I do."

"Repeat it."

"I have to go. It's past my bed time."

"I could drive you to the airport…after spending the night together."

"Let me think about it."

"Think about it? Most men don't turn me down, Declan…and we may never see each other again."

Declan saw a sudden hardness in her face.

"I'm sorry, but I'm an old guy…maybe not up for a one-night stand, no pun intended. A ride sounds tempting, however. We'd both be safe on the road since someone has to drive."

Declan was puzzled by a sudden suppressed mirth in her face and eyes. Then he saluted her and started for the door. Outside, the air hit him and he took a deep breath. Declan took a step and Jenny Rose blocked him. "Not so fast, Mulligan."

"Queen Guinevere — what is it?"

"This." She kissed him. He felt the softness of her lips and probing tongue, and Declan gently touched her breast. Then she pulled away and said, "If you need a ride, call me." Jenny Rose pushed back into the tavern and Declan walked toward the motel.

Inside, sitting on his bed, Declan felt restless and not ready for sleep. Declan quickly packed his small bag. For a moment, he was tempted to call Jenny Rose, this fair creature of an hour. He liked the slight overhang of her upper lip. After staring at the semi-lit courtyard, Declan finally slipped into bed.

Declan dreamed again of the white and yellow mansion, and this time, he was a camera tracking close where he saw Kate in a shining white gown setting a dinner table with new china and silverware and glowing candles. Then he saw a young Michael Mulligan, handsome in his cavalry uniform, and next to him, a beautiful woman with copper-colored hair, dressed in a flowing dress with a tight waist and full sleeves. Was this Maria Burke, the woman he took from Ireland? His ancestor seemed to meet his eyes with a secret challenge. Other long dead guests were entering the large ornate room. Declan began screaming at the apparitions, but they didn't hear him. Suddenly, Kate faced him across the chasm, a slight frown on her younger face, as she closed the window.

Declan woke up with a cry. He stared into a dark motel room, and after parting the curtains, saw the first faint light beginning on the horizon. Declan dialed a number, and when there was no answer, left a message. Panting, he lay back on the bed. By morning, he waited in front of the motel and was surprised to see a cream-colored stretch limo pull into the parking lot. A tinted window rolled down revealing Jenny Rose's smiling face.

"Time to move out, Pilgrim," she said. "Dump your bag in the trunk and get in."

He put his bag in the trunk which automatically closed, and got into the limo. The unseen driver turned toward the freeway and the Harrisburg airport. Declan saw a bucket of champagne and two glasses on a tray.

"Where did you get the money for this? Impressive."

"I have another business, renting limousines. Champagne?"

"I don't drink until after breakfast," Declan told her.

Jenny Rose laughed and poured herself a glass. She wore a short skirt and a loose, low-cut blouse, her thick hair tied back. She wasn't wearing a bra.

"I would've invaded your room last night, but I was too drunk."

"How would you find me?"

Jenny Rose gave him a skeptical look. "I'm a psychic. Your miserable Irish aura is a mile wide. Listen, Declan, I quit smoking, and need to put something in my mouth."

"Lucky me."

"But maybe champagne will do. We should celebrate our lucky meeting. Share these precious final minutes."

"I *do* appreciate the ride."

"Think nothing of it. I *want* to give you a ride."

Looking away, Declan felt Jenny Rose watching his profile; he briefly glimpsed her bare thighs beneath the short skirt and finally looked at her mouth as she tasted the champagne, licking her lips. The limo moved swiftly, smooth and powerful. When they slid together on turns, Declan could feel the old warmth coursing through him. On the music system, Bob Dylan was singing, "I've got a couple more years on you, babe, that's all."

"It's decadent to drink in the morning, but this champagne is so-oo-oo sweet."

"I've had a few shots with beer in the morning," Declan said.

"I bet you have." He glanced away and she said, "Look at me."

"I *am* looking at you."

"Kate is now a free spirit. You may meet her again—"

"I don't believe that—"

"—but until then, she has closed the door…or the window…on you. Time to move on."

"So you had the same dream."

"Perhaps I did." She rubbed his thigh and then kissed his neck. Then she poured another glass of champagne. "Care to join me?"

"Perhaps I could have a drop taken."

She poured him a glass. He never drank in the morning, but sometimes it was fun to break the rules. The champagne had a sharp taste and he felt it rush to his head. They locked eyes and Jenny Rose grinned.

"We have this brief moment, Mulligan."

"True." He gently touched her face. "I made a discovery, last night, about love. It's connected to the cavalry officer standing next to General Farnsworth."

"The old photo you were admiring. I was going to connect with you but pouting Thomas interfered."

"That officer was Michael Mulligan, my great great grandfather—a soldier, horse trainer, scholar, theatre promoter, and an assassin. He was also a romantic."

"Like you?"

"Yes." As Declan undid a few buttons on her blouse, he told the romantic story of his ancestor stealing a tyrannical landlord's bride and escaping to America, making love on the very coffin ship that carried Typhus known as ship fever, unaware his love would die in his arms on Grosse Isle. With strong fingers, Jenny Rose skillfully undid the top of his pants even as Declan's voice continued the story. He could almost see Mulligan and Maria making love. He could see the remote and desolate graveyard with nameless victims. He could see Michael Mulligan's face, a man now abandoned in a foreign land, unable to return home.

"But years later, he *did* return, a sightless old man, with his son and grandkids. He was ready to face judgment," Declan declared. "His crime: falling in love."

Jenny Rose pressed a finger across his lips. When Declan pulled apart her blouse and saw the large firm breasts, he slipped into his best fake Irish accent: "Bejasus, Jenny Rose, but sure you *are* lovely like that Maureen O' Hara." Declan poured a drop of champagne on each nipple and gently took each into his mouth.

"Mulligan, if you stop now—"

"I *have* to finish my story."

"Jesus!"

Declan then explained how Michael Mulligan bought the plantation where he had been a horse groom and ordered the rotting mansion dismantled and burned before the townspeople feasting at his expense.

"Then some Irish tinkers appeared. According to witnesses, he seemed to know they were there though he was blind. He walked toward them."

Jenny Rose licked his neck. Sliding his hand up her thigh, he realized Jenny Rose wore no panties. She suddenly kissed him and moaned in his ear. Declan felt his body responding to the sweet sensuality of the moment. The music had switched to a slow throbbing blues. Eyes closed, the words rushed out of him as he came to the climax of Michael Mulligan's story.

"His granddaughter, Kate, reported they met, they spoke in their own language, then they shook hands and embraced. And finally—"

"Declan, stop talking!"

"Michael Mulligan collapsed and died in his son's arms—his destiny fulfilled."

Jenny Rose pulled away, her red hair wild and suddenly loose, her breasts exposed, the short skirt pushed up her thighs. He felt a breeze over his lap and saw the urgent need in her eyes. Then she reached down and touched him as Declan finished his family history.

"A year later in a remote cemetery, his ashes were poured on Maria's grave, uniting him at last with his long gone love."

"Love yes," Jenny Rose said, bending down, her voice suddenly muffled. "Yes!"

Seconds later, Jenny Rose sat up and ripping apart his shirt, kissed him. She lifted herself and he saw a triangle of reddish hair before she slid onto his lap, posting on his bare thighs as they rode down the highway toward Harrisburg.

Hours later when Declan Mulligan arrived to an empty house, he unpacked his bag and collected the mail. He let the cat out after two weeks inside. On a CD, Dylan was singing about lips dripping with honey, and Declan, with a slight headache, could still taste the sweetness of Jenny Rose. Declan saw the backyard of dry lawn and roses and turned on the sprinklers. Moments later, Declan noticed Kate's worn playing cards spread on the table. He touched the queen of hearts and remembered Kate's quiet concentration as she played the game every morning. Declan spoke aloud to no one.

"Well, Kate, I guess you're not coming back."

Softly weeping, Declan placed the cards in a pack and put them away.

Return of the Exiles

IT was a hot July day when they met at the Hemingway Memorial in Sun Valley, Idaho. The brook was high and fast running underneath the bust of the celebrated writer. Declan carried a chest full of roses from his garden, and Sean Dineen brought some cheese, cups and bottles of red and white wine. Dexter Flanagan stood on the hill, holding his guitar case. Sean Dineen examined Hemingway's bust in profile.

"So this is the monument to old Ernie, eh?"

"That's right," Declan said. "It was here where Kate and I were married 20 years ago."

"I'm glad I made the trip," Sean said.

"It's a nice bust," Dexter said. "I like the inscription, too. I'll have to read Hemingway."

Declan could still see Kate wearing her blue wedding dress with a light-colored hat and veil, listening to him play a Beatle song about loving one person above all other people and things. It had been hot, that day, and after the song ended, they were married, the judge's words carrying above the sound of the narrow running stream. Many of the people from that day were gone, including Kate. Now, he only had a yearly ritual.

"Kate loved roses," Declan said.

Sean Dineen cut some slices of cheese and held up the wine bottles. "Red or white?"

"White," Declan said.

"I'll take the red."

"I have some ginger ale," said Dexter.

He produced a bottle of ginger ale. Then they heard Sami's voice.

"I could use a shot of ginger ale."

Wearing jeans and a tank top, her hair natural brown and held by a red bandanna, she walked down the path toward the monument.

"Our local artist has arrived," Declan said.

The night before, they had attended Sami's opening at a Sun Valley gallery, her brooding but somewhat surreal landscapes greeting guests and admirers. Dexter had provided acoustic folk and blues music for the show. Now Dexter and Sami held hands while Sean passed a cup of white wine to Declan. He then poured red wine for himself. They would eat the cheese after the last rose was sent downstream.

"Wine and cheese. Hemingway would approve."

"I'll have my drink later," Declan said.

They watched as Declan took the roses out one by one and placed them into the brook. "Sweets to the sweet," he said. "Farewell."

They listened to the running water and many birds singing in the trees. Sean Dineen felt moved, watching the floating roses and thinking about Rachel and Priscilla. Did their spirits dwell in the hidden forest places? Declan was also quiet, following the roses as they drifted into the current and disappeared downstream. A small wooden plank ran across the stream and there were cottonwood trees along a forest path. Declan wondered if Kate watched him from behind the trees. Below the monument was a golf course. In the distance, they could hear bulldozers clearing a field for another clubhouse.

Declan held up the last flower, a red and pink long-stemmed Princess Diana rose, and dropped it into the current. The rose turned in a circle and moved in toward the bank where it stopped. They sipped their drinks and watched as the final rose rested on a fallen branch touching a slight eddy of pebble-colored water.

"That last rose doesn't want to leave us," Sean said.

"I think you're right," Declan said. "But Kate won't be denied even one rose."

Dexter and Sami were silent. Then Declan spoke.

"I wonder if I should push the rose out into the stream?"

"Let's wait," Sean said.

"For what?" said Dexter.

"Maybe a sign."

Declan remained silent. They began eating the cheese with their drinks, aware of the rose stuck by the bank. A middle-aged man with short gray hair and wearing shorts appeared on the path, a black Labrador following him.

"Hello," the man said. He turned to the dog. "Come along, Skipper. Don't bother these people."

But Skipper jumped into the brook before the bust and stood in the running water. The dog looked back at the people on the bank. Then he lumbered toward the stationary rose, rippling in the shallows.

"Now Skipper," the man warned. "Don't eat that rose!"

They watched as the big black dog suddenly nosed the flower into the middle of the brook. It was caught by the current and soon disappeared downstream.

"Hail to the skipper," Declan said. He lifted his cup of wine and the others raised their cups. "The journey begins."

"Skipper, you come along right now," the man warned. He looked at them. "He never listens."

The visitor finally turned and walked down the path. The black lab suddenly jumped from the brook, shaking off water, and chased his master around the turn. Declan met Sean's eyes and suddenly began laughing through tears. Sean Dineen started laughing. Then they all hugged each other in a circle while laughing. When the circle was broken, Dexter took out his guitar.

"That calls for a song," he said.

Dexter started plucking a familiar rhythm in ¾ time. Sami took Declan's hand and they began a slow waltz while Sean poured himself another drink.

"If music be the food of life, play on," Sean said.